THE PHOENIX GUARDIAN

The Phoenix Guardian

First edition published in 2012

Second edition published in 2016

Cover art by Daniel Kordek

ISBN-13: 978-1536841756
ISBN-10: 1536841757

To Mel Odom,
my inexhaustible writing professor,
mentor,
and friend

THE PHOENIX GUARDIAN

MAP OF MITHRIS

PROLOGUE

The man strode silently down the sidewalk underneath the moonless sky. He wore a fedora low over his brow, concealing his face. His black three-piece suit blended into the murky night.

Leaves brushed against his feet as he walked past the quiet homes of the peaceful neighborhood. The wind blew through the trees, rustling the heavy boughs above him.

Up ahead, two boys were playing underneath a streetlight. They played with the giddy excitement of children staying up past their bedtime. One of the boys bounced a basketball and jumped into the air to shoot at the small hoop on their driveway.

The ball bounced off the backboard and rolled down the sidewalk toward the man in the black suit. The older boy ran after the ball. He caught up with it in a pool of light underneath a lamppost, a few feet away from the man.

The child picked up the ball hesitantly, uncomfortable in the presence of a stranger, especially so late at night. He scurried back to his brother, but he could not resist venturing a look at the man over his shoulder.

The man raised the tip of his fedora, revealing his face—and the child screamed. He dropped his basketball, ran back toward his little brother, and dragged him to the safety of their porch. The children threw open their screen door and bolted inside.

The man lowered the fedora over his eyes and walked past the house.

A dog, standing in the middle of the street, began to bark at him. Its legs were spread apart, and its sharp ears were straight up, alert. The dog's thin brown fur stood on edge.

The man moved closer. He grinned.

The dog whimpered, stepping back with its tail between its legs.

Still the man advanced, his footsteps making no sound.

Tilting his head thoughtfully, he stopped and examined the dog.

He raised his arm toward the animal. The dog tensed, poised to run. The man snapped his hand across his chest, like a conductor silencing an orchestra. The dog gave a sharp yelp, and its legs buckled. It collapsed onto the asphalt road and did not stir again.

The man walked on. He passed a brick house with a huge oak tree in the front yard. Its branches shrouded the man in greater darkness, making him nearly invisible.

He arrived at a two-story house with a driveway that led around to the back. A cricket chirped in the yard. The man followed the gravel driveway, walking silently toward a wooden porch behind the house.

He climbed the stairs, grasping the banister until he stepped onto the porch and stood in front of the screen door.

A welcome mat lay at his feet. Through the window, he could see a young woman sitting in a wooden rocking chair.

The woman had a plait of brown hair that fell across her shoulder. She held a little girl close to her chest. The girl, who wore white pajamas with soft pink stripes, was fast asleep. The mother rocked back and forth, eyes closed, stroking the child's long brown hair.

A porch light illuminated the man's imposing figure as he watched the mother and her child. The high cheekbones on his pale, gaunt face were clearly visible underneath the light, but the mother did not look outside. She was content to hold her toddler, lost in maternal bliss.

The crickets had stopped chirping.

The man took off his fedora. His suit jacket began to flap, as though it was caught in a high breeze—but the wind had stopped. The edges of his clothing stripped away into nothingness. The man's body faded into the night. Soon he was a dark wisp of cloud against the comfy glow of the porch light.

He glided toward the window, baring his teeth, and then his face melted to join the smoky mass floating in the air. In his new form, he flowed underneath the door.

Inside, the light from the ceiling fan went out. The little girl stirred in her mother's lap.

"Mom?" She looked up to find comfort in her mother's face, but she saw nothing. The entire room had been plunged into swirling darkness, as if someone had dropped black ink into a cup of water.

"Shh, baby, it's okay."

The girl heard her mother's voice, but she could no longer feel her mother's presence—neither her warmth nor her touch.

Then her mother drew a great shuddering breath and cried out in pain. The sound was short and abrupt. The girl dropped to the ground. She screamed loudly, panicking, reaching for her mother but grasping thin air.

Her mother's face came into view. It was deathly pale. The woman's beautiful blue eyes rolled back into her head. The rocking chair collapsed, throwing mother and child to the floor.

The girl tried to scream. She summoned every ounce of sound that her tiny lungs could muster, but no sound came. She felt a terrible weight upon her chest, forcing her to the ground. She struggled against the weight, trying to sit upright, but it pushed her down...down...

Two murky white eyes appeared in front of her. Then a ghastly face formed around the eyes, and a thin red tongue stuck out from between pale, dry lips. Just before the girl passed out from terror, a blinding light flooded the room and washed away the blackness like a tide.

The man in the black suit materialized fully, his fedora back on his head as he stumbled into the far corner of the room and fell against a bookshelf. He shielded his blank eyes from the light, which emanated from a celestial figure.

It was the graceful form of a young woman. Her face was fair but terrifying. Her long, flowing hair shone with a fearful light. The woman pointed at the pale man in the black suit, who opened his mouth to scream, stretching it to a grotesque size. His entire face contorted hideously. The girl put her hands to her ears to shut out his unnatural, high-pitched squeal.

A gaping hole grew in his torso, burning like a flame, consuming the man until he shriveled away into nothingness.

The radiant woman stepped carefully over the child, who was numb with terror, to examine the body of the mother. It lay pitifully beside the broken rocking chair. The woman shook her head, placed her fingers gently on the mother's face, and closed the lifeless eyes.

The girl found that she had recovered her voice. She began to sob. She wanted her mother to wake her up from this nightmare and hold her close. The child reached toward her mother, but the luminous woman stopped her from touching the limp body. She took the girl's hands and caressed them gently.

She spoke, and her voice was firm and reassuring. The girl couldn't understand the woman's words, nor could she recognize her shining features, but her body relaxed when the woman placed a warm hand on her forehead.

Forgetfulness washed over the child, and her mind spun into darkness and slumber...

*

"I warned you to have nothing to do with the mortal, Julius. Mortals die."

"The gods can die too, Ambrosia. Or hasn't our father's illness taught you anything?"

Julius stared at the huge panoramic window that stretched around the half-circular throne room. The glass reflected his tall, muscular frame. His short black hair matched the simplicity of his white toga. Julius stood with his back to his sister, but he could see her flowing robes and blonde hair in the reflection.

Outside, the storm raged.

A polished black floor reflected the surges of electricity jumping from cloud to cloud. Rain beat mercilessly against the throne room, which rested at the top of a colossal skyscraper.

The astonishing height of the building, and its alarming proximity to the tempest overhead, would be enough to make any human quake with fear.

But Julius was a god.

And while he could control the elements outside, he was struggling to control the emotions raging in his soul.

He turned around to face his sister, who was shaking with anger.

"How dare you mention our father! Not when your decisions are killing him!"

Julius tightened his quivering fists, forcing them to remain at his side.

He clenched his jaw. "Be careful what you say."

"I will not!" Ambrosia pointed a finger at her brother. "You have shamed us all by immersing yourself in this uncleanliness!"

Julius grabbed Ambrosia's hand with alarming strength. His broad fingers closed easily around her slim forearm. Fear flashed across her eyes. She shrank backward, trying to wrench her hand free of his grip.

"Ambrosia, learn your place!" Julius clenched his teeth, his blue eyes blazing as his voice rose to a scream. "My wife and daughter died tonight! Burned to death while they slept! Do you think I care to hear *your* grievances?"

Ambrosia struggled to pull free of her brother's grasp. Behind the curtain of blonde hair that fell in front of her eyes, her expression was defiant.

"I am sorry for your loss, brother, but I will not tolerate flippant references to our father's illness—certainly not when the cause of his condition stands before me!"

"Flippant references? The cause of his condition? You're a liar, Ambrosia!" Julius pushed his sister roughly down the steps of the dais. She cried out and stumbled to regain her footing.

"Father was wounded ages ago in the War of Chaos," Julius growled. "He was pierced by Makay's poisoned spear. The poison never left him, and now it may claim his life. If he dies, he dies from the weapon of an enemy—not at the hands of his son!"

A peal of thunder accented Julius's last words.

Ambrosia glared at her brother. Lightning silhouetted his imposing frame.

"The poison may claim his life," she said, "but you broke his heart when you fell in love with a mortal woman!"

Lightning crackled at the edges of Julius's fingers, illuminating the entire room.

"You dare speak of broken hearts?" Julius screamed, sending bolts of electricity rippling along the walls of the throne room, breaking statues and melting the golden trim. "My heart is shattered! My wife and daughter are dead! And if you had let them stay here in the Tower, they would never have died in that human house!"

"If I had let them stay?" Ambrosia laughed in spite of the lightning shattering the air around her. "I never had the authority to let them stay or not."

Julius lowered his hands, and the lightning flickered into nothingness. Trails of smoke filled the room where his lightning had burned the walls and floor. Julius stepped down the dais and pointed an accusing finger in Ambrosia's face.

"You could have helped me. You could have convinced Father to let Jillian stay with me—"

"Do not mention her name to me." Ambrosia curled her lip in disgust. "I was humiliated by your involvement with the mortal. So was our father. The arrival of your offspring only made it worse."

A blinding flash covered the window, followed by a terrific thunderclap. The entire Tower shook violently, throwing Ambrosia off balance.

"My offspring?" Julius took deep breaths, his shoulders heaving as he clenched and unclenched his fists.

He closed his eyes, willing himself to control his anger before he did something he would regret.

Finally, he whispered, "You speak of my beloved daughter, your *niece*, and you refer to her as my *offspring*?"

Ambrosia trembled under her brother's fierce gaze. She looked at the floor.

"I just visited the house, Ambrosia. After you told me about the fire, I went to see for myself. Less than an hour ago, I stood in the ashes of their home. There's nothing left. No trace of their bodies."

Julius lifted Ambrosia's chin, forcing her to look in his eyes.

"They were burned alive. Have you no respect for the dead?"

Ambrosia's eye twitched. Her face was no longer defiant. When she spoke again, her voice sounded small.

"I never hated them, you know. I am sorry they are dead."

Julius closed his eyes, shaking his head and stepping away from his sister.

"You were never meant to be with a mortal," she said. "No god is. That is the law. Father had to keep the law, and so did I. It is a wonder that Father did not physically restrain you from contacting the mortal these last three years."

"And you wish that he had?"

Ambrosia crossed her arms, letting her silence show that she would have liked nothing more.

Julius closed his eyes and ran a hand over his short black hair. White light shone through his eyelids as electricity rippled across the sky.

"That's the law, is it? No involvement with mortals?"

"That is the law. The Pantheon strictly forbids relations between the gods and men. Demigods are dangerous and unpredictable." Ambrosia brushed a strand of hair behind her ear. "I am sorry for your loss, brother. But if you had kept the law, none of this would have happened."

Julius glared at his sister, who had approached him warily.

"We are all under the law of the Pantheon, Julius. The law laid down by the First Gods. That is why Father would not consent to let the human come into the Tower. Gods and mortals are not allowed to mate."

"To mate?" Julius's voice betrayed the slightest tremor. "To *mate*? How vulgar. It speaks nothing of love."

"Love? With a mortal?"

"You could not understand."

"No. I could not." Ambrosia raised her head proudly. "Never with an inferior creature."

Julius clenched his jaw. He walked back up the dais and stood against the window. He watched the lightning dance across the dark storm clouds.

"Fine," he said.

"'Fine' what?" Ambrosia walked up after him, her sandals slapping against the marble steps.

"I will no longer involve myself with humans."

"Very good." Ambrosia nodded. "Then I am sure—"

"Wait." Julius held up a finger. "Let me finish."

Ambrosia frowned, confused.

"I will not concern myself with mankind. At all."

"Julius..." Ambrosia rolled her eyes. "What are you talking—"

"No, listen to me!" Julius yelled, lightning flashing in the skies behind him. "I will not intervene in the affairs of men. Let the rain fall where it will. Let them grow their own crops and fight their own wars. Let them heal their own sick and answer their own prayers."

"If that is your attitude, then it is a good thing you are not the God of Gods."

"But I may be someday." Julius held up a finger. "And on that day, it will be your fault that the humans pray for deliverance and find silence instead."

"Julius, listen to yourself! Do you not know what happened tonight? The humans have started their wars again. Bombers from Teuten attacked the country of Viras. Two thousand Virans were killed—most of them children. Schools, hospitals, homes— all destroyed. And this is only the beginning. Now is not the time to withdraw from humanity! Not for you or any of us!"

Julius shrugged. "You should have thought about that. I've made my decision."

"You are a fool!"

"Remember your place!"

"I am your older sister!"

"And I am heir to the throne! I rule the skies!" Julius bellowed. Thunder boomed at his words. "And I will follow the law. I will not involve myself with mortals."

"This is not following the law." Ambrosia poked him in the chest. "This is immaturity. Are you going to pout and leave the humans to their own devices?"

"How dare you touch me like that." Julius grabbed for Ambrosia, but she slapped his hand aside. She squared her shoulders and turned up her chin in defiance, daring him to strike again.

Julius considered her for a moment. Then he sneered. "I have spoken. Leave me."

Ambrosia walked down the stairs, her robes shining in her fury. She strode down the long white carpet and stopped at the golden throne room doors, which had been left untouched by Julius's rage.

"You may have spoken," Ambrosia opened one of the doors and glared at her brother, "but your word counts for little until you are the God of Gods. And for the sake of Mithris, I hope that day never comes."

Before Julius could respond, a tall, gray-haired god in white robes burst through the door and almost knocked Ambrosia over.

"My lady—I'm sorry." The god caught Ambrosia before she lost her balance. He helped Ambrosia steady herself, then looked around in a panic until he spotted Julius.

"Nikolas, what's wrong?" Julius hurried down the dais, alarmed at the god's frantic expression.

Nikolas dropped to both knees in a bow. "My lord!"

Julius hesitated. "Why do you prostrate yourself like this?"

Nikolas's lip trembled, but he kept his voice steady as he met Julius's eyes.

"Your father, the Great Aurelius, has passed away." Nikolas held his right fist to his chest in a salute. "All hail Julius, God of Gods, Ruler of Mithris!"

CHAPTER 1:
THE GIRL WHO FELL FROM THE SKY

Serena screamed as the figure hurtled toward the ground. Through the windshield, she watched the red and yellow form drop from the evening sky. Serena sped up to the spot where the unfortunate person would probably land—and she almost hit the black car racing in the other direction.

She swerved off the road to avoid the other car, which was speeding in her lane.

"Hey!" Serena sounded her horn. She shot a furious look at the black car in her rearview mirror. In the reflection, she watched the vehicle peel out of sight.

Serena swore at the driver under her breath. Her blue eyes flashed angrily underneath brown hair. Then she turned her attention back to the horrifying spectacle in the sky.

She could make out the figure now. A girl was holding onto a red umbrella, trying desperately to slow her rapid descent to the earth. Her body swayed violently, back and forth, as she attempted to lessen the blow of the inevitable impact.

Serena swore again, out of shock, as the girl crashed into a field of sunflowers beside the highway. Her stomach twisting with anxiety, Serena pulled over to the side of the road and threw her seatbelt off. She stumbled out of the station wagon, feeling nauseous, expecting to see a bloody mess when she found the girl's body.

Pushing aside the tall sunflowers, Serena reached a clearing in the grass where the girl had landed. She was dead or unconscious, but at least she was still...intact.

Serena vomited, shuddering involuntarily, relieving herself of the tension that had built up inside of her. Her knees shook and her eyes were watery. She pushed her long brown hair out of her face and wiped her mouth with the sleeve of her black cardigan.

Serena didn't know what had happened.

Was it an airshow stunt? she thought.

She arched her neck and looked for any sign of a plane. The darkening skies were empty, save for the wispy clouds reflecting the sunset. A breeze blew past her. She rubbed her shoulders against the cold.

Shielding her eyes with her hand, Serena looked at the highway, trying to see if the black car was still anywhere to be seen. The tall sunflowers blocked her view of the road.

Serena knelt beside the girl and bent over her mouth to see if she was breathing. A light flutter of air brushed against her ear. Relief flooded Serena's body. The girl was alive. Serena took a heavy, grateful breath.

The girl, who was lying quite still, wore a yellow raincoat, blue jeans, and shocking white rain boots. She looked about fourteen, and her flaming red hair was strewn across her face. Her right hand was clutching a red umbrella with a crook handle. The canopy was torn in places, and the end was slightly bent.

Serena noticed a small leather-bound book lying next to her. A journal. The smooth brown cover was decorated with a golden bird sitting in what looked like a nest. By some trick of the light, the bird seemed to be shedding feathers. She tried to open it and check for identification, but the journal was sealed by a small golden lock.

The girl's left arm lay across her chest, a golden watch on her wrist. Serena gently raised the girl's arm and checked the time, but she couldn't make it out. The clock was scrambled in a maze of numbers and hands.

Serena took the girl's wrist to feel her pulse. A vein throbbed faintly underneath Serena's forefinger.

The girl opened her eyes and jerked upward, almost hitting Serena in the face.

Serena stumbled back. "Oh my gosh! Are you okay? You fell—" She held her hand up to her mouth, trying to compose herself. "I don't know how you're still alive. What happened?"

The girl stared at Serena with wide, green eyes. She pushed herself up onto elbows.

"It's you?"

Serena frowned. "What?"

"It's you! I knew it was." The girl's face relaxed with—what was it? Relief? Recognition?

"Of course it's me." Serena patted her hand reassuringly while a knot of anxiety twisted in her gut. She had never seen this girl before.

A faint smile started at the corner of the girl's mouth.

Suddenly, the girl put her hand inside her raincoat, searching frantically for something in a hidden chest pocket. She tried both sides of her coat, breathing heavily, her eyes wide.

Serena stood to give the girl some room to breathe. "Is something wrong?"

The girl moaned, turning out pockets and grabbing at the dirt around her.

"What are you looking for?" Serena saw the journal lying behind her. "Oh! Is this it?"

She held out the journal to the girl, who shuddered in relief. The girl took the journal with trembling hands and held it close. Then she placed it carefully inside her coat.

Her chest rose and fell as she tried to calm down and control her breathing. She looked at her watch and frowned. She winced at her damaged umbrella.

Serena knelt in front of the girl. "Who are you?"

The girl shook her head and clutched her umbrella tightly.

"Not now. We're not safe yet." She looked at Serena. "You're being followed."

"Followed? We're out in the country. There's hardly anyone around."

"Trust me. If I can find you, they can too." The girl tried to get up on her knee but collapsed to the ground with a yelp of pain.

Serena reached forward to support her. "Sweetie, I think you need to lie still."

"No." The girl shook her head again. "We need to go now. Help me up, please."

Serena put her arm around the girl's shoulder and helped her stand. The girl's body felt thin and light, but none of her bones appeared to be broken.

They walked through the sunflowers, Serena pushing aside tall stalks with her free arm. When they reached the road, the girl narrowed her eyes grimly and pointed down the highway.

Serena followed her gaze to see a black car off in the distance. It was the same one that had nearly hit her. The car was parked on the road, an ominous silhouette against the horizon.

"Probably waiting until nightfall. They move faster under cover of darkness," the girl muttered. Serena helped her to the passenger door. "He used the car because he was tracking you in the daylight. And now he's weighing his chances."

"Whose chances?" Serena felt a mixture of fear and frustration boiling inside of her. She glanced nervously back at the car.

11

The girl didn't answer. She just nodded gratefully as Serena settled her into the passenger seat.

"We need to get you some medical attention," Serena said. "There are some towns nearby." She opened her door and sat down. "Where were you heading anyway?"

"To Locke City before I found you. But I don't think I'll be flying there anytime soon." The girl patted her umbrella with a wry smile. "That landing was rough. Those crosswinds have it in for me."

Serena stared at the girl. "You were flying your umbrella to the city?" She started the engine. "How? From a plane?"

The girl waved her hand dismissively.

"No planes. I just need an umbrella." She closed her eyes and leaned back into her seat. "I've always preferred umbrellas. They're so stylish."

Serena accelerated the station wagon to seventy miles per hour, wondering how much head trauma the girl had suffered from her crash. Checking her rearview mirror, Serena could see the black car off in the distance. It was matching their speed.

The sun set, bathing the fields in red and orange, illuminating abandoned oil pumpjacks. But the black car's windshield did not reflect the light.

"We really shouldn't be caught out at night," the girl mutter softly, staring out the window. "I'm so tired."

For a few minutes, both girls were silent, and nothing could be heard but the whirr of the engine and the hum of the tires. Serena felt sick again from nervousness.

"I don't understand." She swallowed. "What does that car want with us?"

When the girl didn't respond, Serena turned to see that her head was resting against the window.

She had fallen asleep, her hands still clutching the umbrella to her chest.

*

Serena fought to stay awake. Night had enveloped the world. The car headlights revealed dead grass and bushes on the edges of the lonely highway. Yellow lane divisions flew past underneath her.

From what Serena could tell from her map, the small town of Honeycomb was only a few miles away. They could stay there for the night. Maybe the girl could get medical attention. Serena couldn't tell if she was injured or not, but something had to be wrong. Normal people didn't just survive falls from the sky without a...without...

Serena nodded and then blinked furiously, shaking her tired head. Her eyes were watery from trying to keep them open.

She looked over at her sleeping passenger, who was resting against the window, motionless.

What a strange kid, dressed in a raincoat and rain boots, falling from the sky. Even in her sleep, the girl was holding her umbrella tightly.

Serena glanced in her rearview mirror to see if the black car was still following them. It had disappeared with nightfall, perhaps breaking off the pursuit. Or maybe it was still out there, trailing them with its headlights off.

Fear crawled up her spine. The hair stood up on the back of her neck. Serena shivered involuntarily, wishing that she had more answers about the girl and the black car.

She yawned. Her eyelids were so heavy. If she could only close them for a minute, just to relax the strain.

There. Just rest for a bit...

Serena woke up when something hard hit her on the shoulder. She shook her head, unaware of where she was.

Movement...highway...car...

Someone was yelling.

In her ear.

Her eyes shot open and panic seized her.

"Oh gods!" She grabbed the wheel tightly.

The girl continued to yell. "Speed up! He's right next to us! I can't believe I fell asleep—I can't believe *you* fell asleep!"

Serena wiped her eyes with her hand and brushed her brown hair out of her face. Her mind was racing with questions, but she obeyed the girl and floored the pedal to ninety. The car shook, struggling under the sudden acceleration.

Telephone poles flew by on the passenger side—too close for comfort. She had drifted onto the shoulder of the road. She glanced to her left and saw a dark shape moving alongside them, matching their speed, neck to neck.

The black car.

The glare from Serena's headlights illuminated the front of the car. Its passenger window was right next to Serena's. She swallowed and looked across—

—and there was no driver.

Darkness swirled inside the empty car.

Serena blinked. Was she still asleep?

The girl was still yelling.

"Drive faster! Don't give him any time to come in!"

"Come in? What are you—" Serena shuddered. She felt cold breath, like a finger, touch her cheek and trail down her neck. It caressed her, dulling her senses, feeling her skin down to the shoulder...

Black mist swirled in front of her eyes. A warning siren blared in her brain, trying desperately to rouse her defenses, but the alarm was overwhelmed by a pleasurable sensation of numbness.

She should just relax.

Visions entered her mind. She saw a woman sitting at a kitchen table. Her smile was familiar. The woman put down her glasses and opened her arms to give Serena a hug.

Let go...

Serena was falling through the air. She was free of all anxiety and fear. The touch, whatever it was, didn't feel cold anymore. It felt warm and soft, pressing against her brain until she couldn't feel anything at all...

A voice screamed in her ear.

"Over my dead body! Get out of here!"

Serena was thrown back into her seat and her car accelerated to speeds unknown. The mercurial hand was ripped away from her, and Serena missed its soothing touch...

An uncomfortable weight fell across her chest.

She opened an eye to see the girl clutching the steering wheel with one hand and holding her umbrella with the other. The point of the umbrella glowed on top of the dashboard.

Serena blinked, staring at the speedometer—the needle was struggling past one hundred twenty miles per hour. Serena thought about warning the girl, but she seemed to have everything under control. With the girl driving, Serena could just close her eyes and sleep...

"Don't worry, Serena," the girl said reassuringly. "I can see the lights of the town. We should be safe there."

Serena leaned against the window, feeling her cold, pale skin against the glass. Her face was covered in sweat. Just before she lost consciousness, she saw the bright lights of the town through her eyelids.

Her mind tumbled into darkness, images and questions swirling around in her head...hadn't the girl just used her name? But Serena had never mentioned it...

CHAPTER 2:
THE HONEYCOMB HOTEL

When Serena woke up, she felt pleasantly warm underneath a quilt on a large bed. She opened her eyes to stare at a plain white ceiling, trying to remember where she was.

She rolled onto her left side, where green curtains were drawn over a window. The curtains had a yellow floral design that repeated across her field of vision, making her dizzy.

Serena sat up on her elbows, and the bed-springs creaked in response. She looked around the dimly-lit room with bleary eyes. A round analog clock hung on the wall above a television set, which was set on a polished wooden dresser.

"Where am I? What time is it?" She yawned, rubbing her eyes. The question was to no one in particular, and Serena was surprised when a voice responded.

"You're at the Honeycomb Hotel. It's about four in the afternoon. You slept a lot."

Serena gave a little scream. She grabbed the covers and held them up to her face. A red-haired girl was sitting on the bed to her right, writing in a journal. She was wearing blue jeans, a pink t-shirt, and a kind smile.

Serena eyed the girl warily.

Who was that?

Then she saw an umbrella leaning against a chair. A yellow raincoat was draped over it—

"Hey! You're that girl!" Serena pointed dramatically, raising her voice. The girl seemed taken aback.

"Yes, I'm the girl." She closed her journal and set it on the bedside table. Then she put her hands in her lap and raised her eyebrows expectantly, as if waiting for more questions.

Serena suddenly felt foolish for pointing at the girl and yelling. After all, the girl had driven them to safety, found a hotel room, and let her rest. Serena blushed. She cleared her throat and put her hands under the quilt.

"You're the girl who fell from the sky," Serena said. "And then there was the black car—with no driver! And that terrible hand..." She shuddered, feeling cold in spite of the heavy blankets.

The girl nodded gravely.

"Yes. The Dark Angel. He tried to kill you."

Serena looked up, wondering if she had misheard. "Dark Angel?"

"Yes, a Dark Angel. 'Demon' is a more appropriate word, but I didn't invent the name. Either way, it was sent to kill you. I don't know when it started following you, but someone found out that you're alive, and they want you dead."

Serena shook her head, laughing in spite of the tension building inside of her chest.

"No, sorry. You've got the wrong girl. I haven't done anything wrong, and nobody wants me dead." Serena wrung her sweaty hands underneath the quilt. "What's a Dark Angel anyway? Is this some kind of mob?"

"No, it's not a mob," the girl said softly. "And you know that it wasn't a human in the other car. The Dark Angel disappeared into a mist and came through the window. It tried to enter your mind and kill you. It almost did, but..." She sniffed knowingly and allowed herself a small smile. "Me and my trusty umbrella were here to protect you."

"I see." Serena raised an eyebrow. "And what are you supposed to be?"

"I'm a guardian." The girl smiled, squeezing her shoulders together happily. "Specifically, I'm a Phoenix Guardian."

"Phoenix?"

"It's a bird."

"You protect birds?" Serena squinted, confused.

"Not really, no." The girl furrowed her brow, equally confused.

This is stupid, Serena thought, feeling hot and uncomfortable underneath the quilt.

Something frightening had certainly happened last night, but there had to be a natural explanation for it. Chemicals in the sunflowers messing with her mind, fatigue from the drive—something, anything but this stupid story. She had fallen asleep after all. Maybe it was a dream?

Or maybe she did something to me. Serena shot a suspicious glance at the girl, who smiled pleasantly.

Was the girl dangerous? Had Serena been drugged and kidnapped?

18

Serena's eyes widened with horror. She immediately reached under her white shirt to touch her stomach, groping to feel any scars or bandages.

"What did you do to me? Did you steal my kidneys?" Serena asked hysterically.

The girl snorted, trying unsuccessfully to stifle a laugh. She quickly composed herself when she saw the horror etched across Serena's face.

"I don't want your kidneys." The girl leaned forward, her expression sober. "All that I've 'done to you' is save you from the Dark Angel, rent a hotel room—with my own money," she sat up proudly, "and let you sleep in really late."

She drew her legs up onto the bed and crossed them.

"I hope we can be friends." The girl smiled, her green eyes twinkling.

Serena shook her head, still confused. "And who are you, exactly?"

"Oh!" The girl slapped her forehead. "How rude of me not to introduce myself. My name is Natalie Bliss, and I've been sent to protect you, and to help your Negligent Gods and Struggling Planet."

Serena blinked, examining Natalie's face for signs of a joke.

"My negligent what?"

"Negligent Gods and Struggling Planet. That's part of my job description. I would give you a business card, but I left them all in my other raincoat."

"Gods? You're serious?" Serena snorted. "There aren't any gods—and if there are, then they're dead or asleep. Don't you know about the war? It's been tearing the world apart for years. Where have you been?"

"Where have I been?" Natalie scooted back on the bed, letting her legs dangle over the edge. Serena noticed her mismatched striped socks: yellow and pink. "I've been in the Beyond. And I've heard all about the war. That's where the *Negligent* Gods and *Struggling* Planet come in." She sighed. "Your gods have neglected the affairs of your world for too long. The Pantheon decided enough was enough, so they sent me to take care of things. I can tell you, it's not as bad as some planets I've been to, but—"

"Listen, kid, I don't mean to step on your religion or anything, but I don't care about your gods or your Beyond. But I do want to know how you knew my name last night."

Natalie leaned forward, pausing for dramatic effect.

19

"You're important."

"Important?" Serena made a face. "To who?"

"To whom." Natalie corrected her. "You're important to a lot of people. You have a vital role to play in the survival of this world."

"Oh, back to the gods again? What do they need? A virgin sacrifice?" Serena laughed again. "Are they going to throw me into a volcano?"

Natalie crossed her arms reproachfully. "Of course not."

"So you're on some kind of mission from the Great Beyond to stop a war and save a planet—but not to sacrifice a virgin, correct?"

"Something like that." Natalie nodded. "I'm also here to protect you."

"Naturally, because you're a bird-guardian. And let's see, you came to this planet on that thing." Serena nodded toward the umbrella.

"Actually, I took the trolley until I reached Mithris."

"Ah, right. You took the trolley across the universe, and then you floated down to earth, where you had a rough landing and found me. Then you already knew my name because—the gods told you?"

"Basically."

"Then you saved my life from a poorly-named demon?"

"I did."

"That just about makes you the nicest, weirdest stranger I've ever met."

Natalie cleared her throat. "I'm not sure how I should take that—"

"Oh, and another really good question." Serena rested her chin on her hand. "Even if I believed your mission was to protect me, how did you find me? It's a big planet."

"Not as big as others. And it's not as if I didn't know what country you were in." Natalie rolled her eyes. "I'm pretty good at finding what I'm looking for."

Serena glared at Natalie. "I'm not buying that. This country is huge. You fell from the sky and found me on the first go?"

"Let's just say you're a special person with an indefinable something." Natalie crossed her arms. "I was drawn to you—much like the Dark Angel, actually—but with entirely different motives. I can't say any more right now. You just have to trust me."

Serena gave Natalie a skeptical look. Her voice dripped with sarcasm.

"So after this magical attraction brought you to me, you just happened to recognize me."

"Yep." Natalie smiled defiantly.

Serena frowned. "How?"

Natalie winked. "It's that indefinable something."

"Girl, you expect me to believe that?" Serena screamed, her anxiety boiling over again. "You fell from the sky and recognized me because of my indefinable something?" Serena sat up and pointed an accusing finger at Natalie. "What are you supposed to be, anyway? A fireman with an umbrella?"

Natalie giggled.

"That's funny—a fireman with an umbrella. I've actually never heard that one before."

Serena didn't laugh. She closed her eyes, trying to soothe her nerves, breathing in through her nose and out through her mouth.

"Look," Natalie said softly. "Even if you don't believe me, you have to acknowledge that I've taken pretty good care of you so far. So at least I'm not dangerous, right? You can trust me."

Serena opened an eye and shot a dirty look at Natalie. She glanced at the red umbrella.

Dangerous? Maybe not.

Crazy? Absolutely.

And was it dangerous to be crazy? Probably.

Then Serena's stomach growled and she realized that she hadn't eaten all day.

"I'm hungry. I'm getting something to eat, and then I'm getting back on the road."

"Sounds like a plan." Natalie plopped down on the floor next to the bed and pulled on her white rain boots.

Serena began to get out of bed, and she realized for the first time that she was still wearing her shoes. She had slept in them. Gross.

Natalie caught the look of disgust on her face as Serena set her feet on the floor.

"I would have taken your shoes off when I put you in bed and tucked you in." Natalie looked apologetic. "But I thought that might be weird."

CHAPTER 3:
CLOTTED CREAM AND HOUSE RULES

The restaurant of the Honeycomb Hotel was on the first floor. An elaborate sign, "The Tea Garden," was written in green letters that wrapped around each other like vines. There were poorly-painted impressions of dandelions in the "a's" of the name.

Serena and Natalie waited by the entrance of the restaurant, obeying the "Please Wait to Be Seated" placard for five minutes as Natalie unsuccessfully attempted to wave down a waitress. Finally, Serena stepped inside the rectangular, green-walled room and dragged a round table toward her, plopping down on one of the high-backed spindly chairs.

Natalie sat down gracefully next to Serena, holding her umbrella in front of her with the point facing the ground. She smiled pleasantly at the white-haired waitress who approached the table. The lady scowled at Natalie, threw two menus on the table, and withdrew to a door at the far end of the café.

"Good afternoon." Natalie raised her voice at the waitress's retreating back.

The only other customers were two elderly ladies sitting at the far end of the restaurant. They looked at Natalie, sizing her up and down, and were clearly disappointed by what they saw. After sharing a knowing look with each other, they sniffed loudly and resumed their meal.

Natalie shrugged and turned around to watch the barista making drinks. This lady was younger, with olive-skin and black hair. The barista shared the waitress's haughty attitude, and she was determinedly avoiding eye contact with Natalie.

"Nice place." Natalie raised her eyebrows, perusing the thin white menu in front of her. "Do you come here often?"

"No." Serena picked up her own menu, curling her lip at the excessive prices. "Actually, this is my first time away from Locke City."

"I see." Natalie smiled kindly. "So why did you leave?"

"I've been there long enough. And there are too many people."

"Is it a nice city?"

"I don't think so." Serena glared at Natalie from over the top of her menu. "That's why I left."

"Oh, right. That is, after all, what you just said." Natalie buried her face in her own menu. "Now, what is 'clotted cream'? It sounds like milk from a cow with high cholesterol."

"Um..." Serena said, at a loss for words.

The barista snorted in derision.

Serena blushed. "You know what, how about I just order for us?"

Serena heard the click-clack of the waitress's high heels approaching. She quickly took Natalie's menu.

"What? But I thought you've never been here before." Natalie reached across the table to retrieve her menu, but Serena held it away from her.

"Don't worry, I can order—yes, we're ready, thank you." Serena smiled at the grim-faced waitress, who tapped a pad expectantly with her pen. "I'd like to order two scones—and could we split a pot of tea? Please?" She widened her smile in an effort to look more endearing.

If possible, the waitress's frown fell even further, impressing Serena with her mastery of facial muscles.

"No, you cannot split a pot of tea." The old lady's jaw was set. "That is against house rules. If you don't like house rules, then you may leave." The thought seemed to cheer the waitress up, and she smiled pleasantly for the first time.

Serena's face turned a bright crimson. Her hair bristled indignantly.

"Fine, then we most certainly will leave!" Natalie tossed her red hair behind her head and made to stand.

"No, we're not leaving." Serena narrowed her eyes, breathing heavily through her nose. She would not back down from a battle of wills.

"Fine, then we most certainly will *not* leave." Natalie settled herself back into her seat. She turned up her nose and crossed her legs to demonstrate her immovability.

"We'd like two pots of tea and two scones." Serena forced a smile, aided by a vision of the waitress falling stupidly down a flight of stairs.

Natalie closed her eyes and shook her head resolutely. "I don't want anything."

"You have to order something. It's a house rule." The waitress glared at Natalie.

"Then...I guess we'll have two pots of tea and two scones." Natalie cleared her throat. "Like my friend said."

"Wonderful. That will be right out for you." The waitress's smile turned to a grimace, making her look like she had appendicitis.

Serena checked her teeth for elongated canines—maybe she was a vampire. But the lady turned around too fast for Serena to see clearly.

Noise from the hotel lobby caught Serena's attention. Someone had raised the volume on the television. It was a news broadcast. Serena turned in her seat to see a well-dressed young man in a blue suit reading a paper.

"...fighting continues today in the ruins of Sydney as Viran insurgents launched a surprised rocket attack on a Teuten military base. The Teuten forces were temporarily overrun as the Virans raided their supplies for food and medicine."

Serena heard Natalie readjust her chair in an effort to see the television more clearly.

"Embedded reporter Edward Bridges has said that the Viran fighters have become bolder as the month has progressed, trying to get food for their countrymen outside of Sydney. Since the Teutens occupied Sydney in the spring, Viran refugees have been without food or clean water. Most are suffering from dysentery and starvation. The death toll has escalated well into the thousands."

The waitress reappeared with their food, distracting Serena from the broadcast. The old lady gently placed the two tea pots in the center of the table, setting a plate with a scone in front of each girl.

"You threw those menus on the table." Serena made sure that her mumble was loud enough for the waitress to hear. "Not so rough with that silverware, now are you?"

"This silverware is very valuable." The waitress sniffed loudly. "You girls had better take special care with it. I would have poured the tea in plastic cups instead of our nice china, but that's against house rules."

Serena ignored her, picking up her teapot and filling her cup. The waitress walked away without another word.

Serena glanced at Natalie. "You do know how to drink tea, right?"

"Of course I do." Natalie sat up straight, indignant. "Why in the world would you think that I didn't know how to drink tea?"

"I don't know." Serena shrugged. "You fell from the sky and banged your head, you carry an umbrella everywhere, and you didn't know what clotted cream was." She scooped some sugar into her tea and stirred with her spoon. "I just wanted to make sure you knew how to drink tea."

"Well, thank you for the concern, but I know how to drink tea." Natalie dropped her voice. "It can't be that hard."

She poured a cup of tea and drank it directly—sticking out her tongue in disgust after tasting the brown liquid. Natalie closed her eyes, shaking her head and smacking her lips to rid her palate of the flavor. Then she promptly began scooping liberal amounts of sugar into her cup.

Serena broke off a piece of her scone and buttered it, sighing irritably at Natalie's antics.

"Teuten is bad news." Natalie nodded toward the television in the lobby. "If Viras is conquered, I don't see what will stop them from invading Artema. Your country will be in terrible danger."

"But Artema is a neutral country. Why would Teuten attack here?" Serena took a sip of tea. "And why do you know about the war anyway?"

"Why wouldn't I know about the war?" Natalie narrowed her eyes. "If I'm not from the Beyond, then I'm probably just a local, right? In that case, I would keep up with the news like everyone else. Or perhaps you're starting to believe my story—in which case I already told you how I know."

Serena ignored Natalie's comments. "The Teuten political leaders are scum, but they're not stupid. There's nothing to gain from attacking Artema."

"I don't know about that." Natalie cut her scone in half and spread butter on both pieces. "Gandia has always eyed Artema's agricultural base. There's a lot of oil here too. I wouldn't be surprised if Gandia and Teuten joined forces to attack Artema. Those two countries have always had good relations. We have to hope that Viras will hold out, but we need to be ready if they fall."

Serena shot a look at Natalie, irritated that this strange girl would lecture her on the politics of her world.

She shook her head in annoyance at that rogue thought: *her* world?

No, *their* world. They were from the same one.

"I don't think Viras will last much longer." Natalie stared into space, stirring her tea thoughtfully with her spoon. "It's only a matter of time before Artema is invaded. That's why we have to get our work done quickly." She checked her watch. "Each day, we're running out of time."

Natalie picked up her teapot to pour more tea, but it was empty.

"Wow. That was fast." She opened the lid and leaned over the table to look inside the pot. "Never have so many spent so much on so little."

"Don't worry." Serena stood. "I got the check."

"Aw, thanks." Natalie pushed away from the table and picked up her umbrella, tucking it under her arm. "Does this mean we're becoming friends?"

"No." Serena turned from Natalie and stared at the back of the tea barista, who looked busy mixing a drink, even though the other customers had already left.

"Hey." Serena reached over the counter and tugged on the back of the barista's shirt. She turned and shot Serena a look of utmost annoyance.

Serena matched her gaze. "The tea had no flavor and the scones were too dry. But I have to pay anyway so I'd like to get it over with."

The barista exhaled deeply through her nostrils but said nothing. She tapped the keys on the cash register—a bit harder than necessary. She slid two receipts across the counter to Serena, who shook her head.

"It's on one tab."

The barista scowled. "But I already printed out two."

"Then print out a third." Serena leaned on the bar and rested her chin on her elbow, daring her to argue.

The barista huffed and puffed, but she combined the bills and printed a third check. Serena reached into her pocket, pulled out her smallest denominations of coins, and placed them on the counter one by one.

When Serena was through paying the bill and antagonizing the barista, the girls left the Tea Garden, no longer hungry, but full of righteous indignation at their poor treatment.

Serena stopped at the foot of the staircase.

"Just out of curiosity, how are you getting to Locke City?" she asked.

"By car, of course."

"Well, have a good time. It was weird meeting you." She started up the stairs. "Be careful who you hitchhike with."

"Wait a minute!" Natalie stood on the first step and held onto the railing. "I meant *your* car. I need you to come with me, don't you remember? I'm on an important mission."

"I just *left* Locke City. And you know what else?" Serena spoke quickly, her voice getting sharper with each word. "I think you're crazy, and I don't care about your mission. I don't even like this world. People are trouble. You're trouble—you fell from the sky and I almost died last night!"

Natalie looked mildly impressed at the rate of words Serena had just achieved. Serena marched up to the landing, leaving Natalie at the foot of the stairs. The red-haired girl ran up after her.

"Well, I saved your life too!" Natalie took the stairs two steps at a time to catch up with Serena. "I rescued you from the Dark Angel—and how do you explain him if I'm not telling the truth about my mission?"

"The truth about your mission is that I don't care." Serena glanced over her shoulder.

"No, wait!" Natalie hurried after her. "Of course you care about people. You pulled over to the side of the road and helped me."

"A decision I regret every minute."

Natalie stomped her foot in frustration. "Look, you're just being rude. You do care about people, somewhere deep down inside—"

"What are you, a psychologist?"

"—and this war has got to stop! The fighting is spreading, and your country is going to fall into it sooner or later. People are dying every day. I'm trying to end this war and I need your help."

"You're not ending the war, you're not a good psychologist, and you're not stopping me from driving away." Serena unlocked their room and stepped inside. "You're a little girl. A strange girl—I will give you that—but a little girl."

Natalie straightened up and squared her shoulders. "I'm older than I look!"

"That would place you at what? Fourteen? Fifteen?" Serena snorted. "So at *least* three years younger than me. Like I said, a little girl."

Natalie dropped onto her bed and crossed her arms angrily. But Serena didn't notice because she was scanning the room for her possessions.

"Where did you put my travel bag?" Serena lifted her blankets and felt along the sheets.

"In the bathroom." Natalie nodded over her shoulder. "And you've seen enough to know that I'm more than just a little girl. I have a lot of work to get done, and we're wasting time. I need you to come with me to Locke City. Do you understand?"

Serena disappeared around a corner, her voice echoing in the bathroom.

"I'm not coming—do *you* understand? What's so important about Locke City anyway? Can't you save the world from the Honeycomb Hotel?"

"Locke City is where the gods are."

"Right, in their fancy skyscraper."

"The Tower of the Gods, yes." Natalie brought her knees up to her chest, holding them tightly as she listened to Serena gather her things in the bathroom.

She looked at the analog clock on the wall. It was already six. Then she checked her golden watch, reading the myriad of hands and spinning numbers.

She was running out of time.

"Serena, you have to come back with me!"

"No, I don't." Serena opened the door, holding her travel bag in one hand. "In fact, I'm leaving right now, and I'm going farther away from Locke City, its people, and its troubles."

"Fine." Natalie stood. "Then I'm going with you until you come back with me to Locke City."

"How are you coming with me?" Serena started to close the door and Natalie hurried into the hall. "I'm not going to drive you. I don't even know you. You just fell from the sky."

"Yeah, but I took care of you. You're safer with me." Natalie walked down the stairs after her. "Besides, you still can't deny that you were attacked by something supernatural, and there are more Dark Angels out there. I can guarantee that."

Serena opened her mouth to argue, but then she just scowled. They walked out of the hotel in silence.

Natalie followed Serena all the way to the street, stopping next to the passenger door of her brown station wagon. Serena stood by the driver side, chewing her lip and watching the sun fall to the horizon. She shot an irritated look at Natalie and then opened the driver side door.

A smile blossomed on Natalie's face when she realized that Serena hadn't sent her away yet.

"So, can I come with you?"

Serena's lips were thin, but she did not protest when Natalie opened her door and took a seat.

"Excellent!" Natalie leaned her umbrella against the glove compartment. She clapped excitedly. "The road trip continues!"

Serena ran her hand over the dashboard. There was a dent on it where Natalie had put her umbrella the night before.

"What is this?" Serena slapped the edge of the concave hole.

"Oh." Natalie folded her hands in front of her. "That happened last night when I sped up the car to escape from the Dark Angel. My umbrella has been a bit temperamental since the fall." She lifted the umbrella and tapped the bent tip with her rain boot. "It's nothing to worry about though."

Serena turned her key in the ignition, shaking her head.

"All I know is that you'll be walking if you set my car on fire."

"I said don't worry. This umbrella won't cause any problems." Natalie swallowed and lowered her voice. "I hope."

CHAPTER 4:
NEGLIGENT GODS
AND A STRUGGLING PLANET

"Julius, the gods are all here. The Council has assembled."

Julius turned away from the wide circular window to see Ambrosia standing behind him. He acknowledged her presence with a grunt, and then he returned his attention to the skyline below.

The setting sun peered out from between the sprawling skyscrapers of Locke City. Red sky faded to a murky purple. The moon shone overhead.

The Tower of the Gods stood at the very center of the city, which was on the eastern edge of Artema. Visible only to divine beings, the Tower was enchanted to prevent mortals from flying or walking into the building. Birds and bugs avoided it by instinct, dissuaded by its supernatural power. The massive skyscraper stood in a vacant lot next to the capitol, but humans never gave the building a second thought, accustomed as they were to the presumably wasted space.

Julius stared down at the humans that scurried about the base of the Tower, over a hundred stories below. The miniscule humans lived, worked, and died beneath Julius's feet. He was the God of Gods. What was a human to him?

And yet the memory of two humans still held his heart captive. His right eye twitched at the thought.

"Julius, we need to go now." Ambrosia's voice rang with irritation. She had climbed the marble steps of the dais to stand at his side. "The gods are waiting. They have travelled far for the Assembly. There are pressing matters to discuss."

Julius was silent for a minute. His voice was low when he finally responded.

"I despise the Assembly."

Ambrosia closed her eyes in frustration.

31

"We go through this every year. You have to attend. It is your duty." She crossed her arms. "Not that you have been performing it."

Julius shot his sister a look of annoyance.

"And what's that supposed to mean?"

"That you have neglected to intervene in the affairs of men for the entire fifteen years of your rule."

"I'm a god. What does fifteen years mean to me?"

"Nothing to you, but a lot in the lives of men. Your pouting has cost the humans. Mithris is embroiled in war and they need guidance and protection. Do you not hear the prayers of refugees? Of the dying? Do they not cry out to you?"

Julius flinched for a brief second, but then he turned his back to Ambrosia.

"The pleas of mortals do not touch me. I have nothing to do with them. And why do you care? Humans have never mattered to you."

Ambrosia rolled her eyes. "Julius, that is a lie."

"Are you calling me a liar?"

"Do not try to intimidate me, dear brother." Ambrosia scowled. "You are being ridiculous. You know I care about the humans."

"You said they were inferior creatures."

"Of course they are inferior." Ambrosia raised her voice. "We are the gods—we are the masters, and they are the servants. They are clay! There is a divide between us and them, between the mortal and the immortal." Her lip curled. "Apparently, you still do not understand that."

Julius shook his head. "I'll tell you what I don't understand. Why do you care about the humans if you think they're so useless—if they're just clay? What does it matter if they live or die?"

"I did not say they were useless. I said they have their place and we have ours. And you would do well to remember that. I care about them as much as you do. I do not want to see them suffer, and thousands of them are dying in this war."

"You're the one who told me not to be involved with them."

"I told you not to mate with a human!"

"Shut your mouth!" Julius's blue eyes flashed. "Don't you ever mention such words in my presence again, do you understand?"

Thunder boomed in the darkening skies.

Ambrosia scoffed. "You are still trying to scare me with pageantry? With loud noises? I am your older sister."

"And I am the God of Gods." Julius pointed at his chest. "It's time you treated me with respect." He accented the last word with another peal of thunder.

"How can I respect you? You are a fool. You are a spoiled brat, stuck with responsibility that you are unwilling to carry—or incapable of carrying."

"You hold your tongue!"

"No, you hold your own tongue!" Ambrosia took a step toward her brother, pointing an accusing finger at him. "Do you even know what is happening in the world? Men, women, and children are being killed by bullets and bombs. Refugees are starving to death. They call out to the gods, but there is no one to answer because the God of Gods has hardened his heart!"

"There is a divide between us and the mortals. You said so yourself."

Ambrosia closed her eyes and shook her head. "All of this because you were denied the woman?"

Julius did not answer. He simply set his jaw and matched his sister's gaze.

Brother and sister glared at each other for a few minutes. Several thunderclaps boomed in the distance, but Ambrosia stood her ground.

"Fine. I can see we are getting nowhere." Ambrosia snorted in disgust. She whipped her hair around her before turning to walk down the dais. "Now come along."

"I hate the Assembly."

"They probably hate you too." Ambrosia glanced at Julius over her shoulder as she walked down the white carpet.

"Then I'll kill them."

"That's the spirit. Show some initiative." Ambrosia stopped at the tall golden doors. "Now come on. You are the God of Gods."

Julius crossed his arms stubbornly.

"Father always attended."

"I'm not our father."

Ambrosia raised an eyebrow. "So I have noticed."

She opened the door. "The Council has been waiting long enough. Come join the Assembly."

Julius watched his sister disappear through the tall golden doors, resenting her haughty tone. What did she mean, "Come join the Assembly"?

He would join when and if he wanted to.

A moment later, he decided that he wanted to, and he walked down the carpet after his older sister.

*

The council room lay beneath the splendor of an enormous dome. A mural spread out on the ceiling, depicting vast galaxies of planets strewn among the stars. The expansive chamber had been filled with terraced seats that rose along the walls on every side. Gods and goddesses clad in togas sat on top of plush red cushions, eating fruit and drinking from golden goblets.

All of the deities' voices mingled together as they commented on each other's togas and shared news about their corners of the world. Some of the gods and goddesses flirted with one another, joking and teasing, their faces flushed with wine. Robed angels walked among them, refilling cups and offering plates of fruit.

When Julius walked into the council room through a tall archway, the gods grew quiet and rose to their feet. Julius strode across the floor to a staircase, which he ascended to take his seat on a high-backed throne overlooking the entire room.

Ambrosia was seated on one side of the throne. On the other side was Nikolas, a tall, gray-haired god with sharp hazel eyes. He bowed low as Julius approached. Ambrosia's bow was little more than a nod.

Julius ignored his sister's coldness, nodding to Nikolas with a gracious smile.

"Good day, Nikolas. How are you, my favorite High Counselor?"

"Well, my lord." Nikolas smiled in return, creasing the wrinkles on his face.

Julius sat down and accepted a goblet of wine from an angel. He leaned over to whisper in Nikolas's ear.

"I absolutely cannot stand these annual sessions. Try and hurry through the ceremonies so the fools can get through their arguing, all right?"

Nikolas's smile widened, and he whispered back to Julius out of the corner of his mouth.

"You're just like your father, my lord. He never could abide the Assembly."

"Strange. Ambrosia was just discussing how unlike we are." Julius cleared his throat before taking a sip of wine. "But may he rest in peace."

"In peace." Nikolas closed his eyes reverently, and then he stood. Any lingering chatter immediately stopped, and the council room fell silent.

"Welcome, my friends, from all of your fair countries, islands, and continents across this world." Nikolas spread his arms wide. "Welcome to this Divine Assembly of the Gods and Goddesses of Mithris."

The council members bowed their heads in respect. Julius waved his hand in mock enthusiasm, and the gods took their seats.

"At this time each year," Nikolas said, "when the summer wanes and autumn draws near, we remember our history. We remember where we came from so we may decide where we should go."

Nikolas turned around and pointed high above Julius's throne to the statue of a god in battle armor, who was armed with an enormous hammer. A lightning bolt was engraved on the hammer's head. Behind the slits of the helmet, the god's fearsome eyes stared down upon the Assembly.

"We remember Aurelius, the father of Lord Julius, and the first ruler of Mithris." Nikolas turned back to the Assembly and raised his hands. The light in the room dimmed. A mist filled the air from his fingertips, forming a cloud of lights and twisting shapes. Images appeared in the nebulous mass—faces of warriors in battle, stars forming and burning out, planets coming into existence from the dust.

"We remember the time before Mithris, ages ago, when the Titans betrayed the First Gods and began the War of Chaos." Nikolas dropped his voice, but his dramatic tone was so captivating that he held the attention of every god in the room.

Even Julius had stopped tracing the design on his goblet to listen to the High Counselor.

Nikolas's eyes were wide, glowing in the light of the ferocious combat that played in the swirling mist.

"The Titans destroyed planets and galaxies, spreading death and destruction everywhere they went. But the First Gods, led by Sol, stood against the Titans, fighting for the very survival of the universe."

He twisted his hands in the air, manipulating the vision so that planets flew about them, spinning and exploding in spectacular bursts of fire.

35

"The cost was high—in the final battle, the Titan Invictus cast many of the First Gods into a deep sleep. To this day, they have yet to awaken. Many brave gods were killed—or wounded in the struggle, including Lord Aurelius, who was pierced by the poisoned spear of the Titan Makay. But the sacrifice of these heroes was not in vain. In the end, the Mighty Sol vanquished the Titans and cast them into the Abyss."

The image of a terrifying chasm—of colossal black gates and horrific monsters—flashed in the cloud, sending a shudder through the entire room.

"And so peace returned to the universe." Nikolas lowered his hands, and the scene of a galaxy appeared above, focusing in on one planet. "Aurelius became ruler of our planet, Mithris. He reigned for many glorious epochs until the poison of Makay's spear finally took his life." Nikolas closed his eyes. "And so our first lord passed, fifteen short years ago, according to the lives of men."

Nikolas opened his eyes and clapped his hands twice. The vision cloud faded away, and the lights returned to normal.

"But we do not weep, for in the past fifteen years, we have witnessed the leadership of Aurelius's son, Julius—"

Nikolas was interrupted as a goblet clattered to the floor. The High Counselor looked around the room, startled, his long gray hair falling over his eyes. Finally, he saw Julius, who was staring at his wine goblet as it rolled to a halt on the floor below.

Julius shifted in his chair, clearing his throat but looking otherwise unashamed. Beside him, Ambrosia was blushing furiously. She buried her face in her hands.

Julius clapped. "A wonderful retelling of our history, Nikolas." The sound echoed in the council room.

Nikolas smiled graciously, bowing at the waist, and then took his seat. Julius snapped his fingers, and an angel ran up the stairs with a new wine goblet. He set it on a small table in front of Julius, filled it from a pitcher, and ran back down the stairs to stand at attention once more.

Julius took a gulp from the goblet, and then leaned over to whisper in Nikolas's ear. "I swear, you become more riveting each year. That depiction of the Abyss was *terrifying*. And you've shortened the narrative too—you know how much I appreciate that."

Nikolas nodded, his mouth a thin line. "Of course. Every year, shorter."

36

"One of your greatest services to me." Julius leaned back in his seat and waved his hand impatiently. "Now let's get the politicking done. This meeting has already taken too much time."

Nikolas raised an eyebrow. "You do not want to moderate the Assembly, my lord?"

Julius rolled his eyes, resting his chin on his hand. "Do I ever? You're the High Counselor. Lead on."

"Your word is law." Nikolas bowed again and then stood to face the Assembly.

Julius winked at Ambrosia. "See, dear sister? Nikolas knows his place. My word is law, he says."

Ambrosia forced a smile as she whispered back. "How marvelous. He supports your wish for a shortened council. Maybe he can join you later when you sit on your hands?"

Julius pursed his lips mockingly. Then he took another loud gulp of wine.

"My fellow gods and goddesses of Mythris." Nikolas spread his arms. "Today it is our unpleasant duty to discuss the conflict that envelops our world. To the south, Dridia and Lansrik are locked in a war of attrition. To the east, Teuten has attacked Viras. All over, unrest grows as governments prepare their armies, ready for war to spill over their borders."

Nikolas paused, surveying the room. "I invite your counsel on what action we should take."

Behind him, Julius drained his goblet and began drumming his fingers on the armrests of his throne.

A fat, balding god raised his hand.

"Attik, God of Lawandola." Nikolas held out his hand to the fat god. "The Council recognizes you."

Attik cleared his throat. "My Lord Julius, High Counselor Nikolas, and my divine colleagues, it is my opinion—and it has been my opinion for years, as you well know—that we should allow the humans to continue as they are. They have been created with moderate intelligence, and they have something which resembles free will, making them responsible for their actions." Attik cleared his throat again. "Their actions, for years, have been to wage war against one another. It is not our duty to babysit these creatures. They have leaders who can govern their affairs. Let them sort the matter out."

Attik sat back down to polite applause. Across the room, a slim goddess with short brown hair stood, raising her hand.

Nikolas acknowledged her. "Aga, Goddess of Dridia."

Aga gave a curt nod to Nikolas and then turned to Attik.

"You speak of responsibility and moderate intelligence. The humans are stupid, Attik. Some of them are almost as stupid as you are."

Attik raised his eyebrows and pointed back at himself, mouthing the words, "Stupid? Me?"

Some council members chuckled, but Aga cleared her throat and continued. "The humans are nothing more than animals. Any trace of the divine has been buried deep inside their clay brains." She crossed her arms. "They need to be controlled. Humanity is a failed race. Humans were flawed from the beginning, showing that even the First Gods can make mistakes."

Murmurs ran through the crowd at Aga's words. Some goddesses whispered to each other behind their hands, stealing furtive glances at the provocative speaker.

"The humans have been given too much freedom." Aga narrowed her eyes. "It's time to rein them in."

She sat down, and another flurry of murmurs spread among the council members.

"Dantis, God of Teuten." Nikolas acknowledged a god with burly arms who had raised his hand.

"Aga gives mankind too much credit. The humans are worse than animals." Dantis's blue eyes shone with a cold light. "Humans are evil. They don't just kill each other for food and territory—they hunt each other down for sport. They constantly devise new methods of torture and bloodshed. Look at their bombs and warplanes! They kill the young, the old, the sick, and the pregnant." He shook his head in disgust. "Humans are nothing but trouble and wickedness. They deserved to be punished."

Someone started clapping in a row above Dantis. The muscular god turned around, confused, trying to see who was applauding him. A skinny little god, scarcely more than four feet tall, was standing, sarcasm etched across his face as he clapped.

"Well said, Dantis, God of Teuten." He put his hands on his hips. "Fine words from the god whose country has provoked most of the fighting. I can see that you've been exercising your body more than your administrative skills."

Dantis sneered at the speaker. He pointed his finger threateningly, starting to speak—but was interrupted.

"How will you punish the humans? Send a plague? An earthquake?" The little god held his finger to his mouth in mock-contemplation. "What a great idea. Why don't you just kill the—what did you say? 'The young, the old, the sick, and the pregnant'? The same thing that Teuten has been doing to Viras?"

"Lott," Nikolas said sternly. "You speak out of turn."

"Yes, the little Lott, God of Viras, speaks out of turn. Since when have the gods not punished the wicked with plagues and earthquakes? The humans must be taught a lesson." Dantis glared up at his detractor, who stared defiantly back at him. "And I am not responsible for the actions of humans, Teuten or otherwise. If you're so upset, why don't you go join the fight?"

"It's not the gods' place to join any fight. Our God of Gods has already set that example." Lott jerked his head at Julius, and a few murmurs rose around the room.

Julius continued to drum his fingers, looking bored.

Lott continued, sneering at Dantis. "And you seem to confuse all humans with 'the wicked,' unless you just want everyone dead. But if they're dead, Dantis, there's no one left to learn from your lesson. Extinction isn't very didactic."

Dantis locked his jaw, smoldering in his fury.

The little god curled his lip. "Do you know what 'didactic' means, Dantis?"

"You insolent little monkey!" Dantis roared angrily and started climbing over his seat to reach his opponent. He slipped on the back of his chair, tripping over a goddess who screamed as his heavy bulk fell upon her. Nearby gods came to her aide, pulling Dantis up and restraining him.

Nikolas's voice boomed out over the din.

"Enough! I am disgusted with your behavior!" Nikolas's cheeks were flushed with anger. "Lott, you will sit down and be silent until I give you permission to speak. Dantis, you will calm yourself at once!"

The little god obeyed and sat down, but not before sticking out his tongue and making an obscene gesture at Dantis. The burly god yelled wildly, breaking free of his captors and climbing up the rows. Lott screamed in fright. He crawled up the seats behind him in an attempt to escape.

Nikolas raised his arms, yelling loudly, attempting to restore order to the Assembly. Beside him, Julius sat in silence, staring into his empty goblet. Ambrosia shook her head in disgust.

Julius sighed deeply. "It's a shame."

"What is?" Ambrosia snapped at Julius.

Julius looked lazily at Ambrosia, allowing the goblet to slip from his hands. "The wine wasn't even that good."

Below him, the council degenerated into chaos. More gods joined the fray to stop Dantis from strangling Lott.

"I think we're done here." Julius stood, patting Nikolas on the back. "You did what you could. I'm sure my father would have been proud."

Julius walked down the steps before Nikolas could respond, working his way through the melee of gods and goddesses before disappearing through the tall archway.

CHAPTER 5:
FIRES IN THE NIGHT

Serena and Natalie drove in silence down the highway, following the sun to the west as it dipped underneath the horizon. Bright red hues faded into black as night closed in.

Serena was surprised at how quiet Natalie was. The red-haired girl kept writing in her journal, pausing occasionally to flip back a few pages and read a passage. Serena was enjoying the silence, but after two hours, her curiosity got the better of her.

She glanced at Natalie's journal. "What are you writing?"

Natalie held up the journal close to her chest so that Serena couldn't see any of it.

"I can't talk to you about that right now."

"Why? Is it a secret?" Serena rolled her eyes. "Are you writing about your feelings?" She adopted a mocking voice. "Dear Diary, sometimes Serena is really hard to get along with, but I hope that we'll become best friends and one day we'll be just like sisters."

Natalie's face reddened.

"I said I can't talk to you about it right now." She shifted in her chair so that her shoulder was facing Serena, and then she continued to write.

"You know, I can actually see it better now." Serena looked at the white pages covered in neat pink handwriting. All of the "i's" were dotted with hearts.

Natalie turned again so that the leather-bound cover faced Serena.

"You know, I liked it better just now when we weren't talking."

"Suits me fine." Serena shrugged and turned her attention back to the road.

About two hours later, at ten o'clock, they arrived at the town of Johnson. Honeycomb had been small, but Johnson was a blink-and-you've-missed-it town.

Johnson's most exciting features were a stoplight, a mini-mart, a neon sign, and the road out.

Everything seemed to be closed. Only a small one-story building beside the road still had its lights on. Above it, the glowing pink neon sign read, "The Johnson Inn."

Serena parked across the street underneath a lamppost, and the girls walked across the empty road to the inn.

Inside, a tall boy slouched over the receptionist desk. He had shaggy brown hair that fell over his eyes. Standing opposite the desk were a love seat, a wooden chair, and one door that presumably led to the rooms.

The boy stood up straight when he saw Serena. He smiled, running his hand through his thick hair.

Serena walked up to the desk. "I'd like a room for one, please."

"For two, actually." Natalie corrected her.

Serena turned around.

"What makes you think we're staying together? You have money. Rent your own room. I left Locke City to get away from people, not to find a best friend."

"It's safer if we stay together." Natalie tapped her foot in frustration.

"We're in the same hotel. That's together enough." Serena turned around to face the receptionist, who was looking her up and down. "A room for one, please."

The boy turned around to pull a key off the wall. Each key was on a hook underneath a room number. None of them had been checked out yet. Slow night.

"Room thirteen." The boy handed Serena a key and pointed at the doorway opposite the desk. "It's not unlucky or anything."

He laughed hopefully, but Serena didn't smile.

His expression became serious as he changed tactics, trying to look suave. "If you need anything, my name's Chad. I'll be right here."

Serena flashed him the briefest of smiles before resuming her stoic expression. She went through the door without looking back at Natalie.

She walked down the hallway, passing underneath the few lights in the dim corridor. She stopped in front of number thirteen, which was illuminated by an exposed bulb. She opened the door and stepped inside. Then she swore.

Natalie stood at the other side of the room next to an open window, holding her umbrella.

"Don't use naughty words." Natalie tapped the window, which closed at her touch. "And it's safer if we stay together."

Serena glared at Natalie. The red-haired girl took the bed nearest the window, slipping under the covers and lying down with her back to Serena.

*

Serena had difficulty falling asleep. She lay on her back, eyes open, staring at the dark ceiling. Thoughts swarmed in her mind as she mulled over the absurd things that Natalie had told her. She couldn't deny everything. Something strange had definitely attacked her last night. The Dark Angel.

And Natalie had definitely saved her. She was powerful. Natalie had survived her fall, she had made the car go faster, and she had opened the hotel room window. Serena couldn't explain those things away. As absurd as the situation was, Serena was forced to believe that Natalie might be...

Serena turned onto her side, unwilling to formulate the thought.

Well, maybe Natalie wasn't *crazy*.

Natalie probably thought she was telling the truth.

But she was weird.

Serena's stomach turned uncomfortably.

Natalie had said that Serena needed to save Mithris.

Her planet. Her people.

What did Serena have to do anyway? She didn't want to go back to Locke City. She couldn't really go back to Locke City. People were trouble, they were messy, and they were selfish. She wanted to get away from people.

Natalie had said that Serena was "important." What did that mean? Serena had joked about virgin sacrifice, but who knew? She might actually need to die for her planet. Gods had a habit of planning things that way.

Serena's skin crawled at the thought of dying for others. Humans were filthy, rude, and ignorant. And the gods didn't seem to be much better. If they even existed, they were incompetent, letting the world fall into decay and destruction. Humans were stupid, but stupid children should be supervised better, or they might get hurt. The gods were terrible parents. Negligent leaders.

Images of the ruins of Sydney, of the starving refugees, flashed through Serena's mind. She felt a twinge of pity, but she let a hot surge of anger choke it out.

There are no gods.

She thought about the planes dropping bombs on Sydney, the soldiers gunning down children, and the bloodthirsty politicians condemning the world to war.

Humans.

Serena snorted. If there was a hell, everyone was going. Humans and gods. They were all going to burn.

Serena closed her eyes, stewing in her bitterness against the world, gleaning satisfaction from her resentment toward the gods she did not believe in.

Then she turned onto her back once more and drifted off to sleep.

*

Chad, the shaggy-haired receptionist, stepped outside to the warm night air. He pulled a pack of cigarettes out of his flannel shirt coat pocket. Lighting a match, he cupped his hand over the cigarette to block the wind, and then he tossed the match onto the road.

He let out a puff of smoke, allowing himself a grin. The girls staying at the inn were pretty hot. Or at least the older one was. Chad smirked. There was a lot to admire. He would definitely check her out again in the morning.

He licked his hand and slicked back his hair, thinking of what he might say to her.

Hey baby, what's up? You know, Johnson is a pretty sweet town, when you get used to it.

Chad flicked ashes onto the sidewalk in frustration.

Yeah, right.

Johnson was a dump. He needed to head out for Locke City. There were lots of hot girls there. At least, that's what he had heard from his friend, Regis.

Locke City, the capital of Artema, and the hot-babe capital of the world.

Chad blew more smoke into the sky. There were only a few stars out. He tried to find his favorite constellation. He didn't actually know the name, but if you tilted your head right it looked like a girl.

Man, Chad, do you hear yourself? You're getting kicks from looking at the stars. You need a girlfriend, man.

What a loser. He needed to be cool, like Regis. Chad sniffed and closed his eyes, reliving a conversation in his mind.

44

"Regis, man, I got this job a while longer. I'm saving up money. Stay for a bit and then we'll go together. We can be roommates in the city, and bring girls back home all the time."

"Chad, bro, I can't wait for you. The ladies are calling me. Catch up when you can, okay?"

He flicked more ashes onto the sidewalk.

Regis was a jerk.

Chad looked up again, still trying to locate his constellation. The patch of sky was dark where the cluster of stars normally appeared. Pitch black, actually.

He screwed up his face and concentrated closer on the spot. It was blacker than the rest of the sky, and the patch of darkness was growing bigger. The warmth of the air had been replaced by a coldness that felt...lonely.

Chad *was* lonely.

A bead of sweat slid down from his armpit—he should have put on deodorant.

Chad dropped his cigarette to the ground and stomped on it. What a loser. No girlfriend, probably no chance with the chick that was staying overnight, and now he was freaking out over the dark. Just like a little girl.

The lamppost across the road went out.

The dark silence was suffocating.

He looked up at the sky again. The blackness was growing bigger, as if a massive shape was falling toward him. A shiver ran down his spine.

Then he saw it.

Chad fell to the ground in terror. He had barely begun to scream when the shape enveloped his head. His body thrashed uncontrollably as darkness consumed him. Then he disappeared completely, leaving nothing but a few glowing ashes on the sidewalk.

*

Serena sat up on her elbows, stirred from sleep. She glanced at the window, which was visible between the partially opened curtains.

Across the street, the lamppost had gone out. Serena didn't know why, but the darkness made her hairs stand on edge.

She looked at Natalie. The girl's chest was rising and falling peacefully underneath the covers.

Serena didn't want to admit it, but she felt a rush of confidence from Natalie's calm presence. If she was fine, then Serena should be fine. Natalie seemed to have a good sense of when danger was coming.

Satisfied, Serena settled onto her pillow and pulled her blanket back over her shoulder. She closed her eyes and lay still, encouraging her body to fall asleep.

Think sleepy thoughts, Serena told herself.

Like that ever worked. She turned on her side and then onto her back again.

A feeling of the uncanny lingered inside of her. She wondered if Natalie might be missing something.

Her fears intensified when a warning sounded in her brain. She tensed, and panic seized her heart.

They were not alone.

The room had grown colder. The air seemed to be circulating, but there was no fan in the room.

Serena didn't want to open her eyes. If she did, whatever it was might see her.

But if something was there, she needed to warn Natalie.

Serena summoned all of her courage and managed to open one eyelid just a little. Mist swirled inside the room. A thousand floating particles shone in the faint light from the bedside table clock.

As soon as Serena noticed the light of the clock, it went out. She closed her eyes tightly.

Oh god. Oh god, oh god.

It was standing over her.

Serena felt a weight press tightly on her chest. The Dark Angel had returned. She was about to die.

As her survival instincts kicked in, Serena yelled with all of her might. She filled her lungs and let loose a bloodcurdling scream, trying to wake up the entire county.

But when Serena opened her mouth, no sound came. There was nothing but silence...and suffocating darkness. Sudden memory flooded her mind.

White pajamas with soft pink stripes. A plait of brown hair. A warm embrace. Serena kept her eyes shut, focusing on the images that were marked by a vague familiarity. The weight on her chest increased.

Oh gods!

Unable to keep them closed any longer, Serena opened her eyes.

A tall man with a black suit and a pale, gaunt face hovered over her, grinning wickedly. His tongue traced the edges of his lips as he widened his milky eyes.

Serena tried, with all of her might, to scream and sit upright—to break free and run away. But she couldn't move. She fought against the invisible force pushing her down, straining to move her legs and chest.

But she was frozen.

Inside her heart, a flair of desperation surged and she thought of Natalie's kind face. Natalie was sleeping right next to her, totally unaware of the monstrosity in the room.

Maybe the Dark Angel had already killed her.

Feelings of panic coursed through her brain. No—Natalie had to be alive.

Natalie had saved her once before. Beautiful, sweet, pure Natalie, with her flaming red hair...

The Dark Angel leaned forward, his tongue extended as if to lick Serena's terrified face. His eyes closed with sheer ecstasy.

Oh, Natalie, help me! Serena screamed inside of her mind. As the thought came into being, Serena sat upright and screamed out loud.

Immediately, the room ignited with fiery light. Natalie stood on top of her bed, her umbrella pointed at the Dark Angel, fire pouring from its bent tip.

Natalie jumped onto Serena's bed and stood over the terrified girl, forcing the Dark Angel back toward the window. Columns of flames shot from the tip of Natalie's umbrella. The Dark Angel shrieked hideously as the heat enveloped his body.

Streams of fire wrapped themselves around the fiend, illuminating his grotesque features and devouring his tall, dark form. But the Dark Angel thrust his hand at Natalie, and a flow of cold, blue fire issued from his outstretched fingers.

The flames grappled above the bed, blue and red, setting Natalie's sheets on fire.

The Dark Angel screamed, licking his teeth and shuddering with the thrill of the fight. He forced Natalie against Serena's bed, causing her to fall onto it. She pushed herself back up with one hand, urging the umbrella toward the Dark Angel with the other, straining to resist the tide of blue flames.

The Dark Angel's fire intensified, and Natalie cried out in duress. She glanced back at Serena, her face full of fear. Without thinking, Serena rushed forward and put her hands on Natalie's shoulder. Natalie immediately turned back toward the Dark Angel, yelling and throwing her strength into pushing him toward the window.

Caught off guard by this burst of strength, the Dark Angel fell back against the glass. Natalie stepped toward him, holding her umbrella with both hands and pointing it at his chest. The Dark Angel wailed under the onslaught of bright red flames. He dissolved into a swirling black mass and burst through the window.

Flames fell from the dark shape as it disappeared into the night.

Natalie turned from the window to look at Serena, red hair falling over her ash-stricken face.

Smoke filled the room from the burning bed sheets.

"Are you okay?" Natalie's voice cracked.

"Natalie! The fire—your umbrella!" Serena pointed to Natalie's side, where her umbrella was still pouring out flames.

Natalie's eyes widened. "Oh, no!"

She lifted the umbrella and adjusted the crook handle, but in doing so she pointed it upward and set the ceiling ablaze.

She frowned. "That usually works. It must be really broken." She flicked the umbrella with her wrist, and the movement ignited the blaze further.

"Put it out, Natalie! Put it out!" Serena raised her voice above the crackling flames that danced around the room.

Natalie tried once more to stop the flow of fire, flicking her wrist again and kindling the growing conflagration. Then she abandoned her attempt, grabbed Serena, and rushed out the door.

Flames still gushed from the tip of her umbrella. Natalie kept it pointed behind her as they ran down the hallway, spreading fire with each step.

The blaze rushed after them, consuming the walls and doorways of the dim corridor. Natalie held Serena in front of her with one arm, and the older girl was astounded by the strength with which Natalie kept her upright.

The red-haired girl slowed for a split second to kick open the hall door, and then she threw Serena around the corner and jumped herself, narrowly avoiding a fireball that rushed out of the hall and incinerated the receptionist's desk.

The girls burst out of the inn doors, and Natalie dropped her umbrella on the sidewalk, leaving it pointing in the building's direction. She dragged Serena, who was coughing violently from the smoke, across the street and away from the licking flames. Moments later, the inn collapsed, groaning under a shower of sparks. Fiery debris rained on the sidewalk.

Natalie waited until the destruction had settled before running across the street to examine her umbrella, which was still spouting spurts of flame. She stomped on the tip with her rain boots, and the umbrella issued a last fiery burst before stopping.

The girl waited for a minute, standing above it with her arms crossed. Finally, she picked the umbrella up and held it loosely at her side. She examined the charred remnants of the Johnson Inn and shook her head. Then she turned around, walking back to where Serena was lying against the curb.

Natalie stood beside Serena but didn't look at her.

"Are you okay?"

"Yes, under the circumstances." Serena sniffed, wiping her nose with the sleeve of her cardigan. "Thanks for saving my life."

"I shouldn't have been in such a deep sleep." Natalie shook her head in disgust.

"Yeah, well, you were tired." Serena shrugged. "And you woke up. We're still here. Thanks."

"Yeah, you're welcome." Natalie continued to avoid eye contact. She looked up at the stars, rubbing her neck and frowning. "I...need to apologize though."

"For what?" Serena looked up at her, watching the burning remains of the inn in the girl's green eyes.

"Well, for a few things. Like...I probably seemed a little weird when we met."

Serena snorted. She couldn't help it—but she felt a twinge of regret when Natalie dropped her head in shame.

"Okay, I guess that's obvious. Another thing is that my umbrella is definitely broken." Natalie held her umbrella in front of her and made a face.

"I can see that." Serena watched a few sparks drift up lazily from the umbrella tip.

Natalie stared glumly at the inn. A few embers were eating away at the wooden post that held up the neon-pink Johnson Inn sign. It flickered momentarily and then collapsed onto the sizzling ruins.

Serena raised her eyebrows. "I can't believe that sign stayed up so long."

"I can't believe I destroyed that inn." Natalie groaned. "And that poor receptionist..."

"He wasn't there when we came out." Serena swallowed, feeling sick in her throat. "I hope he got away...but I wonder if the Dark Angel..."

She shuddered and covered her face with her hands.

Natalie sat down and put her arms around Serena, who surprised her by leaning back into the embrace.

"Did something happen back there, in the hotel?" Serena clasped her hands in her lap. "When you were fighting the Dark Angel—and you looked at me. I put my hands on your shoulder..."

"Yes, I think you helped me," Natalie said quietly.

"How?" Serena examined her palms.

"Well, friends are always a comfort when you're fighting against the forces of darkness." Natalie patted Serena's arm.

Serena shook her head. "I think we both know it was more than that."

Natalie nodded, and the girls sat in silence under the stars.

"There are things about me I don't understand anymore," Serena whispered softly. She shuddered. "And I'm scared."

"I know." Natalie closed her eyes, feeling the warmth of Serena's face against the night, which had grown cold.

"I just don't understand..." Serena's shoulders trembled, and Natalie felt a drop against her cheek. "Someone's trying to kill me."

Serena lowered her head, teardrops glistening in the light of the dying flames.

"I want the answers, Natalie." Serena looked up into the girl's green eyes.

Natalie nodded. "Then we need to go to Locke City. All of the answers are there. And you'll hear them the way you need to...from the people who need to tell it."

Serena sniffed, wiping away tears with her forearm. She got to her feet slowly, taking a deep, shuddering breath.

"Okay, then we'll go."

Natalie rested her chin on her knees. She glanced at Serena out of the corner of her eye, feeling a surge of respect for the eighteen-year-old girl. Serena had survived two attacks by Dark Angels in the last twenty-four hours. She had been thrust into a dangerous world of divinities that she had never believed in, and she was holding her own.

There was a long way to go, but Natalie felt confident that this girl was the right one for the job.

Both jobs, in fact.

Natalie managed to smile at Serena, who was watching the sky.

The older girl raised an arm to point at something that Natalie could not see.

Serena's jaw dropped. "We need to go now."

Natalie lifted her head slowly. The night breathed cold air upon them without wind. Above her, stars faded and splotches of darkness appeared in their place, blacker than the night itself.

"Can we outrun them?" Serena swallowed.

"We'll have to try." Natalie closed her eyes, feeling the fatigue of her aching body. Her muscles tensed as they prepared for flight. "Go!"

Both girls shot to their feet and ran to Serena's car. They opened the doors and jumped inside, starting the engine and roaring down the street as the remaining lights on Johnson Main Street winked out.

CHAPTER 6:
DEMIGODDESS

Through the car's rearview mirror, Natalie watched darkness envelop the few remaining lights of Johnson. She strapped on her seatbelt as Serena raced the station wagon down the highway. Her heart beat rapidly. Wiping her sweaty hands on her jeans, Natalie took deep breaths, trying to remain calm.

"How many of them do you think there are?" Serena's voice shook as she brushed a strand of hair behind her ear.

"No idea." Natalie leaned forward to look at the sky through the windshield. The stars were blinking out overhead. An invisible brush was painting the sky black, sweeping over the car and passing in front of them. It didn't seem possible that they had escaped one nightmare only to fall into another.

"How fast can we go?" Natalie looked at the speedometer, which was pushing eighty miles per hour.

"A little faster than we are now." Serena gripped the steering wheel tightly as she accelerated past ninety. The car began to shake from the strain, the engine complaining with a loud hum. "Is there any chance that you could do your umbrella-speed trick again?"

"None." Natalie shook her head, looking at the dent her umbrella had made the night before. "Not unless we want to set the car on fire and deprive the Dark Angels the satisfaction of killing us."

She looked out her window, trying to discern the shapes of the Dark Angels pursuing them. Thick black curtains pressed against the car, obscuring every feature of the surrounding landscape. The only light that Natalie could see came from the glare of the headlights and the glowing buttons on the dashboard.

Natalie tapped her umbrella nervously on the floor.

"If your umbrella can't help us outrun them," Serena asked, "will it be any use in a fight?"

"Maybe. But it would be suicide to use it unless we were out of the car." Natalie bit her lip, running a hand down the battered umbrella. "If they stopped us, I could probably take a few of them with me before this thing exploded into a raging fireball." She swallowed. "I'm not sure what you would do after that, unless you can run really fast."

"So what are our choices?" Serena tried unsuccessfully to keep the panic out of her voice. "What are we going to do if they catch up?"

Natalie tilted her head, running a hand through her hair.

"We'll try not to let them catch up."

Something hard slammed into the driver side of the station wagon. Serena screamed. The headlights caught a dim shape flying alongside them before it disappeared again into the night.

Natalie placed a reassuring hand on Serena's shoulder.

"Just keep your foot on the gas and your eyes on the road."

"I can barely see the road!" Serena shrieked.

A mercurial shape swooped in front of them, trailing over the windshield before disappearing. A pale, grinning face lingered in the air where the apparition had been a moment before.

Natalie reached inside her raincoat and pulled out her journal. She slid her finger across the lock to open it.

"Are you going to write about this?" Serena asked indignantly, looking at the leather book.

"Sometimes that helps," Natalie muttered, flipping through the pages.

She scanned the neat pink handwriting, looking for something that could save them. The answer might be simple, floating around in her mind...just out of memory's reach.

"Remember." Natalie closed her eyes—opening them immediately as Serena screamed again.

A man in a black suit was draped across the driver side of the car, holding onto the roof with his right hand. His face pressed against Serena's window. She tried to shake him off by stepping harder on the accelerator. The car veered left and right, shaking as it hurtled down the highway.

Natalie heard the tires squeal and caught the scent of burnt rubber. But the Dark Angel held on, the tip of his fedora pasted against his ghost-white forehead. Natalie's tongue stuck to the roof of her mouth as she tried to avoid the milky gaze of the Dark Angel. Then he lifted his head from the window, letting loose an inhuman howl that froze Natalie's blood in her veins.

She tried to shut out the sound as her heart rate accelerated. The Dark Angel's lugubrious cry grew louder, and Serena shrieked in panic.

54

"He can't come inside if he still has his hat on, Serena!" Natalie said urgently. "They're toying with us first. Just try and hold the car steady. I'm thinking—oh heavens!"

Natalie jumped in her seat as another Dark Angel slammed against her window. The demon's cheek was inches from hers, and his breath fogged the outside of the glass. Bulbous pimples dotted the Dark Angel's sallow face. His mouth brimmed with sharp yellow teeth that scraped against the car.

Two thuds on the roof informed Natalie that more Dark Angels had joined. Howls issued from above, filling the night with the unnatural noise.

She closed her eyes, holding her watch close to her ear, letting the rhythmic ticking of the clock soothe her mind.

Her umbrella could not work—it was too volatile. What else did she have in her raincoat? Natalie searched her pockets inside and out. Pink pen, birthday candles, coloring pencils, a ball of rubber bands...

Serena shuddered next to her, and Natalie opened her eyes at another animal-like scream. The Dark Angel on the driver window was beating his head against the glass, spit flying from his mouth.

"Calm down, baby, it's okay." Natalie curled up in her seat, trying to shut out the grotesque noises.

"Why doesn't he just do the mist thing?" Serena raised her voice above the din. "Why is he trying to force his way in?"

"I think the first one was trying to read you—to find out who you were." Natalie held her head in her hands, trying to answer Serena while images and memories flashed in front of her mind's eye. "These Dark Angels will kill us outright...when they stop playing with us."

A Dark Angel beat his head against the passenger window, making Natalie jump again. The demons above them were pounding mercilessly on the roof. She wiped her sweaty hands on her jeans, trying to exorcise her nerves—to think straight. She felt handicapped without a working umbrella.

Natalie glared at the pink handwriting of the open book lying in her lap. The words, "Never forget who you are. Write it down. Write it on your heart," shone out from the white pages.

Natalie had written it down, but even now, she was still trying to connect...

What did she need to know?

She pressed her knuckles against her forehead, needing the words to become alive. The answers were beyond her grasp, immaterial power hidden somewhere on the page.

Or was it something Serena needed to know?

"You said the Dark Angel was trying to find out who I am." Serena's voice interrupted Natalie's thoughts. Tears were running down Serena's face. "And who am I, Natalie? You know I'm ready to believe you, so tell me who I am! I need to know before I die."

The Dark Angels knocked hard against the glass, like ceaseless hammers made of flesh and bone.

"You're important, Serena." Natalie fought to keep her voice steady. "You're important to this world—so important that you're not going to die here. We're going to get through this. I'm going to remember how to get us through this and you're going to learn all the answers at Locke City!"

"No, no." Serena shook her head. "I need to know now! Tell me who I am!"

Natalie swallowed, grasping her knees as if to brace herself for impact.

"You're a demigoddess, Serena! You're the daughter of a god!"

"Daughter of a god?" Serena's eyes widened. She leaned forward in her seat, gasping as though a weight hung from her neck. "A demigoddess?"

An enormous black shape slammed into the windshield. Natalie screamed, and her journal fell onto the floor. A Dark Angel stretched across Serena's view, blocking the road. He beat the glass with his left fist, holding on with the other hand. The demon's pale eyes stared down upon Serena.

"Serena!" Natalie grabbed her friend by the shoulder. Serena's chest was rising and falling from heavy breathing. "Hold on, we're going to get out of this!"

Natalie pulled her umbrella up from the floor, twisting it around to point at the Dark Angel in front of her. The umbrella might kill them both, but "might" was better than the certain death they faced in the next moment.

"No, not yet!" Serena threw her hand in front of Natalie, hitting her arm. "I need to know more. I'm the daughter of a god!" Serena said, her voice rising hysterically. "And my mother—she was a woman? A human?"

Natalie nodded urgently. "Yes, she was a human."

"But what was her name?" Serena sounded like she was hyperventilating. "What was my mother's name?"

"I don't...I can't..." Natalie searched her lap for her journal. "Just hold on...where is it?"

She leaned over to feel the floor at her feet. Her hands closed around the book, and she threw open the pages, scanning them quickly. Serena's breathing had increased to such a frequency that Natalie thought she would pass out at any moment.

"It's somewhere near the...there! That's it—Jillian!" She held the book up to Serena's face, her index finger pointing at the name.

Serena fell silent at the sound of the name.

She turned slowly to read it, and Natalie gave a cry of fright. Serena's blue eyes shone with a supernatural light.

"Jillian?" Serena let out a long breath, strangely calm. "My mother's name..."

The howling and pounding of the Dark Angels had faded from Natalie's ears. All that she could hear was Serena's voice.

"Yes, Jillian." Natalie tried to swallow, wincing as her parched throat resisted the attempt. She gripped the edge of her seat.

"Memory is strength." Serena's voice was soft and distant. Natalie watched, with some uneasiness, as Serena's brown hair lifted slowly from her shoulders, caught in a wind that Natalie did not feel.

"Yes. Memory is strength," Natalie whispered, blinking and wondering if she had fallen into a daze. "Or at least, good memories can be strong. All memories can be powerful...but some are dangerous."

She cleared her throat, realizing that Serena had continued to steer the car from the beginning of her trance. A shiver ran down Natalie's spine.

Serena nodded.

"Memory is strength," she repeated.

Then Serena turned her head to the Dark Angel lying above her. She closed her eyes and whispered a word.

"Jillian."

Blinding white light shattered the night like a bullet through glass, and the station wagon rocketed forward.

The Dark Angels were ripped away from them, thrown to the night in all directions. Natalie watched white flames consume the apparitions as they hurtled through the air at alarming speeds, burning up like comets entering the atmosphere.

The unnatural howls lingered in the air for a moment...and the demons flickered out of existence.

Then the night fell silent.

Bright stars winked above the girls as the veil of darkness lifted.

Natalie gaped at Serena—then the red-haired girl grabbed the wheel to stop the car from going off the road.

Serena was slumped against her window, eyes closed. Her skin was pale and running with sweat. All of the color had drained from her lips. Natalie could feel a cold aura emanating from her friend's body. Serena whispered softly, her breath like fog in the air.

"I remember...I knew...oh, Mom..."

Then she grew quiet and did not stir.

Tears brimmed on the edges of Natalie's eyes. Her body ached with fatigue and stress, but the trouble was not over yet—the car was still moving dangerously fast. The needle on the speedometer was broken, hanging limply below the numbers.

Natalie reached over Serena's lap, pulling her foot off the accelerator and allowing the car to slow down. Then she grabbed Serena's shin and—groaning slightly as she stretched across the seat—she pushed Serena's foot against the brake pedal.

The station wagon veered off the road, rumbling underneath her, but Natalie kept it close to the highway by steering with her right hand.

Finally, the car came to a halt. Natalie took a deep breath and fell back into her seat.

Oh, god, she thought.

She corrected herself. *Demigoddess.*

Natalie closed her eyes. They were safe.

Chapter 7:
A Vacation to the Country

Charles Finch opened his tired eyes to see the multicolored lights of the balloon lamp on his desk. His mother was gently shaking his legs. The six-year-old rubbed his face with small fists.

"Charles, it's time to get up. We need to get you dressed."

The boy groaned and pulled the covers over his shoulder, rolling onto his right side to face the wall. His mother tousled his thick black hair playfully and took off the sheets.

"I know it's early, kiddo, but you need to get up." She stood and piled the covers at the foot of the bed. "We need to get you to the train station."

Charles drew his bare feet close to his body and curled into a ball to preserve his warmth. When he realized that the effort was in vain, he swung his legs over the side of the bed and allowed his mother to dress him.

She sat on one knee, fitting knee-high green socks and black shoes onto his feet. Charles's mother had short black hair tied into a bun behind her head. She wore a heavy jean jacket and a white scarf around her neck.

Charles stared at the lamp on his desk, amusing himself by looking at the brown bear that held blue, red, and green balloons. A light bulb shone inside each one. The bear was smiling as his feet lifted up from the round wooden base.

Charles raised his arms, allowing his mother to put a warm green sweater over his white shirt. The little bear was flying, just like the planes he had seen on television the last few nights. He liked to see the planes—fast fighters with roaring engines, and huge bombers that flew close together, covering the sky. Charles liked the fighter planes the best because his daddy was a fighter pilot.

Charles didn't just like planes, however. Tanks were a favorite of his, and the news had shown plenty of those recently. Charles would love to ride in one of those tanks that had the big rolling wheels—just like bulldozers. He wanted to drive the tank like a big monster truck and fire the big gun on the front. It made a lot of noise.

"Per-kooow!" Charles made a tank-firing sound with his mouth as his mother finished tying his shoes.

"What's that, sweetie?" she asked absentmindedly, opening his brown backpack and filling it with socks and underwear.

"I'm a tank." Charles repeated his artillery-fire, adding a dramatic pointing gesture. He recoiled his arm after the shot, just like he had seen the tanks do on TV.

His mother placed a warm beanie on his head and frowned.

"Tanks are dangerous, Charles. Why don't you pretend to be something else?"

"Okay." Charles put a finger to his mouth and thought. "I could be a fighter plane, like the one Daddy flies." He made a buzzing sound with his lips, moving his hand in front of his face like a plane.

"Maybe you could be something friendlier than tanks or jets." His mother zipped up his backpack. "What about a bus? Or a train? You're going to ride a train today."

She looked at the mechanical flip clock beside Charles's bed, reading the time by the blue, red, and green light of the lamp. It was two in the morning.

"We need to get to the station. Come on." She took his hand and steered him toward the door.

"Wait!" Charles wrenched free of her grasp and ran to the end of his bed where a teddy bear had fallen onto the floor. "Don't forget Eugene."

"Of course not." She ruffled his hair as he ran back to her side, holding Eugene. "Now let's go, honey. The train leaves in forty-five minutes."

"Why am I going on a train again?" Charles yawned, trailing his hand along the walls of the dark hallway. He let his hand bump against the cabinet doors lining the corridor.

"Mommy told you before, remember?" His mother tried unsuccessfully to stifle a yawn herself. "I said that you might get to take a vacation to the country sometime soon. Didn't you say that you would enjoy that? You like trains, right?"

"Yeah, I like trains." Charles nodded. "And I want to see the horses in the country. There are lots of trees and forests for adventures."

He sniffed loudly and wiped a hand across his nose.

His mother bent down in front of him, pulling a tissue from her pocket and wiping his face.

"Well, hopefully you can have some nice adventures with the horses in the forest." Charles noticed that his mother's voice shook. A drop of water sparkled on her face and fell to the floor. "Daddy called from work and said that now is the time for you to take a vacation to the country."

"Mommy, I think you need a tissue too." Charles held his mother's hand in front of his face, grasping the tissue that protruded from her fingers.

"No, Mommy's fine." She gave him a watery smile and wiped her face quickly with the back of her hand.

Mommy opened the front door, ushering Charles outside. The two were greeted by the brisk early morning air.

Standing on the front doorstep, Charles could see the moon reflecting on the water of the Saint Martin harbor. The street sloped down from his house to the Saint Martin Bay, which lay on the eastern edge of Artema. A hundred little ships could be seen anchored on the dark shoreline.

Charles reached out his hand to the sky, holding the moon between his thumb and encircled index finger.

He closed his fist and blocked the moon from view. "Poof! The moon is gone."

"What?" His mother locked the front door and turned around, staring first at Charles and then at the moon. "No, I think the moon's still there, sweetie."

"Nope, it's gone. I have it in my hand." Charles stuck out his tongue in concentration. "It's really heavy."

"Mmhmm. But you're really strong, just like your daddy. Let's go." His mother held his hand and walked him down the steps to the street, where she unlocked a blue car and placed Charles in the back seat.

"Will Daddy be at the train station? Or is he still at work?" Charles yawned again as his mother buckled his seatbelt.

She walked to the other side of the car and stepped in quickly, rubbing her shoulders to generate warmth.

"No, baby. Daddy wishes he could come, but he has to talk to people about some important decisions."

Charles frowned.

"That sounds boring. Why can't he just come anyway if it's boring?" Charles stared out of the window as they drove down the street, trying to see inside the thin houses that squeezed together beside the road. To his left, he saw the moon glitter on the water between passing buildings.

His mother slowed down as they reached an intersection.

"Daddy can't leave his work because he's doing important things."

The headlights of the truck behind them illuminated their car. Charles turned around to see that a long line of cars had grown in their wake.

"Are they taking a vacation to the country too?" Charles raised his eyebrows at the drivers honking their horns. He leaned forward in his seat hopefully. "Can I honk our horn?"

"No, Charles." She glanced at him in the rearview mirror. "Sit back in your seat, okay? Mommy needs to concentrate. There's a lot of traffic."

Before them, drivers in every direction waited impatiently for their turn. Charles noticed that the stop light did not seem to be working. It was flashing yellow.

"Mommy, I think the light is broken."

"Shh, sweetie." His mother waved a hand absently at the back seat.

One car ran the intersection, darting across Charles's field of vision. A chorus of horns and angry yells filled the air. Cars started forward and then stopped, confused by the lack of direction.

The truck driver behind Charles blasted his horn, making the six-year-old jump.

"Hey lady, go already!" A man in a sleeveless shirt stuck his head out of the truck. "What are you waiting for, an invitation? We're trying to move here!"

Charles held Eugene close with both hands, squeezing the teddy bear as the man leaned into the truck's horn.

"Are we going to be okay, Mommy?"

"We'll be fine, Charles. Don't worry." His mother swallowed and started the car forward, but another car cut across them.

She stepped on the brakes. This time she sounded her horn, which elicited another chorus of noise. Once again, the other drivers hesitated on whether to go. Taking her chance, she accelerated through the gap to escape the angry chaos of the intersection.

They reached the train station a few minutes later, finding a parking spot after circling the lot twice. Charles grabbed Eugene and jumped onto the curb when his mom opened the door. She grabbed his backpack from the seat and looped it around his arms, fussing with the sweater at his neck and waist. Then she took his hand and walked him across the dimly-lit parking lot to the red-brick station.

Inside, Charles was surprised to see that the building was bustling with people. He and his mother walked straight down a center aisle toward a kiosk. The aisle was flanked by rows of benches, which were occupied by parents and their children. Charles stared at a little boy sleeping in his mother's lap. The woman stroked his blonde locks as tears rolled down her cheeks.

"Mommy, why is that lady crying?" Charles pointed at the woman, but his mother quickly put his hand down by his side.

"It's rude to point, Charles." She escorted him up to the kiosk, where they stood at the end of a long line.

Charles continued to gaze around the room, noticing that a lot of people looked sad. He leaned back to take in the tall, arching ceilings and latticed windows. When the sights overhead lost his interest, Charles redirected his attention to the tiled floor.

He stepped playfully on the black and white checkered floor, stomping on the black squares while avoiding the white ones. He walked around his mother in this way, stepping on black squares while they moved forward in the line.

Minutes later, he heard his mother say "Charles Finch," but not to him. The boy looked up, realizing that they had reached the front of the line. An elderly lady with white hair and spectacles leaned over the counter to look at Charles. She gave him a warm smile.

"Hello there, Charles. Are you excited for the train ride?" The lady handed his mother a white card, which she filled out and tied around Charles's neck so that it hung loosely on his green sweater.

"Make sure you don't lose this, okay, Charles?" His mother tied another white paper onto the handle of his backpack. "It's important."

Charles nodded, examining the card around his neck. It read, "Finch, Charles. 1940 Trafalgar Street, Saint Martin 824. Son of Devin and Deborah Finch."

"They spelled my name wrong, Mommy. It's backwards. 'Finch, Charles.'"

"Don't worry, it's fine." She steered him away from the kiosk and toward the benches, trying to find a seat.

"If this is important, why don't you just hold onto it, Mommy?" Charles looked up at his mother.

She swallowed and blinked, but did not answer him.

They walked past sleeping children and large suitcases, looking for an open spot.

"Mommy?" Charles tugged on her white skirt. "Mommy, why don't you just hold onto this paper?"

"Oh, look, there's Emma Kitchen." His mother pointed. "Dolores!" She waved to a woman in a red cardigan, who waved back and motioned for her daughter to look up.

Charles followed his mother's gaze and saw his friend, Emma, a six-year-old girl with curly brown hair. She waved at him as they drew nearer. Charles noticed that she also had a white paper tied around her neck.

"Hey, Charles. Look what I drew." She held up a white paper that depicted three stick figures on a long train.

Charles assumed that the figures were a daddy, a mommy, and a girl. The sky was a haphazard black with spaces for yellow dots.

"I just finished it." Emma pointed to a box of coloring pencils on the seat. "We've been at the station for a while. Aren't you excited that we're going on a train?"

Seeing Emma made Charles forget about the confusing paper and the angry drivers. He felt his sense of adventure rekindle. Emma beckoned him to lean close, and then she whispered in his ear.

"And we get to stay up really late!" She grinned mischievously.

"Yeah." Charles's face brightened for a brief moment. Then he frowned. "But we had to wake up really early."

"It's like the same thing." Emma rolled her eyes.

"I brought Eugene." Charles held up his teddy bear and flapped the stuffed animal's arms. He let Emma hold Eugene. She gave him a tight squeeze.

"He's so fluffy." She smiled, playing with the white ribbon around the teddy bear's neck.

"Charles, Emma." His mother beckoned them to sit down.

Emma handed Eugene back to Charles, who climbed into his mother's lap. He looked into her face and saw that she was crying again.

Charles felt a cold, unfamiliar sensation sweep through his body. "What's wrong, Mommy?"

"Charles," his mother wiped her eyes with a damp tissue. "You need to go to the country and be very good, okay?"

Charles nodded. "Okay, Mommy. When is Daddy going to come stay with us?"

"Oh, baby." Mommy swallowed, running a hand through his black hair. "Daddy is going to have to stay here. And," her lip trembled, "Mommy has to stay here too. She has to keep going to work and building planes so Daddy can fly them."

Charles widened his eyes in surprise, jaw dropping. He turned to look at Emma, who was sobbing into her mother's red cardigan. Emma's mother blinked furiously through misty eyes, rocking the little girl back and forth in the seat.

Charles's mother took his face in her hands as he started to cry. His eyes brimmed with warm tears that streaked down his face.

"You and Emma be good, okay?" His mother tried to smile. "It will be an adventure, right? Just like you said? And nice people are going to take care of you and the other children."

"But," Charles stuttered through short sobs. "But why do I have to go away?"

"Dangerous things are happening at home. Daddy and his friends have to fight some bad guys." She held him close to her chest. "But don't worry. Nice people will take care of you until you can come back home."

Charles hugged her, feeling her thick jean jacket against his body. He soaked in the security of her hand rubbing his back, of her warm face on his head.

His mother whispered a prayer.

"Dear gods, please protect my son." Her breath fluttered against his short hair. "Please protect us all in these dangerous times."

Charles wished the embrace could have lasted forever, but the train whistle sounded. All around them, people started getting up from their seats. His mother patted his head, picked him up, and set him on the checkered floor.

"Time to go, Charles." His mother wiped her eyes with a clean tissue. She took his hand and led him past the kiosk and toward the train track. Emma and her mother followed.

The mothers stood with their children in line to get on the train. A conductor with thick glasses and a black mustache smiled at the children as they ascended a small stepstool into the passenger car. Parents waved and wiped away tears, standing by the side while their children boarded. One woman wailed loudly when her boy got on the car. Another lady helped the disconsolate mother away from the line, speaking softly to her.

When Charles reached the stepstool, his mother handed a ticket to the conductor, who punched it.

"Here you go, lad." The man winked and gave Charles the ticket. Charles turned to face his mother, and she bent down to hug him. He grasped her arms, feeling the tough texture of her jean jacket.

"Other people are waiting, ma'am." The conductor's voice was kind but firm.

"Right, of course." His mother stood and smiled, ruffling Charles hair fondly. The boy looked into his mother's face. Her brown eyes shone down at him.

"I love you, Charles." She stepped aside, allowing Emma's mother to give a ticket to the conductor.

"I love you too, Mom." Charles wiped his wet eyes and waved from the door of the passenger car.

When Emma boarded, she and Charles ran to find a window seat in the passenger car. They could see their mothers fighting against the crowd of people to locate them. They waved and blew kisses when they spotted their children, mouthing "I love you" and "Be good."

The whistle sounded again, and the train started to roll by the platform. Charles waved at his mother until the pillars and walls enveloped her familiar face. A lump grew in his throat as the station lights were whisked away by the darkness.

Charles sat in the window seat next to Emma, propping up Eugene in his lap. He felt the fuzzy pads on Eugene's hands while bright lampposts passed by. The lights on the shoreline shone as the train snaked away from the Saint Martin Bay and into the heartland of Artema.

A young lady in a dark blue uniform entered their car, holding a clipboard.

"Hello, dears. What are your names?" She leaned over and smiled at Emma and Charles. "Let me check your tags."

Emma allowed the lady to examine the paper hanging around her neck.

"Emma Kitchen. Very good. Thank you, darling." She marked a sheet with her black pen. "And what's yours, young man?"

"Charles Finch." The six-year-old held out his tag to the young lady. "Someone spelled my name wrong on the paper. They wrote Finch Charles but that's backwards."

The young lady examined the card and laughed.

"Don't worry. I'll take care of it. Thank you, sweetie."

The young lady was very pretty, and Charles blushed as she smiled at him and moved to the next row of children. He watched her small blue hat move above the seats before him. His stomach turned slightly when he saw that her hair was tied in the same bun that his mother wore.

Charles swallowed and looked out at the night. He couldn't see anything in the dark, but right now, he liked the emptiness.

Beside him, Emma stared at her color drawing. She had been very quiet since they had been in line for the train. When Charles tore his gaze away from the window, he looked at the paper in Emma's lap. It was marked by splotches of water.

"Hey," Charles whispered, placing Eugene's fuzzy face against Emma's arm. "Maybe this will be an adventure, right?"

Emma did not respond. She gazed at the ground, blinking her red eyes.

CHAPTER 8:
SERENA'S STORY

Natalie woke up to see a clear blue sky through the car windshield. She moaned in pain—the car seat felt uncomfortable against her back. She sat up from her slouch and yawned, making her jaw pop. She groaned, rubbing it with the palm of her hand.

She blinked her heavy eyes and checked her golden watch for the time. When she remembered that her watch didn't tell normal time, she managed a giggle that sounded strange in her sleepy throat.

Natalie looked at the girl sleeping beside her. Serena was slumped against the steering wheel. The eighteen-year-old was breathing steadily through her nose. She had drooled on the sleeve of her cardigan. Brown hair fell across her face, which still looked pale and worn after last night's events.

No wonder, Natalie thought. For a mortal, the discovery of divine power was nothing short of traumatic.

Natalie stretched her arms in front of her, blinking in the light that poured in from above. She looked out the windshield, trying to identify the position of the sun.

They had been driving west...and the sun rose in the east...so if the sun wasn't in the west yet, then it was probably before noon.

That's good. Natalie sniffed. She would have been sad to miss lunch.

She opened the passenger door and stepped onto the crusty brown grass beside the road. Yawning again, she stretched down to touch her toes, and then she swung her arms from side to side.

"Excellent. Let's go." She clapped her hands together. "Serena! Time to wake up! It's morning, and we need to see if this car can still drive."

She stepped back into the station wagon. "Serena!"

Serena groaned and buried her face in her arms.

"Come on, sunshine." Natalie nudged her elbow. "Rise up."

Serena shrugged Natalie's hand off, making a noise like a disgruntled cat. She turned away from Natalie and leaned her head against the window with a thud.

Natalie sat up straight, placing hands on hips.

"Well, I suppose the demigoddess isn't much of a morning person. Maybe I'll just sit tight until she feels that it's an acceptable time to wake up?"

Natalie waited to see if the sarcasm had any effect on Serena. It didn't. She looked at her watch. Then she punched Serena in the arm.

"Ow!" Serena flinched. "Why did you do that?"

She opened her eyes, rubbing the sore spot. Then she jumped in her seat.

"Oh gods! What happened last night?"

"A lot." Natalie crossed her arms. "Glad to see that you're awake."

"Oh gods!" Serena repeated, her eyes wild. She ripped off her seatbelt and hugged her legs tightly.

"Whoa, are you okay?" Natalie leaned back to give Serena some space.

"What happened?" Serena pulled anxiously at her hair.

"You fought off the Dark Angels." Natalie reached a comforting hand toward Serena, but the girl knocked it away. "Hey! You found out that you're a demigoddess, remember?"

"This has all been a nightmare!" Serena pointed an accusing finger at her. "What are you doing with me?"

"Serena! I'm not doing anything with you." Natalie slapped her knees in frustration. Did they have to go through this every time Serena woke up? "You're learning about who you are. Don't you remember what happened the last two nights? Don't you remember your mother's name? Jillian?"

Instead of responding, Serena threw her door open and bolted outside. She ran to the back of the car—and beyond.

"Serena!" Natalie shouted. "What are you—come back!"

She groaned in frustration, jumping out of the car and into a sprint.

"Serena, come back here!"

Serena was running full speed along the side of the road—to who knows where.

"Unbelievable!" Natalie hissed between sharp breaths.

Her rain boots pounded against the asphalt road. She caught up to Serena next to an oil pumpjack and tackled her around the waist. Serena yelped in surprise, and they fell into the grass. Natalie landed on top of her with a groan.

Serena pushed Natalie off and scooted a few feet away. She rose unsteadily to her feet—only to stumble and fall again.

Then she collapsed in a sobbing heap.

Natalie held her breath, poised to resume the chase if Serena took off again. But the girl folded over her knees, burying her face in her jeans.

Natalie watched Serena carefully, but she didn't move.

Overhead, the grasshopper pump turned slowly, humming and creaking, the walking beam nodding up and down. The noise seemed to have a soothing effect on Serena.

After a few minutes of silence, she started picking at the grass.

Natalie crawled closer, hoping the movement wouldn't upset her friend.

"Hey?" she ventured. "You okay?"

Serena didn't acknowledge her. Her face shone with tears. Natalie reached out to take the grass from Serena's tussled hair. She paused to gauge Serena's reaction, but the girl didn't resist her touch.

Natalie slowly picked out the blades of grass.

"Are you okay now?" she whispered.

Serena nodded, resigned. Her skin was still very pale.

"So you remember what happened last night?" Natalie asked, speaking with her soft hospital room voice. "You remember who you are now?"

Serena looked away. When she spoke, her voice was a whisper. "I don't want it to be true."

Natalie gave her a pitying look. "I'm sorry."

"I want out!" Serena pulled angrily at the grass, yanking huge tufts from the ground. She threw a clod of earth and grass, spraying the air with dirt. Then she buried her face in her hands. "I don't want any more Dark Angels."

"I think we've seen the last of them." Natalie looked up at the sun and shielded her eyes. "Don't worry."

"How can you be sure?" Serena yelled. "How can you say, 'don't worry'?"

Natalie fell back onto her elbows, surprised by Serena's raw emotion.

"I'm not positive." Natalie brushed grass off her raincoat. "But I'm pretty sure that they're not coming back. My instincts tell me that assault was all or nothing. And they got nothing."

She sat quietly for a few minutes, letting Serena rip out chunks of earth until she got bored. When Serena finally grew still, Natalie risked conversation again.

"Listen..." she eyed Serena warily, as if her friend was a bomb that could explode at any moment. "We need to see if the car still works, okay? And we should probably get some food. I'm hungry. Are you hungry?"

Serena shook her head. Natalie thought she looked like a little girl—sitting in the dirt with torn grass all around her.

She offered her hand to help Serena to her feet.

The girl took her hand and stood, and she didn't let go. So they walked hand-in-hand back to the station wagon. They stepped onto the asphalt, which was hot from the midday sun.

Natalie took in their surroundings. Plains stretched out as far as the eye could see. The flatness was occasionally interrupted by a bush, or a shriveled tree, or a pumpjack, but there was no elevation, and certainly no buildings to be seen.

Natalie looked up and down the road for a car, but to no avail.

She whistled softly. "If there's a middle of nowhere, we sure found it."

She helped Serena—who was being temporarily cooperative—into the passenger seat.

Natalie walked to the driver side and took a breath before getting behind the steering wheel.

"So how do we start this thing?" She patted the dashboard hesitantly, hoping not to spook the car.

Serena was looking out of the passenger window.

"You need keys," she said.

"Right, of course you need keys." Natalie nodded, trying to convince Serena that she knew what she was doing. "I've seen you use those keys before, to start the engine."

Serena turned and examined the red-haired girl with mild interest. "Did you turn off the car last night?"

Natalie pursed her lips. "Turn off the car?"

"Yes. Did you turn off the engine and take the keys out of the ignition?"

Natalie narrowed her eyes, scanning the steering wheel for signs of an ignition.

"I know I did something." Natalie leaned against the window, resting her chin in her palm. "And I don't see any keys...or an ignition. So I probably did something else."

Serena pointed to a spot next to the steering wheel. Natalie followed her gaze to see a horse keychain dangling from a pair of keys.

"Ha!" Natalie slapped her forehead. "How could I have missed it?" She pulled out the key and held the horse up to her face. "You like horses too? I love horses."

Serena turned away and began staring out the window again.

"I have the keys..." Natalie jingled the keys in front of her. "And now what?"

"Put them back in the ignition and start the car."

"Right. I'll just do that." She glanced at Serena out of the corner of her eye, looking for guidance, but Serena was gazing at the road, her eyes half-closed.

Natalie grumbled under her breath. "I probably shouldn't have taken them out to begin with. Here goes."

She tried to fit one key into the ignition. It didn't work.

"Lucky there are only two options. Only two! Only two options!" she sang happily, trying to make their situation better by sheer optimism.

She stole a look at Serena, who rolled her eyes.

Natalie tried to put the remaining key into the ignition. After a few tries, it fit. Natalie gripped the steering wheel, waiting to hear the engine roar.

No sound. She honked the horn hopefully, causing Serena to stir and look at her.

Natalie dropped her head in disappointment. "I think the car is broken."

Serena did not respond, but she reached over and turned the key in the ignition. The engine puttered loudly and the car shook.

"You did it! It's working!" Natalie clapped her hands.

The engine gave a terrible cough that shook the car again. It made a noise like the slamming of a door—or the smashing of paint cans—and then it fell silent.

"Oh, it's broken." Natalie buried her face in her elbow. "Too much magic."

Serena closed her eyes and fell back against her seat.

"Yep. It's broken."

Natalie rolled her fingers on the dashboard, feeling the dent that her umbrella had made two nights ago. What a shame. The car had a good run.

She looked at her watch. Tick tock.

"Looks like we have to walk." Natalie unbuckled her seatbelt and opened the door. "I hope there's a town nearby. I'm really hungry. And we'll be thirsty soon."

"There's some food in the back." Serena waved her hand unenthusiastically.

Natalie leaned around her chair to examine the backseat. Jackets, shirts, and paper bags were strewn across the seats and the floor. She opened the bags, sorting through them until she found one with dried fruit, bananas, and peanuts. After giving a cry of delight, she lifted the crinkled bag over the seat and into her lap.

"Yay, food." Natalie smiled. Then she scanned the backseat again. "Nothing to drink though?"

Serena shook her head. "I think we're out of water."

"Well, you're a demigoddess. Maybe you can do a rain dance, right?" Natalie paused, waiting to see if her joke drew a smile. No luck. "All right, let's go. We've got a long walk ahead of us."

Serena didn't move, so Natalie walked around and opened the door for her.

"Come on, friend." Natalie waved her hands, beckoning her to come out.

Serena closed her eyes and groaned, but she unbuckled her seatbelt nonetheless.

"Now! Which way do we walk?" Natalie put her hands on her hips, looking up and down the road. "We're trying to get to Locke City, so..." She looked at the direction the car was facing. "We've been going this way since we left Johnson, and you were driving away from Locke City, so we probably want to go that way. East."

Natalie slapped her forehead. "Ha, of course, because Locke City is on the east coast."

She started down the road. After a few seconds, she realized that Serena wasn't following. She jogged back to her friend, who was slouching against the station wagon.

"Come on, Serena." Natalie failed to hide the impatience in her voice. "We really need to go."

Serena reluctantly stepped away from the car, and they began walking down the highway together.

Faced with the prospect of a long march, Natalie realized just how hot the sun actually was. She took off her yellow raincoat and slung it over her shoulder. Then she opened her umbrella to block the sun.

A ray of sunlight peeked through a hole in the canopy.

Natalie sighed. "Everything's breaking."

She tucked the handle awkwardly under her arm as she opened the bag and pulled out some dried fruit. The umbrella slipped, flopping in front of her and hitting her knees.

"Ow! Can you hold this?" Natalie handed her umbrella off to Serena without waiting for an answer.

She tossed some fruit into her mouth and then took the umbrella back. Natalie crunched on the sweet preserved pineapple and smiled. Other things might be falling apart, but Natalie would make sure that *she* operated at full capacity.

They walked along the highway for over an hour, bearing the heat of the sun. Serena endured it silently. She took off her cardigan and tied it around her waist. Natalie tried to entertain herself by pretending the cracks were canyons that she had to step over. She wove in and out of the yellow lane divisions, pretending to be a car. Occasionally, she made a honking noise, screeching and hopping to the side as if she was dodging oncoming traffic. Her umbrella swayed ridiculously above her, like a red parachute on a stick.

Serena was not amused. She plodded alongside her overenthusiastic companion, who occasionally turned around to make sure that Serena was still following.

The older girl surprised Natalie by breaking the silence.

"Why didn't he ever come looking for me?"

"Excuse me?" Natalie tripped over a crack at the sound of her friend's voice. She recovered her balanced and looked back at Serena.

"My father, he was a god." Serena crossed her arms. "Or is a god. Why didn't he ever come looking for me?"

"I don't know." Natalie frowned. "Maybe he just didn't know that you were still alive."

"But he's a god." Serena squinted, her face expressing disbelief. "How can you be a god and not know everything? I thought the gods were in control of what went on—and for that matter, how could he be a god and let his wife die? And why did he even get involved with her in the first place?"

Natalie swallowed, twirling her umbrella and feeling more than a little overwhelmed by the enormity of the questions.

"Well," she said. "I'm sure that he would have come looking for you if he knew that you were alive."

"How can you be sure? Do you know him?"

"Well, no. But he seems like the...I mean, I would imagine that he would."

"Look, if you don't know, just say so." Serena quickened her pace and caught up with Natalie. "Whether he knew about me or not, he never came for me."

Natalie noticed that Serena had exchanged disbelief for angry skepticism.

"The gods don't know everything." Natalie swallowed. "Some gods in the Pantheon are pretty sharp, but you get your share of idiots everywhere. Some planets have nothing but fools to govern them. The gods of Mithris seem to be along that line—they're making a mess of the world."

"That's for sure." Serena scowled. "I wonder if my—if this god—is the one responsible for everything, or if he's just a minor god."

She kicked a rock off the side of the road and watched it bounce across the dirt. Little dust clouds rose into the air before it skidded to a halt.

Natalie let the questions linger in the air, unsure whether she could address them.

"If my father didn't know that I was still alive, how did you know?" Serena shot an accusing look at her.

The red-haired girl raised her eyebrows.

"Your name was on file at the Pantheon database."

"How?"

"Someone must have registered you after your mother died. All living demigods and demigoddesses are required to be registered at the Pantheon."

Serena frowned. "So my father must have known that I'm still alive. And he never even bothered to come looking for me."

"Well, your father might not have been the one who registered your name. But obviously someone knew about you and your mother, and they took the time to mention that you were still alive. Gods aren't supposed to get involved with mortals, but hiding a demigoddess worse than confessing, so it's a good thing that your name was registered."

"What happens if a demigoddess remains unregistered?"

"Whoever's responsible—the God of Gods, most likely—can be severely disciplined." Natalie adjusted the raincoat on her shoulder. "Even though demigods and demigoddesses only have a touch of the divine, they can become very powerful. Some are a force to be reckoned with. You know that—you saw last night what you could do."

Serena shook her head. "I don't know what I can do. Last night was terrible." She shivered. "I felt—I still feel—sick and tired. I never want to do that again."

Natalie shrugged. "You may need to. That saved us."

Serena lowered her head. "No. I hate it. I would rather live a normal life than be divine. A lot of good this has done for me. My mother is dead and my father doesn't care."

Natalie shot Serena an exasperated look. "You don't know that."

"Isn't it obvious? My name was on some *database*!" Serena shook her hands in front of her face. "You and whoever sent you took the time to look for me, so why couldn't he? Why didn't someone send him a letter or something if he didn't know?"

"Well, the Pantheon is really bureaucratic." Natalie cleared her throat, looking embarrassed. "If no one from Mithris ever asked about you, then no one would have volunteered the information. It would have remained available but untouched."

Natalie's heart fell at the mingled grief and fury on Serena's face.

"Hey, your father could have assumed that you died with your mother...depending on how much he knew about the situation."

Serena pulled her sleeve over her hand and wiped her face.

"How did my mother die, anyway?"

Natalie stared at the ground. "The records say that it was Dark Angels."

"Figures." Serena brushed a strand of hair out of her eyes. "They're the cause of all this trouble."

"Not quite. There has to be someone giving the orders, or the Dark Angels wouldn't attack. Someone has to release them from their coffins."

"Coffins? Good god." Serena stuck out her tongue in disgust. "They sound like real winners. Who has creatures like that anyway? What are they good for?"

"Good for? Nothing. They're totally evil, and they're among the most dangerous creatures in the universe."

77

"I noticed." Serena shuddered in spite of the heat. She wrapped her arms around herself. "But why have Dark Angels if you're the good guys? I mean, aren't the gods supposed to be the good guys?"

Natalie tilted her head back and forth, considering the question.

"It's not that clean-cut. Every now and then the gods feel that they need to use deception or murder to achieve their ends. The Dark Angels were created in the War of Chaos—along with a host of other nasty creatures—to help the First Gods defeat the Titans."

"The Titans?"

"The First Gods who rebelled against the other First Gods. The Pantheon might be sketchy on the good side, but the Titans are definitely on the bad side."

"Figures."

"Anyway, after the war was over, some gods argued that the Dark Angels should be destroyed or locked in the Abyss. Others thought they were useful to have around."

"Classy." Serena curled her lip. "And these same gods set up the laws?"

"Yes, but they occasionally find reasons to break them. A lot of them feel that the ends justify the means."

Serena ran a hand through her hair. "But I thought gods were supposed to be good. Aloof, maybe, but good."

Natalie shrugged. "They keep the universe running."

"And they let my mother die!" Serena threw her hands into the air indignantly. "They let this war happen."

"Specifically, the gods of Mithris did that." Natalie raised a finger. "And the humans are the ones fighting the war. Not the gods."

"Yeah, but good leadership starts at the top."

Natalie conceded Serena's point with a nod. "It's a big debate. Human free will versus divine intervention. The gods have debated those issues since they created mankind—and humans have killed countless trees writing about it." Natalie frowned. "And countless other humans too, come to think of it."

"Are there other planets with humans?" Serena asked.

"Of course. Lots of solar systems have humans."

"And is each planet in the same mess?" Serena stared accusingly at Natalie, as if she was in charge. "War and destruction and death?"

"It varies from planet to planet. But the human condition is generally the same, yes."

"And the gods just keep letting it go?" Serena asked incredulously.

"Yep. The universe rolls on."

"But does the system work?"

"Who's to say?" Natalie looked at Serena with a strange expression, as if daring her to question further.

Serena dared. "It doesn't work here. Makes me wonder if anyone has it figured out."

Natalie avoided Serena's gaze, hoping that the difficult questions and heavy accusations would stop soon.

She shook her head and considered the irony. A few days ago, Serena had been the unsociable one. Now, after the recent interrogation, Natalie wanted some time alone.

"So where are you from?" Serena asked, unwilling to give Natalie a break. "I mean, originally. What's your story?" She pointed at Natalie's raincoat, where her journal bulged out of a pocket. "Is it all in there?"

Natalie grabbed her journal protectively. "Yes, I have a story. I wrote it down...am writing it down..." She glanced at her watch—the movement was like a twitch. She looked away quickly, suddenly self-conscious. "We need to pick up our pace. Find another ride to Locke City."

"Hold on. You're not getting away that easily." Serena put her hands on her hips. "What's your story? Let me see the journal."

She reached for it, but Natalie stepped away.

"No." Natalie stared from Serena to her outstretched hand.

"I've seen you writing in it." Serena rolled her eyes. "I know that you're writing about me."

Natalie shook her head furiously, blushing. "I don't want to talk about it right now. It's not the time."

"Time!" Serena yelled, waving her arms angrily. "It's all about time with you, isn't it? Time and secrets! What's with all of the secrecy? What's on the clock?"

Natalie bit her lip.

They had stopped walking and were standing in the middle of the road. Natalie looked up at the sun. It was no longer at the top of the sky but had drifted lazily off to the west. The sun still beat down upon them. It had to be early afternoon.

What's on the clock indeed.

"Fine." Natalie wiped sweat from her face—including one particular drop that had fallen from her eye and traced its way down her cheek.

"What?" Serena leaned close. "Fine what?"

"Fine, as in 'I'll tell you my story' fine."

"Excellent. It's about time we got some more answers from you."

"But," Natalie held up a finger, "I'll only tell you my story if you tell me your story first."

"Me?" Serena stared incredulously at Natalie. "Why should I tell mine first?"

Natalie raised her nose defiantly. "I told you something last night."

"Last night—oh, right!" Serena slapped her sides in frustration. "Sure! You told me something last night that saved our lives! That was a real heart-to-heart!"

"I told you something out of my book—a memory."

"A memory?" Serena eyed Natalie with a strange interest. "You told me my mother's name. That was your memory? You knew my mother?"

She snatched at the journal, but Natalie yanked it away just in time.

"I didn't say that!" Natalie held Serena off with her free hand. "Stop it, Serena! I didn't say that I knew your mother!"

"But you have her name from your memories!" Serena insisted, grabbing Natalie and trying to tale the book.

"I wrote it down from the database!" Natalie pushed her away. Serena stumbled backwards and fell.

Natalie stood over her friend, shaking her head. "Goodness! Calm down!"

Serena glared at her.

"Information still counts as a memory," Natalie said. "I've given you something important. Now I want to know more about you."

"Hmmph," Serena said.

They eyed each other warily.

Finally, Natalie offered her hand. "Are you going to behave?"

Serena nodded and took Natalie's hand. She stood, and a sly grin spread across her face.

Natalie didn't like that smile. She turned and continued down the road. Serena followed.

"So are you going to tell me something from that book?" Serena pointed at the journal.

"You first." Natalie waved over her shoulder.

"Fine." Serena rolled her eyes. "And then you'll tell me something?"

Now it was Natalie's turn to grin. She beamed in triumph, pleased that she was getting her way.

Serena sighed. "What do you even want to know?"

"A lot, actually," Natalie said excitedly, jumping into fact-finding mode. "For example, what have you been doing for the past fifteen years? And how did you not know that you were a demigoddess?"

Serena sniffed in derision. "Aren't you the deity expert? How are people supposed to discover that?"

"I'm no expert on your personal experience, and discovering the divine essence is different for each individual," Natalie said, sounding academic in spite of herself. "A lot of people discover their identity through moments of intense stress, as you did. That discovery can be precipitated by some kind of object or feeling."

"Or a memory. Like my mother's name."

"Right." Natalie nodded. "But were there any moments in your childhood when you discovered power in yourself?"

Serena scratched her head. "Nothing comes to mind."

"No strange abilities or knowledge? Sometimes demigods will set stuff on fire or levitate objects or other things like that. Anything like that ever happen with you?"

"Never."

"Interesting." Natalie pursed her lips in thought. "Perhaps the trauma of your mother's death suppressed your powers until her memory brought it all flooding back."

Serena's face darkened at the mention of her mother's death. She shrugged. "I guess. I don't know."

"So who did you live with?"

"A lady."

"A single mom?"

"I didn't say that she was a mom, but I lived with her."

Natalie raised her eyebrows curiously. "Just you and her?"

"Just us." Serena nodded. "She's a professor at Locke University."

"What's her name?"

"Professor Danette Glen. She teaches history."

"And did you know that she wasn't your real mother?"

"Yes. She told me that I was adopted from an orphanage."

Natalie's eyes widened. "An orphanage?"

"Yes, an orphanage," Serena answered irritably. "She told me I was adopted as soon as I was old enough to handle that information. Professor Glen always liked to be up front about things."

Serena stared off into space, expressing an emotion that Natalie couldn't read.

"Professor Glen was just a straightforward woman. A good teacher—but to the point."

"And how was your life with her?"

"It was decent. I guess. Professor Glen is one of the top professors at Locke University. She works hard. All of my needs were provided for." Serena played with the sleeves of her black cardigan. "I got a good education at school and nice things at home. I never had reason to complain, except that we never left Locke City. Not even for a vacation to the country. That's why I hate the city so much. I've been stuck there for eighteen years."

"Why didn't you just take a trip yourself?"

"I didn't have a car, and Professor Glen always got upset when I asked if I could take a train somewhere." Serena rolled her eyes. "She apparently couldn't fathom why I would want to leave."

"Didn't you have a car? When did you get that one?" Natalie pointed in the direction of their abandoned car.

"Oh..." Serena hesitated. "I got that car not long before I left."

Natalie narrowed her eyes. "How 'not long before' are we talking about?"

Serena looked away, chewing on her lip.

Natalie's jaw dropped. "You stole Professor Glen's car?"

"I didn't say that," Serena snapped.

"But you did, didn't you! You were sick of being cooped up in the city! You just stole her car one day and started driving!"

Serena scowled. "So you're telling *me* the story now?"

Natalie put her hands on her hips. "I can't believe you stole the car!"

"Well, it's a good thing I did, with those Dark Angels hunting me!" Serena raised her voice defensively. "If I hadn't left the city in time, I could have been dead!"

"Or maybe they started hunting you *because* you left Locke City." Natalie pointed an accusing finger at Serena. "Ever think about that?"

"What?" Serena blinked.

"Have you heard of geographic magic?"

"What?"

"Of course you haven't." Natalie waved her hand impatiently. "But geographic magic refers to a spell centered on a certain location, like a city. Of course, the spell will be stronger if the location has magical potency—like Locke City, since it holds the Tower of the Gods. Geographic magic has a variety of uses. Concealment is one of them. It's possible that whoever registered you at the Pantheon also provided for your protection in Locke City by casting a geographic concealing spell."

"And what would that do?"

"Basically, as long as you stayed in Locke City, you would be undetectable to any gods or supernatural creatures."

"But when I left..." Serena bit her lip.

"The concealment lifted. You became detectable. Not like a flashing beacon—but anyone who was searching for you in that area could have found you. That's how I found you along the highway. I traced your demigoddess essence—your 'indefinable something.'" Natalie pursed her lips. "Obviously, the Dark Angels did too. They must have caught your trail right after you left Locke City. Why else would they have waited fifteen years to attack you? Your enemy waited for you all that time, hoping you might turn up. And you finally did."

Serena wrung her hands nervously. "But you don't know for sure that's what happened, do you?"

Natalie shrugged, her expression grim. "It's a good guess. We won't know for sure unless we ask Professor Glen—who I've decided we should visit anyway."

"What?" Serena hurried after Natalie, who had started walking again. "I don't think you understand. I didn't leave Professor Glen on the best of terms."

"Right. You stole her car."

"I can't just walk back into her house again like nothing happened!"

"You won't. You'll apologize to her, and I'll be there with you."

"What? But—" Serena broke off into incoherent noises of frustration.

"I can't believe you were just left in an orphanage after your mother died," Natalie said. "Do you remember the orphanage at all?"

"Remember? No, but," Serena sputtered, "I mean, I was really little. I don't see what that has to—"

"I don't think there ever was an orphanage," Natalie interrupted. "My guess is that whoever rescued you as a child placed you directly in Professor Glen's care. We need to find out who that rescuer was. We'll talk to the professor and find out whatever she knows. It will give us something to work with before we get to the Tower. Maybe she knows who your enemy is." Natalie arched an eyebrow at Serena. "It would be nice to know who wants us dead before we walk into the front lobby."

Serena fumed, tying her hair into a ponytail to do something with her hands. She glared at Natalie but was unable to come up with a good retort. She had to content herself with crossing her arms and making disgruntled noises.

*

The girls trudged along the highway, Natalie deep in thought, Serena blocking the sun with her hand. A few trees interrupted the grassy plain, but the rest of their view was full of flat earth stretching out to the horizon.

Natalie examined Serena. Although the girl was still upset, she looked healthier. Her skin was reviving a little, the sun having restored some of the color and warmth to her face.

Natalie glanced over her shoulder to check (for the hundredth time, it seemed) if there were any cars.

Her eyes widened, and she came to a dead stop.

"Have we been invaded, Serena?"

"I don't think so. Why?" Serena turned around to follow Natalie's gaze.

"Because those tanks sure are going somewhere in a hurry." Natalie pointed down the highway. A column of dust was billowing on the horizon. "And I hope they're on our side."

CHAPTER 9:
RELUCTANT PASSENGERS

The girls stepped off the road to let the tanks pass. A long line of trucks and jeeps followed in their wake.

Serena watched the military vehicles speed by. "Where do you think they're going in such a hurry?"

"Don't know..." Natalie eyed the big olive-green tanks apprehensively.

The first few vehicles sped by without stopping, but then a truck pulled out of line. It drove alongside the road, directly toward the girls. Two young men in green uniforms sat in the front seats. The truck bed was covered with a tarp.

As soon as the truck stopped, three uniformed men with rifles jumped out of the back. Before Serena and Natalie could react, they had been surrounded.

The soldiers raised their weapons.

"Hands up!" A clean-shaven young man motioned at them with his rifle.

"Who are you?" Serena raised her chin defiantly.

"We said 'Hands up!'" One of the soldiers moved closer until the barrel of his gun was inches from Serena's chin.

He did not look much older than she did, but there was grim determination in his stern blue eyes. He seemed ready and able to pull the trigger.

Serena and Natalie raised their hands.

"Who are you?" he demanded.

"We're from Locke City," Serena said. She glanced at the tag on his chest, which read "Clayton."

"What are you doing here?" the soldier pressed.

"We're—" Serena hesitated.

"Road-tripping," Natalie supplied.

Serena and Clayton both looked at Natalie. To her credit, she kept a straight face.

"Road-tripping," Clayton repeated.

Natalie nodded. Serena nodded too.

"Right," he said skeptically. He jerked his head at one of the soldiers. "Private Jones, search them."

"Yes, sir." Jones stepped forward and grabbed Serena.

"Hey!" she protested, caught off guard. The young man started to pat her down, and she slapped him across the face. "Don't you dare touch me!"

Jones wiped his face with the back of his hand. He glared at Serena but retreated, still aiming the gun at her.

He lifted his chin toward Natalie's umbrella. "What's that?"

"It's an umbrella," Natalie answered simply.

He narrowed his eyes. "What's in your pockets?"

"Balloons. Rubber bands. A journal." She tilted her head. "What's in *your* pockets?"

"Uh..." Jones looked from Natalie to his superior. "Your orders, corporal?"

Corporal Clayton studied them for a minute before reaching a decision.

"All right." He lowered his rifle. His soldiers followed suit. "Put them in the back of truck and let's move out."

Jones and the other man slung rifles over shoulders and grabbed Natalie and Serena by the arms.

"Put us in the truck?" Serena repeated, wrenching her arm away. "What's this all about?"

"Miss, don't you understand that we're in a state of national emergency?"

"Emergency?"

Jones and the other private snorted in derision.

"Where have you been, miss? Do the words 'Teuten' and 'Gandia' mean anything to you?"

Serena scowled. "Yes."

"Well, they bombed us yesterday," the corporal said. "Teuten has conquered Viras and allied with Gandia. They're trying to soften us up for an invasion. It's working too—Albia and Saint Martin were devastated last night."

"Albia and Saint Martin?" Serena's eyes widened in shock. "Devastated?"

"Devastated," he repeated grimly. He grabbed Serena's arm and steered her toward the back of the truck. "More cities will burn if the air force doesn't get its act together. The Teutens use some mean incendiary bombs." He grunted. "The military is stretched and casualties are high all around. We don't want

86

people running around the country unaccounted for, do we? Gotta watch out for civilians—and spies!"

"Our car broke down in the highway—how could we be spies?" Natalie asked.

"I didn't say you were spies." Clayton helped the girls to a wooden bench. "You trying to tell me something?"

"No, we're just teenagers—but this is stupid." Serena cast an angry gaze at the interior of the truck.

"Rules are rules." The young man grinned, tilting back his helmet. "Everyone has to be accounted for, and the roads need to be clear."

He swung up the truck bed door.

"Where are you taking us?" Natalie asked.

"To Hamilton, where we can get you on a train and away from danger."

Natalie slapped the side of the bench in protest. "But we need to go to Locke City!"

The corporal shook his head. "Sorry, miss, but Locke City is under heavy bombardment right now. Children are being evacuated from all of the coastal cities."

"We're not children!" Serena growled angrily.

"Of course you're not." Clayton winked. "But either way, we're taking you to Hamilton, where you can ride a train to someplace safe."

"But we need to go to Locke City!" Serena made up a lie on the spot. "My little brother might still be there!"

"Look, miss, children are being evacuated, okay? You can meet up with your kid brother at the train station in Hamilton, or wherever they send you to." He held up his hands, raising his voice above Serena's protest. "A lot of young people are getting moved around, and it's not easy for anyone. We're doing this for your own safety, you understand? We can't just let you wander into a warzone."

He grabbed a few water bottles from his pack and tossed them to the girls. "Have some water—and make it last. It's going to be a long trip." He patted the small door to the truck and shouted to the driver. "All right, let's head out."

Natalie heard a door slam, and then the truck lurched forward to rejoin the convoy. She opened a water bottle and took a grateful sip. It wasn't cold, but it was the first water she had tasted all day. That made it wonderful. Natalie closed her eyes and drained half of the bottle before putting it away.

Serena drank her own water quietly, glowering at the faces of the men driving the truck behind them. The two soldiers grinned. One of them winked. Serena blushed and turned to face Natalie, who was examining her golden watch.

Serena pointed at the strange hands on the clock. "I'm guessing that we're running out of time."

Natalie withdrew her arm when she realized that Serena was watching her. "We're always running out of time."

She pulled her sleeve over the watch and tucked her hands inside her coat pockets.

Serena looked at the line of trucks in their wake. "So do you want to tell me what that watch is all about?"

Natalie shook her head. "Not yet."

"Why not?" Serena scowled, putting her water bottle under the bench. "You said you would tell me some of your story, and we have all of the time in the world."

Natalie rolled her eyes, and Serena sighed impatiently.

"I mean, relatively speaking. We're running out of your weird clock-time, but this truck ride will give us a while to talk."

"Let's talk about something other than my time." Natalie shifted in her seat and sat up straighter. She rubbed her left forearm self-consciously, feeling the watch band.

"Fine." Serena looked at the thick green tarp above them. She gave an exaggerated smile. "At least we have a ride now."

"Who are you and what have you done with Serena? I thought you were the pessimist. Find something unhappy to say."

Serena shrugged. "Nah, I was getting tired of walking."

"We'll be soaked if it rains." Natalie pressed her hand up against the flimsy fabric.

"Maybe this is waterproof material." Serena ran the tips of her fingers against it. "I don't know what they normally have in these trucks. I've never been in a military convoy before."

"I have, but not like this one." Natalie kicked the wooden floor with her rain boot. "Second rate."

*

The convoy traveled through the night, stopping only when the sun crept over the horizon at dawn. Scores of engines puttered in unison as the vehicles slowed to a halt.

Natalie could hear the soldiers getting out of their vehicles, groaning and yawning while they stretched. A weary-eyed Private

Jones walked to the back of the girls' truck. He lowered the door so Serena and Natalie could get out.

They stretched their sore limbs, grateful for a chance to stand.

"Corporal says take five minutes to get some privacy in the bushes." Jones helped Serena down first. "But don't think about running off. You don't want to abuse your privileges, and you wouldn't get far anyway."

Serena wandered off into the semi-darkness. Natalie took the Jones's hand with her left, still holding the umbrella with her right.

"You don't need your umbrella, miss. No rain clouds out this morning."

"Oh, thanks, but I think I'll hold onto it." Natalie smiled.

"But—"

"Just let the young lady do what she wants, Jones," Clayton grunted, leaning against the truck and shaking his head at the private.

"But sir—"

"Didn't I just give you an order, private? We're wasting time."

Clayton pushed his helmet back and cupped his hands around his mouth to light a cigarette. The match illuminated the black stubble on his face.

"Let them do their business so we can get back on the road."

"Yes, sir." Jones answered sheepishly, allowing Natalie to walk into the darkness—but not before she had shot him a look of triumph.

She stumbled along, half-asleep, trying to find a bush a reasonable distance from the road.

"Don't go far!" Jones yelled.

"Shut *up*, Jones!" Clayton barked. "They heard you the first time. They'll come back before we leave. Those girls don't want to walk any more than you do."

Serena and Natalie were back in the truck a few minutes later. Serena appeared pale and worn again.

"Are you okay?" Natalie asked worriedly.

Serena leaned against the side of the tarp, caressing her stomach. "You still have any of that food?"

Natalie searched inside her coat and pulled out a squished banana.

"Oops," she smiled weakly, placing the banana on the bench beside her. "Don't worry, I'll eat that one."

She handed Serena the bag of dried fruit. The older girl grabbed a handful and began munching on it, blinking in the soft red light of the rising sun.

"It could be a pretty day," she muttered. "If only I wasn't so tired and this country wasn't at war."

"At least we're together, right? With friends?" Natalie examined the squished banana, trying to figure out the best way to peel it. "Things will get better when we find a way to—" She paused, looking around to see if any soldiers were around.

But the truck behind them had started up its engine, and the convoy was on the move once more.

"...when we find a way to Locke City," Natalie finished.

Serena smiled briefly before zipping up the food bag and handing it back. "You do realize that I don't want to be a hero."

Natalie tucked the bag inside her coat pocket. "What do you mean?"

"I mean I'm only going to Locke City for answers."

Natalie could not prevent her eye from twitching. "I still don't understand."

"Listen, Natalie." Serena lowered her voice, leaning close so that her face was inches from Natalie's. "I think that you're a nice person. You've done a lot for me. I want to know more about my past—but not so I can save the world. I want to put these demons to rest so I can move on with my life."

She leaned back, undoing the knot in her ponytail.

"Maybe you didn't hear," she let the hair fall over her shoulders. "But I've already been through a lot, and I don't feel like I owe the world anything." She closed her eyes. "It's not like the world has done much for me."

Natalie's jaw dropped. "What do you mean? This is your world—*yours*, not mine. You *have* to help! And how can you say that the world hasn't done much for you? Professor Glen adopted you—took you in and raised you!"

"Yeah, and we were such a cozy family," Serena said bitterly. "And now you're saying she probably lied to me about the orphanage. Who knows what else she lied about?" She scowled. "Nothing is what it seems."

"No." Natalie frowned, looking Serena up and down. "Nothing at all."

90

CHAPTER 10:
THE HIGH COUNSELOR

The great doors to the throne room opened, stirring Julius from his nap.

He rubbed his eyes, blinking in the dying sunlight that shone over Locke City. The skyline was different now—a number of buildings had been destroyed in the Teuten air raids. As night approached, the streets were quiet and the lights were dark. Locke City held its breath, nervously anticipating the bombers that would return tonight.

Julius heard someone walk up the marble steps behind him.

"Who's there?" he yawned.

"It is your faithful counselor, Nikolas."

"Oh, hello." Julius swiveled his chair around lazily to face the older god.

Nikolas bowed respectfully, his gray hair falling over his face. "My lord, all but twenty of the council members have returned to their principalities. The remaining delegates seem to be...enjoying one another's company in the suites. But they will be gone tomorrow."

"Finally." Julius rubbed the bridge of his nose wearily. "Company is such a headache. I need peace and quiet."

"Yes, my lord. And allow me to repeat my sympathies about the Assembly. I am terribly sorry it did not go as planned—"

"Didn't go as planned?" Julius snorted. "It was a total disaster. I will admit, however, that this Assembly was far more entertaining than any I can remember."

"Yes." Nikolas cleared his throat. "Dantis and Lott were entirely out of line."

"They were the most disruptive elements of an entirely unhelpful council." Julius waved his hand dismissively. "I'm sorry to have put you through that."

"It was my duty. I live to serve."

"Yes, you do." Julius smiled. He stroked the lion's head sculpted into his armrest, gazing thoughtfully at the golden decoration. "But tell me, Nikolas, what do you think about the current situation?"

Nikolas hesitated. "You have decided not to intervene, my lord."

Julius sighed. "I already know what I think. I asked what *you* think. You advised my father for countless millennia, and I'm asking you to advise me. So please. Advise."

"Well, my lord, the situation has recently changed. War has come to Artema—"

"Yes, I know that." Julius rolled his eyes. "I saw the planes bombing the city. I can see the damage from here." He swept his hand in the direction of the skyline. "War has come—but to the humans. Not to us."

"Yes...to the humans."

"Your advice then?"

Nikolas frowned. "The humans are acting naturally. As it is, they expand into each other's territory unchecked. Without intervention, this violence will only continue."

"And what do you think of that?"

Nikolas folded his hands and stared at his interlocked fingers. "The humans have great capacity for good and evil. But they are, in many ways, like children. Without guidance, they follow their own impulses, which are immature and short-sighted. They must be guided. The humans cannot preserve their own system. They did not create it, and they cannot maintain it."

Julius drummed his fingers on the armrest. "So what do you think I should do?"

"I think mankind will eventually destroy itself if you do not intervene."

"Destroy itself?" Julius raised his eyebrows, pausing for a long moment before speaking again. "Duly noted. Thank you, Nikolas. I will consider what you've said."

He waved his hand to indicate that Nikolas was dismissed. The High Counselor bowed, retreating down the steps of the dais. He paused when he reached the bottom.

"My lord," he asked, "what do *you* think about the current situation?"

"What do I think?" Julius laughed, shifting in his seat. "Do you really want to know?"

Nikolas inclined his head. "Earnestly."

Julius gripped the lion armrest. A frown creased his forehead. "I don't care about the current situation."

"Don't care about?" Nikolas walked slowly up the marble steps. "Or don't care for?"

"I don't care about it. The humans and their wars are of little concern to me. Even if they destroy Locke City, or all of Artema, the world will go on. The planet will spin and the seasons will change. The Tower of the Gods remains untouched." Julius shrugged. "It's the natural order of things that civilizations rise and fall. And if humanity suffers extinction, so be it. They're inferior creatures."

Nikolas raised an eyebrow. "Is that what you really think, my lord?"

"It is. There is a divide between us and the mortals. I don't intend to cross it. They can handle their own problems, just like we handle ours."

Nikolas paused before responding. "That almost sounds like your sister."

Julius's face darkened. Nikolas swallowed, dropping his gaze to the floor.

"Forgive me, my lord. I spoke out of turn."

"No." Julius stood suddenly. Nikolas flinched and took a hesitant step back, but Julius did not move toward the counselor.

Instead, he walked behind his throne to the panoramic window. He folded his hands behind his back, staring at the skyline.

"No, you're right. That is my sister speaking." Julius's lip curled. "It has been my sister speaking for fifteen years."

Nikolas approached Julius cautiously. "What do you mean? Does Ambrosia advocate isolation?"

"Not in so many words, but yes."

"How strange. It seems to me that she wants to be involved in the affairs of men."

Julius scoffed, not bothering to disguise the bitterness in his voice. "Don't let her fool you. Involvement with mankind is the last thing my sister has ever wanted."

"Ah." Nikolas bowed reverently. "I should have remembered. I am sorry."

Julius clenched his jaw, trying to focus on the sunset before him—but feeling instead a sharp twinge in his heart.

"It's not your fault."

"I wish I could have done more at the time."

"There's nothing you could have done," Julius whispered, a slight catch in his throat. "Their homes are so fragile and easily destroyed. Fires or floods. And the humans themselves, my wife, my daughter...so fragile." He shook his head.

"I wish I could have convinced your father to let them stay here."

Julius reached out to hold Nikolas's shoulder. "Thank you for saying that, my friend. But it wasn't your place. There's nothing you could have done."

He watched the sun dip completely out of sight.

"Did I ever tell you how I met her?"

Nikolas blinked in surprise. "No, my lord."

"It was eighteen years ago. About three years before my father died." Julius closed his eyes. "He was so ill back then. I couldn't stand the sight of him looking so weak..." He cleared his throat, embarrassed. He glanced at Nikolas. "I can trust you, can't I?"

Nikolas raised his eyebrows. "Of course, my lord. I have served your family since the War of Chaos. I've known you and your sister since—even before your mother—"

"Left us here with Father, yes." Julius smiled bitterly. "She wasn't much of mother. Or a wife. But my father wasn't much of a husband, was he?"

Nikolas avoided Julius's gaze. He stared at the sunset, his expression unreadable. "Your father was a mighty warrior."

"Well, that's something, I guess." Julius scowled. Then he shook his head, ridding his mind of the thought. "But I almost forgot my story. One day, over eighteen years ago, I decided that I had to leave the Tower. Ambrosia was pestering me about something or another. Father was sick. I couldn't stand it any longer. So I took the Portal and envisioned going someplace beautiful. Nowhere far—somewhere in Locke City—but somewhere I could get some peace."

Julius smiled, closing his eyes and allowing the memory to wash over him. "And I found myself in a beautiful garden. I remember it so well. The sunlight shone on me through the trees, bathing me in warmth. Flower petals floated to me on the wind—all of nature embraced my presence. It soothed my soul. And then—"

Julius's eyes widened. He took a sharp breath, just like he had when he first saw her.

"There she was. A daughter of man. She was clothed in a simple green dress—all the more to accent her stunning beauty. Her long brown hair cascaded over her slender shoulders. She saw me—and her blue eyes twinkled at me like stars." Julius shook his head. "She can't have been human. She was more beautiful than any goddess I've ever seen. She bewitched me. When she spoke to me, her every word was a melody to my ears."

Nikolas stared out of the window, standing still as a statue, listening to the tale of Julius's love.

"And I knew in that moment that she had to be mine." Julius's voice was so uncharacteristically passionate that Nikolas stepped back in surprise. "It wasn't right that someone so beautiful should be kept from me. And I thought, 'Perhaps the humans are not so different after all.'"

Julius stared into the night as the stars appeared in the sky. "And she loved me. It was over in a moment. We were captivated by each other."

Nikolas averted his gaze, clearly embarrassed. But Julius didn't care. He closed his eyes and inhaled deeply.

Jillian's face swam across his mind, her brown hair teasing him...but then the brown hair glowed, brightening to a blonde head, and the vision of an angry sister replaced his lover.

A shadow passed across Julius's face, and he scowled, turning to Nikolas.

"But Ambrosia couldn't leave it alone. I simply couldn't be in love with a mortal."

Nikolas swallowed. His eye twitched.

"Father couldn't let her stay in the Tower, could he?" Julius growled. "But what did he know about love? All he knew was war and honor—rules and laws! If they had just let us be, my family would still be alive!"

Julius screamed, slamming his fist in the hard floor. Shards of black obsidian flew into the air, and Nikolas jumped in fright.

Julius withdrew his fist, leaving a small crater in the ground. He straightened himself up again, his shoulders heaving. He wiped sweat from his brow and glanced apologetically at Nikolas.

"I'm sorry that you had to see that, my friend. I said too much. I should have let you go earlier. That was improper."

"No, my lord." Nikolas held up his hands. "That is, after all, why I'm here. I may not understand all of the duties and feelings of the God of Gods, but I have served one all my life. You can always trust me with whatever you have to say."

Julius nodded gratefully. "Thank you, Nikolas. And you can always trust me."

Nikolas bowed, understanding this as his time to leave. He started down the marble steps before stopping at the bottom once more. "As it so happens, there is one last thing that I wanted to discuss with you."

Julius sighed. He walked around his throne and fell into the chair.

"What is it?" he asked, straightening his robes at the shoulder and rubbing his forehead wearily.

"I..." Nikolas hesitated. He brushed his long gray hair out of his eyes. "I have heard dangerous whispers as of late."

Julius rested his chin in his hands. "Dangerous whispers?"

Nikolas glanced behind him, making sure that the doors were closed. "Whispers from those in the Assembly who want us to be more involved in the affairs of men. From those who question your leadership."

Julius gripped the lion armrests tightly. "And who might be the gods guilty of such treacherous whispers?"

Nikolas hesitated again, as if struggling to come to terms with something in his mind. "Anyone who thinks they could be a better ruler of Mithris. Anyone who hungers for power."

"A better ruler? Than me?" Julius tightened his fists. "Who would be so arrogant? Why would you say such a thing?"

"They are not my thoughts, my lord." Nikolas held up his hands. "And I do not even know if any serious threat exists. As I said, there have only been whispers. But I spoke my mind too plainly. Please forget what I have said."

Julius rose to his feet. "No, you had a reason for saying it! Tell me," he implored, walking down the dais. "What do you know?"

"Just...guesses. Guesses and observations."

"But who?"

Nikolas wrung his hands in obvious discomfort. "I can't say, my lord."

"Tell me!"

"It's only speculation!"

Julius threw up his hands in dismay. "Then why bring it up?"

"Because it's worth being careful, my lord." Nikolas lowered his voice to a whisper. "Surely you see the wisdom in that? I have been following someone for some time."

"Who—"

Nikolas held up a finger. "I cannot say who just yet. I don't want to be the god who prejudices you against anyone. I couldn't live with that—but neither could I live with the thought that your life might be in peril! I have known of rulers who have been overthrown by their council—assassinated with Dark Angels by their closest companions."

Julius nodded, urging Nikolas to go on.

"All I can say—and mark me closely, my lord," Nikolas stared intently at Julius, "is that you must be careful of anyone who undermines your authority."

"Of course." Julius nodded, his mind racing. "Of course..." He stroked his chin anxiously. "I will consider everything you've said."

"Very good, my lord. I shall continue to keep a sharp eye, and to follow the one whom I suspect."

"Very well." Julius stepped forward and grasped Nikolas's hands firmly. "Together we will stamp out any treachery."

Nikolas met his gaze. "And preserve the safety of Mithris."

Julius let Nikolas go, and the older god strode across the long white carpet toward the tall doors.

The counselor's words rang in his ears like hammers. He turned and looked at the night sky, his chest tightening with anxiety.

Gods assassinated by their closest companions...

Be careful of anyone who undermines your authority...

...anyone who undermines my authority.

Julius's stomach twisted in angry knots. Ambrosia undermined his authority.

He snorted. That was an understatement. She was the epitome of insolence. She always questioned him.

But was it malicious?

Not really. She was just being...Ambrosia.

But she belittled him. She was ashamed of him, and she probably thought she could be a better ruler.

A nervous energy crept up his arms. Ambrosia was his closest relative. She was next in the line of succession.

Would she ever overthrow him?

Surely not...

But Dark Angels...Nikolas had mentioned gods who had been assassinated by Dark Angels.

Hadn't his father kept Dark Angels down in the Crypt?

Julius swung his chair around.

"Nikolas?" he called out, a sliver of unease in his voice.

Nikolas stopped by the doors. "Yes, my lord?"

"Are there any Dark Angels in the Crypt?"

Nikolas tilted his head in reflection.

"I believe there are."

"And could anyone release the Dark Angels?"

Nikolas shook his head and smiled reassuringly.

"Not without your knowledge, my lord. You are the only one with the keys. The Crypt was one of your father's best kept secrets. No one else besides your sister has any knowledge of it."

"Right." Julius swallowed. "Thank you."

Nikolas bowed as he walked out. The throne doors shut with a dull boom.

Julius hurried to the door after him, listening until Nikolas's footsteps faded away. He reached into his robes, feeling a set of bronze keys in an inner pocket. Then he opened the door and set off quietly down the hall. The Crypt might be a well-kept secret, but he would make absolutely sure that the Dark Angels still rested in their coffins.

Then he would discover who the conspirators were, and they would join the Dark Angels in darkness and slumber.

CHAPTER 11:
THE TRAIN STATION

The girls arrived at Hamilton as the sun set on their second day of travel. Thick curtains of red light fell across the town's gray buildings. Tall billboards with tattered advertisements punctuated the darkening horizon.

Serena looked out of the truck, noting a black and white sign that read "Hamilton." A gray brick courthouse was off to her right. The courthouse was the largest building in the town. In its shadow were a brewery, an abandoned theater, and a coffee house. A few cars dotted the surrounding parking lots.

Natalie leaned forward to see past Serena as the truck came to a stoplight. "Not a lot of people."

They made a quick right turn and the truck swayed, throwing Natalie back onto the bench.

The tires rumbled as they crossed over the railroad tracks to the Hamilton Train Station. They pulled into the gravel parking lot next to a few other trucks. A large blue and green train was already in the station.

"Only two passenger cars." Serena frowned. "That's not a lot of room. I wonder why they're running short."

"Goodness gracious!" Natalie stuck out her tongue. "What a color scheme."

"There's nothing wrong with blue and green." Serena sounded offended. She gave Natalie's yellow raincoat an appraising look. "Just because you like to dress like candy corn."

Natalie stifled a giggle. "I like candy corn."

"Well, each to her own," Serena said. Private Jones lowered the small door and helped her out. "Besides, I like the engine—it's diesel."

"Steam engines are better." Natalie waved off the private's hand and jumped out of the back. Her rain boots scrunched on the gravel. "They have more character."

"Diesels have plenty of character. And they're more powerful."

Natalie shrugged. "Each to her own. How do you know so much about trains anyway?"

Serena snorted. "What do you mean, 'how do I know so much?' Anybody can see that it's a diesel engine."

"Not many girls would take the time to learn that." Natalie twirled her umbrella absentmindedly.

"Well, I like trains, okay?"

"The station is over there," Private Jones interrupted, pointing at the building directly in front of them.

Serena eyed him quizzically. "Thanks?"

"Y-you're welcome," he stammered. He met Serena's gaze and blushed.

An uncomfortable warmth rose up in Serena's chest. He was looking differently at her than before—when he had pointed a rifle in her face.

He cleared this throat. "I hope you have a safe trip."

"Thanks," Natalie said brightly.

Serena just nodded.

"Our convoy is moving on," he pointed awkwardly at the truck. "So...have a safe trip."

"Thanks," Serena said curtly. "You too."

Private Jones nodded. His Adam's apple bobbed up and down in his skinny, unshaven neck.

Why was he extending this awkward exchange?

"Uh..." he scratched the short black hair under his helmet, drawing attention to a forehead pimple. It reminded Serena how young these soldiers were. "I hope you find your little brother," he added.

Serena gave a start, momentarily forgetting about the pimple. "My what?"

Confusion wrinkled Jones's face. "Uh...your brother?"

She betrayed herself with surprise before remembering her lie from the other day. She was about to salvage the situation when Natalie jumped in.

"Yeah, your brother," she said. "Jimmy...Bob."

"Jimmy-Bob?" Serena and Private Jones repeated.

"Yes," Natalie affirmed, with admirable conviction. "Jimmy-Bob."

Jones looked at Serena, who turned a shrug into a fervent nod. "Yes. Jimmy-Bob."

When the soldier didn't look convinced, Serena pressed on.

"My side of the family doesn't normally call him Jimmy-Bob. Her side does. We've been...estranged."

Jones raised an eyebrow. "Estranged?"

"Yeah," Serena cleared her throat awkwardly. She grabbed Natalie and pulled her into a stifling hug. "But now we're back together!" She gritted her teeth with forced happiness. "And we'll find Jimmy-Bob and everything will be okay."

Jones opened and closed his mouth.

"Yeah," he finally said. "Yeah! I hope you do."

"Well, thank you so much," Serena said, steering Natalie toward the station. "We'll just head into the train—"

Jones held out his hand. "Oh! Before you go, I was...I was th-thinking..." he started stammering again.

Serena's smile froze on her face. Was this guy going to ask her out?

Fortunately, Corporal Clayton appeared from around the truck and rescued them from death by awkwardness.

"Jones!" he barked. "Get your butt in the truck! We're pulling out in ten minutes."

The private snapped to attention. "Yes, sir! Butt in the truck, sir!"

He retreated sheepishly toward the passenger side. He paused at the door to steal a look at Serena, but the corporal glared him into the truck. Jones stepped inside and shut the door, a look of resignation on his youthful face.

Corporal Clayton turned smartly and tapped his helmet respectfully at Natalie and Serena.

"Ladies," he said. "Have a safe trip. Stay out of trouble."

"Yes, sir," both girls repeated.

He walked to the truck and opened the driver door.

"Oh," he added to Serena, "and I hope you find your little brother."

Serena forced another smile. "Thank you."

"Yes, sir," Natalie agreed with a straight face. "Little Jimmy-Bob, sir."

Clayton nodded and pulled himself into the truck.

"Jimmy-Bob?" Serena hissed as they walked away.

"At least I *remembered* you had a little brother," Natalie hissed back. She nudged Serena in the ribs. "I think Private Jones likes you."

"Don't care."

"You don't like a man in uniform? I thought he was rather fetching. When he wasn't about to shoot us."

"Oh shut up," Serena snapped. She pulled away from Natalie and stalked toward the train. "I'm going to look at the diesel. I'll meet you in the station."

"But I want to look at it—"

"I said I'll *meet you in the station*," Serena said, squeezing Natalie's shoulders meaningfully.

"Ooh." Natalie frowned. "I see."

"Thanks," Serena said, releasing Natalie with a light shove toward the station.

After making sure that Natalie was actually going to the station, Serena almost skipped to the tracks. She stepped in front of the engine, and excitement filled her chest. The engine was loud, but she relished the noise.

Serena gazed at the blue and green markings that stretched around the engine. Blue and green were the colors of the Arteman Express. She used to see the Express all the time when she visited the train yard after school.

She stepped off the tracks and picked up a loose railroad spike, remembering how she would collect them back home. Serena smiled. She loved the train yard.

Occasionally, the engineers would let her up into the engine to drive one of the trains into the station—carefully supervised by their veteran hands, of course.

"Trains, trains..." She caressed the railroad spike in her hand, finding momentary relief in her nostalgia.

But she realized that very train yard was being bombed in Locke City. Her face darkened.

She dropped the railroad spike. It fell to the ground with an empty clatter.

*

Serena walked back to the front of the station to rejoin Natalie, who was wrapping herself in her yellow raincoat. Serena pulled on her black cardigan, suddenly conscious of the colder weather.

"Come on into the station, ladies!" A soldier waved at the girls and pointed to the entrance.

Serena and Natalie followed the soldier's orders, walking onto a wooden porch and into the station.

When they entered, Serena was surprised to see that the building was full of children. Dozens of boys and girls sat on the benches. White tags hung around their necks. Other children surrounded vending machines, eyeing sodas and candy bars hopefully. A few tired young ladies in blue uniforms leaned against the wall or sat on benches. One attendant was sleeping, her arm slung over her eyes to block the light.

Natalie beamed. "Don't you love children, Serena?" She clapped her hands in excitement.

"No." Serena frowned. "I didn't like them when I was a child, and I don't like them now."

Natalie opened her mouth in shock. "Why not?"

"They're dirty, loud, annoying, unthankful, and whiny." Serena curled her lip. "Shall I go on?"

"I think they're just too cute." Natalie grinned. She walked up to a little boy and leaned over, hands on her knees. "What's your name?"

The boy took a step back, putting a finger to his mouth shyly.

"See?" Serena laughed. "Kids. They don't like you."

Natalie reached inside her coat and pulled out a bunch of balloons, which inflated and rose through the air on white strings. The boy laughed in delight. He reached for a balloon—but then hesitated. He looked into Natalie's eyes for reassurance, and she nodded. The boy smiled gleefully and took a red balloon from her hand.

Soon Natalie was surrounded by children. A few of the young ladies in blue uniforms rose from their seats to see what the matter was, but they relaxed when they realized it was just a girl handing out balloons. The sleeping attendant didn't stir at all.

Serena laughed to herself. Those ladies didn't know where the balloons came from, and they didn't care. They just wanted a break.

She moved away from the commotion to find a corner where she could be alone. She thought she had found an isolated bench, but then she saw a little boy walking in her direction. He held a teddy bear in his left hand, and blue and yellow balloons in his right. Serena tried to ignore the boy, but he continued until he stood in front of her.

"Hi." The boy held the yellow balloon out. "My name is Charles Finch. You look lonely."

Serena crossed her arms. "Why do you think I look lonely?"

"Because you're sitting by yourself."

"There are other people sitting by themselves." Serena nodded at some of the uniformed girls.

The boy shrugged and sat down next to her. The bench was small, so Serena was unable to scoot away from him.

She groaned inwardly. The mere presence of children made her feel uncomfortable, but sitting quietly next to one was even worse.

She sighed, resigning herself to conversation. "So how old are you?"

"Six and a half." Charles held up a hand and a finger to show his age.

"And a half?" Serena repeated skeptically. "It's either six or seven. There are no halves allowed."

"Of course there are." Charles frowned. "My friend Emma is only six. I'm six and a half. How old are you?"

Serena made a face. "How old am I? You can't ask a girl how old she is."

"Why not?" It was Charles's turn to make a face. "I wouldn't know how old Emma was if I didn't ask her. Unless I went to her birthday party and I saw it on the cake. When's your birthday?"

"I don't share my birthday with strangers."

Charles held out the yellow balloon again. "If you took the balloon, then maybe we would be friends. What's your name?"

Serena tried to suppress a smile. "My name is Serena." She stole a glance to make sure Natalie wasn't looking, and then she accepted the balloon. "Thank you."

"You're welcome."

"Such nice manners, Charles," Serena managed a brief smile. "Your mother must have taught you well."

"Yes, she did." Charles stuck his head up proudly. "She's very smart and very pretty. And so is my daddy. I mean," he corrected himself, "he's very smart and handsome—not pretty." He looked down at his feet and blushed. "You're pretty though."

"Well, thank you, Charles." Serena hid her amusement by staring at the ceiling through the yellow balloon. She was secretly glad to have a balloon—she just hoped that Natalie wouldn't spot her with one of *her* balloons.

That would be more than Serena could take.

"So where's your mother?" she asked.

"She's back at home." Charles swung his legs back and forth under the bench, still looking at the floor.

"And where's home?"

"I'm from Saint Martin."

Serena felt like a block of ice had slid down her throat and into her stomach. The hair rose on the back of her neck.

"Saint Martin?" she repeated, remembering what the soldiers had said about the city.

Devastated.

Incendiary bombs.

In her mind's eye, she saw the city consumed in a ball of fire—a mother crying out for her son as she disappeared into the flames.

Serena tried to swallow, but her throat had gone dry. She looked down at Charles's black hair, which shone in the station lights.

"Your mother didn't come with you?"

"No, she works at the factory." Charles bounced his teddy bear in his lap. "She needs to stay there and work so Daddy has airplanes to fly."

Serena turned her head away quickly, hoping that Charles did not see the look of horror on her face.

"But she'll be okay," he said confidently.

Serena summoned her nerves and put on a brave face. "Yes, I'm sure she'll be okay."

Charles stopped bouncing his teddy bear. "She prayed to the gods that we would all be safe," he said softly. "So we'll all be safe. I'm taking a vacation to the country while my daddy fights the bad guys, and then I'll go back home."

Serena listened to the conviction in the boy's voice, and her stomach turned. If he only knew.

Something touched her hand, and she gave a start. Looking down, she saw that Charles had taken her hand in his.

She responded to the boy's touch, holding his hand gently in her own. Tears were welling up in Charles's eyes and spilling onto his lap.

Half an hour ago, Serena would have immediately left a crying boy.

But now she found herself giving one a hug.

"It's going to be okay," she whispered, feeling the warmth of Charles's green sweater against her black cardigan.

Charles didn't answer. He just let himself be held.

His tears dripped onto her jeans, creating small watermarks in the denim.

Serena blinked, wondering what on earth she was doing. But it felt natural and right.

And human.

"Hey." She swallowed, feeling obligated to lift the boy's spirits. "That's a nice bear you have. What's his name?"

"This is Eugene." Charles sniffed, wiping his nose with the back of his hand. "He's my friend."

"Hello there, Eugene." Serena gave him a watery smile, touching Eugene's fuzzy paws. "He's a very nice bear."

Charles nodded.

The train whistle sounded, and both of them looked up. The young women in blue uniforms rose to their feet, calling for the children to get ready to leave. They herded the kids toward the doors, helping them pick up their stuffed animals and bags. A parade of balloons made its way out through the main door as the children took Natalie's inflatable presents with them.

"Looks like your train is about to leave, Charles."

"Yeah," Charles said softly.

Serena got up from the bench, surprised to find that she had to wipe her eyes. They must have been sweaty from the ride in the truck.

She cleared her throat, feeling uncomfortable now that the moment of emotion was over. She resorted to swinging her arms by her sides as she waited for Charles to get up. But the boy didn't move.

He was staring intently at Eugene, as if deciding something. Then he untied the white ribbon on Eugene's neck and held it out to Serena.

"What's this?" Serena put her hands on her knees, leaning down to Charles's eye level.

"It's for you." Charles blushed, nodding at the ribbon.

Serena took the silky white ribbon into her hands.

"My mommy said that nice people would take care of me until I got home." Charles stared at the floor and shuffled his feet awkwardly. "You're very nice."

Serena gave him a hug, blinking back something. Maybe tears this time. She sniffed as she let him go.

Charles smiled, and then he bounded off past the rows of benches to the doors. One of the blue-uniformed ladies slapped her forehead in shock.

"Where have you been?" the woman exclaimed, taking Charles outside, his blue balloon floating behind him.

Serena followed after them, past the shafts of light which cut through the ceiling windows. Without the children, the room felt dull and empty. Only a few older travelers remained, talking quietly among themselves as Serena walked by.

Out of the corner of her eye, she saw Natalie leaning against a post. Her arms were crossed, and she was smiling the biggest smile that Serena had ever seen. Serena pretended not to notice, even though Natalie had obviously noticed everything.

Serena stood in the doorway of the station and watched the children file onto the train. A black-haired boy stopped at the stepstool and looked back. It was Charles. Serena waved. He motioned for a little girl with curly brown hair to turn around.

"Must be Emma," Serena said out loud to herself.

The little girl waved too, and then the two children were ushered onto the train.

Charles ascended the stairs and disappeared around a corner, his balloon bumping against the ceiling. Serena rubbed her arms as another evening breeze picked up. Across the train tracks, some soldiers were smoking cigarettes and laughing among themselves.

"Hey missy!" one of them called out. "You best get inside the station. It's gonna get cold. Your train will be here later. This one's full, but the next one should have more than two cars."

Serena nodded curtly to indicate that she had heard, then continued to stare at the children's passenger car. The train whistled again, and the engine started forward.

"You were quite the favorite with the kids."

Serena gave a start. Natalie had joined her on the porch.

"I don't know. You were doing fine yourself." Serena watched the train pick up speed and pull away from the station.

A blind opened at one of the windows, and a small hand waved until the train was lost in the glare of the sunset.

The girls stood in silence for a few minutes. Natalie stared down at the porch, scuffing the wooden floor with her rain boot. The children had been so cute...

"I hope those kids'll be okay." Serena wiped her face with her sleeve, blinking furiously.

"As safe as anyone, I think." Natalie sighed. "They're going away from the fighting." She looked at Serena out of the corner of her eye. "But they won't really be safe until the war is over."

Serena turned away and said nothing.

"Serena, I've told you before how important my mission is. The world needs more than just a girl looking for answers." Natalie crossed her arms. "The world needs a hero. Those children need a hero."

There was a long pause, and then Serena walked back into the station.

Natalie followed her to a bench in an empty corner of the building.

"So..." she cleared her throat. "How are we going to get to Locke City? They think we're children and they won't let us on the eastbound train."

Serena tied Charles's white ribbon in her hair. "Then we'll let ourselves on."

CHAPTER 12:
DESCENT INTO DARKNESS

A long hall stretched out in front of Julius, wrapping around an expansive wall decorated in enormous bas-reliefs. The artwork depicted his father, Aurelius, in various scenes of glory. The powerful portraits were painted with startling realism. The center of the piece showed Aurelius fighting Makay, the fearsome Titan. Makay was piercing Aurelius with his poisoned spear, but Aurelius was standing firm in the fray, poised to strike back with his shining hammer of lightning.

In the actual battle, Aurelius had held his own against Makay in spite of the wound, remaining at his post until he could be relieved. Even then, Aurelius was reluctant to withdraw. His comrades had forcibly removed him to save his life before the poison could kill him on the battlefield.

Julius walked on the white carpet of the hallway, trailing his hand against the golden walls opposite the bas-reliefs.

He sighed. Even in death, the legacy of Aurelius cast a long shadow. He was a legend in war and politics. It was a shame that his talents had not extended to marriage and fatherhood.

Or helped him to understand the love between a god and a mortal.

Julius followed the hall until he arrived at an elevator. A short moment later, the doors slid open silently and he stepped inside. He rolled a series of black dials to select the third level below ground. Wiping sweat from his brow with the back of his hand, Julius watched the black dials count down the floors.

A short time later, the elevator opened to reveal a small antechamber. Massive chains crossed a rough stone door, and a huge lock rested at their center. Julius pulled the ring of bronze keys from inside his robes, fumbling through them until he found the right one.

He put the key into the lock and turned. There was a click, and then the lock vanished into mist. Julius put the keys back into his pocket as the chains rattled loudly, withdrawing into holes at each corner of the entrance.

The door opened, and a draft of cold air grabbed at Julius's chest. He immediately wished that he had worn more than his robes. He held his hand against the door, trying to let his eyes adjust to the darkness before venturing in.

He had not been down here in fifteen years, but the Crypt was as unnerving as he remembered. His only other visit had been after his father's death, when Nikolas had given him control of the keys.

A chilly mist wrapped around his feet and filled the chamber. The blackness before him looked uninviting—and yet it breathed seductively against him, exciting morbid thoughts and fears.

The Crypt held all manner of unspeakable creatures that the First Gods had used in the War of Chaos. The hair stood up on the back of Julius's neck when he considered the beings that resided here. He wished his father had never condescended to use such abominations.

Julius's skin crawled whenever he remembered that Dark Angels slept in their coffins over a hundred stories below him.

So he usually didn't think about it.

But Julius had kept them, because even he might need to use deception or murder at some point—for the greater good. Julius could not deny the Dark Angels' extraordinary powers. They were cold-blooded killers, unparalleled in ruthlessness and efficiency.

Far above the Crypt, at the top of the tower, Guardian Angels played the counterpart to their lethal brethren. Guardian Angels were used for personal protection, but Julius hated the thought of relying on anyone for his own well-being. He rarely used them.

With a twinge of apprehension, Julius realized that his eyes were as adjusted to the dark as they could be. There was no more excuse to delay.

He roused his nerves and stepped into the Crypt.

An ominous hiss sounded behind him, and the light of the elevator was reduced to a thin slit. It ran down the aisle in front of him like an arrow shaft, revealing a smooth dusty floor. Julius fashioned a sphere of light and waved it ahead to illuminate his path. He walked cautiously down a series of stone steps, guided by the orb's blue light. His footsteps echoed in the vault, making him cringe. Who knew what he might disturb down here?

To the left and right, coffins were stacked upright against the walls. His light cast deep shadows underneath them. He thought that he heard faint voices all around him, wisps of air that brushed against his forehead. He shivered.

The long aisle made a sharp right into a cavernous room. Even with the light from his orb, he could see neither the walls nor the ceiling. Alone in this enormous chamber, Julius's breathing sounded heavy in his ears. He wanted to close his eyes, to shut out the unnatural darkness that cowed at the edges of his blue light.

Chains rattled off in the distance. Moans reached his ears from near and far. He shuddered at one particularly close wail and quickened his pace along the paved walk. If he didn't leave the path, he would be fine. Or so he hoped.

Something screamed, freezing his blood.

It lasted for an entire minute, rising to a frightening screech. It ended abruptly, overwhelmed by the clanging sounds of many chains.

Silence again.

Julius felt as though his heart was beating inside of his throat. His breathing was ragged and hoarse.

The path widened to encircle an enormous grate in the ground. He halted before walking over it, but his abrupt stop knocked a rock through the large holes, sending the stone ricocheting against the sides of the pit.

The stone echoed for a long time. Julius held his breath, wondering if the creatures of darkness would be alerted by the noise and attack. However, the massive chamber around him had grown silent. Not a single moan, not one clink of a chain, could be heard.

The stone hit bottom with a rocky clap.

Julius swallowed apprehensively. Maybe there was nothing down there—

A deep growl, like enormous stone slabs grinding against one another, broke the silence. The ground underneath Julius's feet shook, and dust fell onto him from the high ceiling. A dazzling flash of fire shone from the depths—and faded as quickly as it had appeared.

Julius blinked in pain. Spots popped in front of his eyes from the unexpected light. He walked quickly around the grate, making a mental note to ask Nikolas what was down there. He didn't know what it could be. Whatever it was, it didn't seem safe.

Then again, nothing down here was safe.

Julius continued walking, ducking under a low arch to enter the passage to the Dark Angels' vault. Inside, the air was musty, but he was relieved to see walls again. The size of the larger room had made him feel naked and exposed.

He trailed his hand along the sides of the wall, grateful for the protection. The passage had been hewn out from the rock, and the walls grew coarser as he progressed. Julius stepped forward cautiously, in case there were any loose slabs concealing holes.

It disturbed Julius to think that, of all the creatures his father had kept in the Crypt, the Dark Angels were the farthest away from the entrance.

He arrived at the vault and entered, sweeping his gaze across the coffins. They lay in rows on either side of a center aisle.

And they were all open.

Julius's heart leapt into his throat. Someone had been here first.

Someone had unleashed the Dark Angels.

Julius peered inside the nearest coffin. Empty black space yawned back at him. The darkness seemed to fall down forever, making him dizzy. Without thinking, he lowered his hand to feel the bottom of the sarcophagus.

Cold, dead stone met his touch. An image flashed across his sight—a grotesque white face with a blank eyes and a fierce grin.

Julius pulled his hand back with a shudder. He blinked furiously, trying to erase the disturbing vision.

A chill ran down his spine. This place was pure evil, and these creatures had been released into the Tower.

Released to kill him.

But who had released them? Nikolas said that Ambrosia was the only other person who knew about the Crypt.

Ambrosia...

She resented his leadership, but would she stoop to such depths? Would she assassinate him with these demons? Julius's tongue stuck to the roof of his dry mouth.

No.

Ambrosia could never murder him. She was his sister. And as far as he knew, she had never been in the Crypt.

Someone else, surely...another god...

His chest grew hot with anxiety.

Would Ambrosia kill him for the greater good? To save Mithris?

Julius shook his head, trying to dismiss the thought. Ambrosia wouldn't betray him.

But someone else *had* betrayed him.

He walked past the first coffin and examined the others. There were thirteen, all empty. One or two had fallen off the rectangular pedestals, and their broken fragments lay scattered across the floor.

Julius surveyed the room, allowing the blue orb to circle his head. He stood motionless for a few minutes, gazing upon the thirteen open coffins. He clenched his jaw, allowing his anger to overcome his fear, breaking the tension and filling him with power.

He had been betrayed. Someone had stolen the keys to the Crypt, used them, and returned them—thinking that Julius would never notice. Someone had unleashed the Dark Angels.

Julius flexed his fingers, fury coursing through his veins.

He didn't want to believe that Ambrosia was the traitor. And he hoped—for her sake—that she was not.

Julius would show no mercy to those who betrayed him. No matter what ties they held, his enemies would suffer the fullness of his wrath.

The Dark Angels might be the most powerful creatures in the Crypt, but Julius was the God of Gods. He ruled Mithris, and he would kill any god or demon who threatened his rule.

Julius walked back through the rough-hewn passage. He ducked underneath the low archway, leaving the musty vault and entering the cavernous room. The darkness around him stirred, but Julius refused to show any fear. He strode confidently across the paved walk, the blue orb shining the way before him.

He was the God of Gods.

The creatures of the Crypt kept their distance.

STEVEN THORN

STEVEN THORN

CHAPTER 13:
A MATTER OF ADJECTIVES

Serena had fallen asleep against the wooden interior of the train station. The back of her head ached when she woke up to Natalie's excited whispers in her ear.

"The train is here!"

Serena blinked, feeling dizzy as the dim ceiling lights came into focus. Natalie tugged on her arm.

"What?" Serena groaned, rubbing the back of her head. "Ouch! Why did you hit me?"

Serena massaged her shoulder where Natalie had punched it. The red-haired girl did not look sorry.

A whistle sounded.

"Serena, we have to go." Natalie indicated the door with a nervous glance. "Come on."

She offered her hand and pulled Serena to her feet. Around them, the other passengers were gathering up their belongings.

Natalie and Serena followed an elderly couple outside. It was late at night—or early in the morning. They stopped onto the porch in time to see the train pull into the station. The lights of the engine cut through the gathering fog. A rush of cold wind overran the station, and Natalie drew her raincoat close.

The train was coming from the west. Natalie noted the two engines on each side of the cars. They were pointed in different directions, one east, the other west.

"All right, everyone in!" a soldier yelled, walking toward the porch.

Natalie stifled a gasp as Serena pulled her behind a stack of boxes. The soldier stepped onto the porch a moment later, but the girls were safely hidden in the shadows.

"Quickly now." The soldier waved his hand, hurrying the few passengers out of the door and down the stairs. "We need to get these supplies up to Locke City."

"Locke City?" An elderly lady clutched the scarf hanging around her neck. "But we just left Locke City to get away from the fighting! I thought we were going west!"

"Of course you are, ma'am." The soldier helped the lady down the steps. "I should have been more specific. This train is going to separate. Your passenger car is going west to safety, and we're heading up to Locke City."

The soldier motioned at three boxcars attached to the eastbound engine.

"That's our ride," Serena whispered to Natalie, standing on tiptoe to peek over the boxes. "We've got to get on one of those cars."

She edged over to the side of the porch, where she climbed over the railing and dropped into the shadows. She motioned for Natalie to follow. Natalie jumped, and they crept toward the tracks.

The passengers boarded their coach as Natalie and Serena moved through the darkness, trying hard to muffle their footsteps in the gravel. It wasn't working, and Natalie cringed with each noisy footfall. But the soldiers hadn't noticed them yet.

A few feet from the train, they heard someone coming. Serena held up a hand, and they knelt on the ground. It was one of the train engineers.

"He's going to uncouple the—"

"I know what he's going to do!" Natalie hissed. "Be quiet!"

Hidden in the darkness, they waited until the engineer uncoupled the passenger car and the boxcar. Then the girls watched the westbound engine pull away from the station.

"Now's our chance!" Serena grabbed Natalie's hand and pulled her toward a boxcar.

Natalie's heart pounded nervously. The train was sitting in a pool of light from an overhanging lamppost, and their side of the car had no opening. Checking to see that no one was watching, they ran across the tracks and crept toward the door on the opposite side.

Serena tried the handle. It was locked. She swore, slapping the side in frustration.

"Keep it down—and don't swear!" Natalie held a finger to her lips. "The soldiers are close by."

The sound of footsteps approached, and she fell silent. The soldiers stopped on the other side of the car, just across from the girls.

"We ready to pull out?" one soldier called.

"Smith is using the toilet in the station. He'll be right out."

"Well, tell him to hurry up. They need this ammo back at the city. The anti-aircraft guns are gonna be hot for the next few nights."

Serena's panicked voice brought Natalie's attention back to the door.

"What are we going to do? The door's locked!"

Natalie frowned, scratching her head in thought.

"Oh!" Her eyes lit up. She pointed her umbrella at the door.

"Whoa!" Serena raised her hands. "You're not going to blow it up, are you?"

"No." Natalie rolled her eyes. "That would attract far too much attention. I'm going to unlock the door."

"Isn't your umbrella broken?"

"Yes, but this is simple magic." Natalie sniffed. "It's a matter of adjectives."

Serena stared blankly at Natalie.

"All I have to do," Natalie said slowly, as if she was explaining arithmetic, "is add a prefix to the locked door, and make it unlocked." She faced the door. "And here we go! *Un*locked."

She tapped the door twice. The response was a satisfying click. Natalie tugged at the handle, which slid open easily. The inside of the car was dark and piled with boxes. Natalie climbed in.

Serena gaped. "How did you—"

"Come along, dear, before they see us." Natalie pulled Serena inside the car with surprising strength.

"How did you do that?" Serena asked.

Natalie closed the door behind them.

"A simple prefix." She smiled, pleased with the attention. "I did it at the hotel with the window. 'Locked' to 'unlocked' isn't that hard. It's just two letters. Now, adding 'flying' would be something else..."

"I'm surprised that worked," Serena said. "What with your umbrella being broken."

"Oh, this ol' girl still does all right now and then." Natalie smiled fondly at her umbrella.

She looked up at the sound of the soldiers' voices. The men were checking the doors, making sure they were shut.

"Natalie!" Serena whispered. "You need to lock it again before they realize something's wrong."

"Oh, right!" Natalie tapped the door sharply.

There was a sound like the splintering of wood.

Natalie pursed her lips. "Oops."

"What do you mean, 'Oops'?"

"I might not have closed the door the way I wanted to."

"Shh, here they come!"

The soldiers had reached their car.

Serena held her breath, but her worry was for naught. The men tugged roughly at the door handle, and it didn't open. They walked by without stopping.

Moments later, the train began to move. The boxes around them shifted. Natalie fell over, sliding comically across the floor to the back. She braced herself against a crate to keep from moving the length of the car a second time. A pile of boxes fell over, and Serena yelped in surprise.

"Okay, let's settle down," Natalie said. "Contents occasionally shift during transport." She took a deep breath. "By the way, where are you now? I can hardly see a thing."

"Over here."

In the moonlight filtering through the door, Natalie caught a glimpse of Serena waving. Her voice sounded nervous.

"Natalie?"

"Yes?"

"I think you should try to unlock the door again."

"Now? While we're moving?"

"I want to make sure it will open when we get to Locke City. I don't want to be stuck and then get caught by the soldiers."

"All right. If it will make you feel better." Natalie rose unsteadily to her feet, then fell back to her knees as the contents in the boxcar shifted.

"This will be difficult," she muttered.

"It will make me feel better."

"So glad I can help." Natalie crawled along the floor, avoiding a box that slid in front of her to slam against the side. "They should tie these crates down better."

Natalie backed up against the doorway, stretching out her feet, ready to deflect any enemy boxes that might attack. She twisted around to tap the door with her umbrella. The door shuddered, and there was another horrible sound, like the crunch of a broken pencil sharpener.

Natalie tried to pull the door open, just a bit, but it wouldn't budge.

"Shoot."

"Well?" Serena asked, although her voice betrayed that she already knew the answer.

"We might be stuck." Even though it was dark, Natalie avoided Serena's eyes.

"But you could blast us out, right?"

"It would alert the soldiers."

"But we might be able to outrun them! Better than being discovered."

Natalie was silent. She leaned her head against the door, reading a box label in the dim light.

"Your umbrella can still do fireballs, right?" Serena insisted. "You can get us out."

"I'm not sure that a fireball would be advisable." Natalie pulled a crate toward her and slid the top off.

Through the dim moonlight, Serena could see the glinting points of tall metal shells.

"Anti-aircraft rounds," Natalie said softly. "No blasting out. We're stuck."

*

Hours passed as the train rolled along. Natalie had been trying to read her journal by the moonlight. It was slow going because they had gone through a wooded area, and she could only see the pages every few seconds. But she had been focusing on a particular page for a half hour now.

She sat up suddenly. "I've got it!"

Serena had been resting, her knees folded in front of her. She jerked her head up at Natalie's voice.

"What?" Serena sounded hoarse against the clinking of the rails. "You know how to open the door again?"

"Even better—I might have something that can patch up my umbrella."

"That's great. Then you can open the door." Serena yawned with fatigue, but she felt a spark of excitement. She crawled toward Natalie, pushing aside the crates that had slid between them. "What do you have to do to fix your umbrella?"

Natalie put her journal back inside her coat.

"The first thing I need to do is repair the torn bits to make the canopy whole again." Natalie opened her umbrella, whacking Serena's forehead in the process.

"Good grief, Natalie!" Serena rubbed at her head. "You almost took out my eye!"

"I'm sorry. It's dark!" Natalie hissed. She felt along the canvas until she had her hands at two holes.

"So repairing the holes will restore all of the power?" Serena watched Natalie grasp the fabric tightly.

"The tip will still be bent. But without the holes, the rain won't be able to get my head wet."

Serena rolled her eyes.

"Don't think I couldn't see that!" Natalie aimed a reproachful kick at her.

Serena drew up her legs to avoid Natalie's foot.

"Sorry." She stuck out her tongue. "I thought it was dark."

"You're so immature." Natalie shook her head. Then she frowned in concentration on the umbrella. She looked comical, her arms spread across the open umbrella as it rested against the floor.

"How exactly are you going to repair it?" Serena had adopted a hospital bedside voice, as if Natalie was performing surgery and could not be interrupted.

"I'm thinking repair-y thoughts," Natalie answered in her own whisper. "Encouraging thoughts."

"Encouraging thoughts? For an umbrella?"

"Everybody likes a good word now and again. You should try it sometime."

"So when will your umbrella be fixed?"

"I don't know." Natalie shrugged. "This train isn't stopping any time soon, so what's the rush?"

"Well, if all you had to do was think encouraging thoughts to lift your umbrella's spirits, why didn't you do it beforehand?"

"I couldn't remember how to fix it."

"You couldn't *remember*?"

"I have a lot to keep track of, okay?" Natalie raised her voice, shattering the bedside protocol.

"It seems like umbrella-repair would be pretty high on that list." Serena crossed her arms and matched Natalie's tone.

"Sometimes things get a little scattered. That's why I write them down."

"I noticed."

"I'm pleased to have made an impression."

There was a long pause. Both girls glared at each other through the darkness, and then Natalie returned her attention to the repair. Serena returned her attention to the questioning.

"So after you fix this and the umbrella tip, no more problems?"

"Thought-Repair is like magical duct tape. It's hardly foolproof, and it won't be as good as new. I really need a professional repairman, but this is the best I can do at present."

Serena sighed in frustration, then swore when a box slid into her back. She whirled around and punched the wooden crate with her fist. She was rewarded with cuts on her knuckles.

"I told you to stop saying bad words." Natalie shook her head. "And you're being too noisy with the boxes. I'm trying to concentrate."

Fingers stinging in pain, Serena let Natalie alone. She scooted into the nearest corner to find a place where she wouldn't be hit by boxes. She listened to the sound of Natalie's fingers scraping against the tight fabric of the umbrella. Then she slowly drifted off to sleep, her head resting against a crate loaded with anti-aircraft shells.

*

When Serena finally woke up, red light was filtering through the cracks in the door. She rubbed her eyes wearily and yawned.

"Is it finally morning?"

"Nope. Guess again, sleepyhead."

Serena looked around to find Natalie. The red-haired girl had moved to the other side of the car and was sitting on a crate. She was holding her umbrella between her legs.

"Not morning? Then what time is it?" Serena yawned again, stretching her arms.

"It's evening." Natalie raised her eyebrows, waiting for Serena's reaction.

"I slept for a whole day?"

"Just about—and good thing too. I needed a lot of time to concentrate." Natalie patted her umbrella and smiled. "Fixed! Or patched up at least."

"Huh, who would have thought?" Serena rose precariously to her feet, swaying with the train. She grabbed a stacked box for support.

Natalie frowned. "Who would have thought what? That I would repair it?"

"Well, that too." Serena shrugged. "But I didn't think I'd sleep all night and day." Her stomach growled. "And I'm starving."

Natalie tossed her the bag of dried fruit. Serena caught it and scowled at the few remaining pieces.

"I guess I should thank you for saving these." She popped the remaining fruit into her mouth.

"You should, and you're welcome." Natalie winked. "This is what, the third time you've slept in? I was fine on my own, by the way. Just concentrating. Without you."

"You know you missed me." Serena rolled her eyes and threw the empty bag away.

Her box suddenly fell onto the floor, and she gave a little scream. She stumbled against the wall before falling over another pile of boxes.

"You should probably sit over here." Natalie patted an empty space on her big crate.

"What makes there any steadier than here?" Serena brushed her hair out of her eyes. It felt oily. "Ew, I'm disgusting."

"Can I quote you on that?"

"Oh, shut up." Serena stuck out her tongue. "We haven't showered in days."

"I applaud your concern for hygiene, but you should probably get over here before sliding boxes give you a concussion." Natalie nodded at her umbrella. "I'm anchored over here. These boxes won't be sliding."

Serena walked toward the front of the car, negotiating her way through the moving maze of crates. She pulled herself onto Natalie's box with a grunt.

"Anchored, huh?" She plopped beside Natalie and leaned against the wall.

"Yes ma'am." Natalie smiled. "And good evening to you, since I wasn't able to say good morning. You might like to know, by the way, that we're at the outskirts of Locke City."

"We are?" Serena sat upright. A thrill of fear and excitement shot down her spine. "How do you know?"

"The buildings." Natalie pointed outside. "And I saw a sign that said Locke City was about seventy-five miles away."

"Really? How long ago was that?"

"About seventy-five miles ago."

Serena punched Natalie playfully in the arm, and then she leaned forward to see through one of the larger cracks in the wooden door. Houses and shops came into view, appearing with more frequency as they rode along.

"Any idea how far we are from the train station?" Natalie peered outside with her.

"Not sure. I never rode a train into the city before, and I'm not even sure where this is."

"I see." Natalie tapped the floor with her boot. "Well, we still need to figure out how we're going to get out of the boxcar."

"You fixed your umbrella, didn't you? Can't we just unlock the door?"

"I broke the door, remember?"

"Oh, right." Serena sighed. She slapped the door in resignation.

A tremendous boom sounded above them, and Serena dropped to the floor, swearing loudly.

"What was that?" she exclaimed, covering her head with her hands.

"Um," Natalie swallowed. "That was probably thunder. At least, I hope it was."

Natalie stuck her face against the door and squinted through a hole. The red light was fading, to be replaced by dark gray clouds.

"Ouch!" she pulled her head away from the door, blinking her right eye furiously.

"What happened?" Serena grabbed her friend's shoulder.

"Oh, it's just starting to rain." Natalie rubbed at her eye. "Nothing to worry about. But that was definitely thunder."

Natalie stopped rubbing her eye as a terrible howl rose up all around them. Serena's muscles tensed. The siren grew louder and louder. She held her breath, and a feeling of panic gnawed at her nerves.

"Air raid siren," Natalie whispered.

"Oh gods, not now." Serena clutched her white shirt at the neck.

Now they heard distant booms that could not be mistaken for thunder. The boxes shifted once more, but Natalie kept them away with a swift kick.

Raindrops pattered on the roof.

The sound of the bombs grew louder.

123

Serena leaned against the door, looking toward the city to see flashes of lightning across the sky, and bursts of red, orange, and yellow on the ground. The train plowed further into the city, into the heart of the storm.

Serena shuddered. "We're in a boxcar with a bunch of explosives...and we're getting bombed."

"I know, just stay calm." Natalie held up her hand. "We've got to get out of the train before it gets hit. I don't like the idea of those pilots having fun with a moving target."

The girls sat still, listening to the harsh, unnerving sounds of thunder and explosions.

The minutes crawled past, and the noises got louder. Sweat poured down Serena's brow. She felt sick. The boxes shook and trembled. Bombs squealed on their descent to earth. The explosions rattled the ground like wrecking balls.

Serena closed her eyes—not praying, unwilling to seek assistance from any gods. But she told herself that they were getting closer to the station—that the train was slowing down.

"I think the train is slowing down." Natalie tapped her shoulder.

Serena opened her eyes. Her jeans were crinkled where she had strangled them.

"Oh, good." Serena tried to swallow, but her mouth was cotton dry. She coughed. "Now we just have to figure out how—what's that?"

She looked up as the chilling wail of a falling bomb sounded directly overhead. It was a high, unearthly screech against the surrounding booms.

"Oh gods, Natalie! It's coming right for us." Serena breathed fast, her voice rising to a squeak. She looked around the car. "All of these shells are going to blow up if we get hit!"

"I know, just keep your head." Natalie joined Serena next to the door and pulled her close. She opened her umbrella, shielding them from the rest of the car. "Hold tight!"

"What are you doing?" Serena shrieked.

"Saving our lives!"

They heard a deafening roar in front of them, and the force of the explosion blasted against the umbrella. Serena saw the brightest hues of orange and yellow through the fabric, and then her world went black.

CHAPTER 14:
WELCOME BACK

Serena opened her eyes to see burning skyscrapers around her. Searchlights combed the dark clouds above. Rain pelted her face, and someone was dragging her across the wet ground.

"Natalie?" Serena asked. Her voice sounded slurred to her own ears.

"Shh, I got you."

Serena blinked against the downpour. The roar of planes shook her bones. The cold wind chilled her body. Sirens wailed in the distance, melting together with the cries of falling bombs. She gasped as a nearby building collapsed in flames, releasing molten beams of steel onto the ground. But Natalie kept a firm grip on her, holding her under the armpits and pulling her to safety.

Around them in the train yard, piles of coal were burning, sending plumes of smoke into the night sky. Serena felt the heat of the blazing fires. Red, orange, yellow, and black swirled together to cloud her vision.

"Here, I've got to lift you a bit."

"What?" Serena shook her head, feeling dizzy. Then she yelped with pain as Natalie pulled her under the shelter of the Locke City Train Station.

Serena felt a sharp pain in her arm. She looked down to see that her black cardigan was damp with blood. She cried out in fright, her heart rate accelerating.

"Shh, it's okay, it's okay," Natalie whispered, pulling a bandage out of an inside coat pocket. She held up the arm and examined the wound. "The sight of the blood is probably worse than the actual pain. I know it hurts, but I don't think anything's broken."

Serena stared at her hand and flexed her fingers. The cut on her arm stung like fire, but she could still move everything. She turned her head away while Natalie wrapped the cut.

"Can't you just heal me with your umbrella?"

"I'm not sure if my umbrella's up for that." Natalie shook her head. "I wouldn't want to risk healing unless it was absolutely necessary." She let the arm rest gently in Serena's lap. "You should be okay though. Just be careful with it."

"Thanks." Serena swallowed, using her good arm to wipe sweat from her dirty face.

Natalie ducked as another bomb landed perilously close. The station roof shuddered, showering them in a thin layer of dust. Serena looked around the inside of the station. Benches and chairs were strewn across the floor, covered in papers that flew about the room. Chunks of the ceiling rested on the floor beneath the holes they had left.

Serena held her throbbing head.

"What happened?" she asked. "Did the train get hit?"

"Ha." Natalie smiled grimly and rose to her feet. "If the train itself had been hit, we would be dead—I can't cover us from all sides. As it was, a bomb landed dangerously close to the tracks." She nodded at her umbrella, which was black and sooty. "Thankfully, I was able to shield us from the blast."

A huge explosion sent Natalie back to her knees. The ground shook violently, and Serena covered her face from the ensuing flash of light. Massive shapes were tossed into the sky in front of them.

"Okay, *that* bomb definitely hit the train!" Natalie yelled over the din.

Through the station doors, Serena watched the remnants of their train crash to the ground.

Someone screamed outside. It was a young man's voice.

"Help me! I'm burning!"

"Oh, gods." Serena covered her mouth. "It's one of the soldiers. How did he survive that first bomb?"

"He won't survive for much longer out there." Natalie's face went pale. "I'll be right back—stay here."

She rose to her feet and held up a warning hand at Serena, but it was unnecessary. Serena had no desire to move.

She listened to the man's shrieks. They got louder...and louder.

Serena felt a terrible cold trace down her back. The chill was quite at odds with the fires raging around her. She held her breath, watching through the station doors as Natalie dodged burning piles of wreckage and ran to the source of the cries.

Then came the horrible wailing noise. The screeching bombs grew louder and louder and—

"Natalie, look out!" Serena screamed.

Natalie did look out. She dropped to her feet and covered herself with her umbrella.

There was another blinding flash and a roar.

More debris piled in front of Serena, and Natalie disappeared.

Serena opened her mouth, her lungs filling and emptying—she screamed for Natalie, but no sound came to her ringing ears.

If Natalie was dead...

She covered her ears, her wounded arm aching terribly as unseen planes dropped death and destruction onto the train yard, her childhood playground.

A deafening silence rang inside her head, a high-pitched buzz that popped incessantly.

"Natalie," she repeated over and over, until her words sounded in her own ears and she could hear the flames and sirens again. She let out a shuddering sob. "Natalie!"

Serena rose unsteadily to her feet and grabbed an overturned chair for support. She waited for a minute, allowing her legs to stop shaking enough for her to move. Then she walked out from under the station. She passed a pile of charred train cars. She stepped over flaming debris and tangles of concrete and steel.

Serena slipped on the wet dirt, caking her knees and forearm in mud. The grime wet her bandage and she swore—then corrected her language automatically.

Oh, Natalie.

Serena stumbled to her feet again, making her way toward the spot where Natalie had covered herself with the umbrella. Her heart beat fast against her chest. Sweat poured down her face.

Natalie was nowhere to be seen.

"Natalie!" She stepped over what remained of the train tracks, avoiding a sharp, broken rail that stuck up dangerously into the air.

Their boxcar had been blown to smithereens. All that remained of the train was an empty, flaming shell of the engine. She approached it cautiously, holding up her muddy arm to block the heat from her face. The young man's voice had come from somewhere over here...

There was a violent cough. Serena jumped in shock.

When she recovered herself, she turned around slowly, dreading what she might find.

A red umbrella emerged from a pile of dirt and rubble. Natalie coughed a few more times, pulling herself from the wreckage. She lost her footing on the wet debris and stumbled to the ground at Serena's feet.

Serena knelt beside her. "Oh, Natalie!"

She wrapped Natalie in an embrace. Tears streamed down her face as she felt her friend's heart beating against her own.

"You're alive!" Serena caught her breath, wiping away tears and dirty hair from her own eyes.

"'es...m'alive," Natalie answered, muffled by Serena's shoulder.

She sniffed loudly, laughing with relief. "Next time, don't just leave me, okay? If we have to go, let's go together."

Natalie's eyes glistened. "Okay." She took a deep breath. "I'll try."

"Oh, you silly. Your face is all muddy and wet." Serena pulled her clean sleeve over her wrist and wiped Natalie's cheek. She realized the pointlessness of her attempt as she smeared mud on Natalie's face.

"I guess I'm a little muddy too." Serena dropped her hand, disappointed, but Natalie laughed. The red-haired girl pulled a pink handkerchief from an inside pocket and wiped both of their faces.

They sat next to each other for a moment, oblivious to the sounds of bombs falling farther and farther away. The rain continued to pour, drops of water tracing muddy lines down their sooty faces.

But Serena didn't care. They were back together again.

And somehow, she realized with an unfamiliar twinge in her heart, being together had become very important.

"We should probably go. I guess you can stand?" Natalie rose to her feet, holding out her hands for Serena.

Serena took her hands and stood, blinking against the relentless downpour. Then she realized that the screams of the young man had stopped. The burning...the bomb...

"Oh, no." Her breath caught in her throat. "What happen to that soldier?"

"Serena, I think it's too late." Natalie took Serena by the arm and tried to lead her away from the train wreckage.

"No, but I heard him—I know he was around here. Didn't you see anything?"

"There's nothing to see," Natalie insisted.

"But—" Serena looked back at the burning frame of the engine.

There was something lying in the shadows next to it.

"Someone's over there," Serena gasped, pulling free of Natalie and stumbling over tangled steel toward the shape.

"No, Serena! Don't go over there." Natalie's voice rang out, stern, frantic—older than Serena had ever heard before.

But Serena had already seen it. Him.

He was barely recognizable anymore.

Serena's stomach turned and her knees weakened. She lurched forward involuntarily. Bile rose in her throat. She threw up.

"Oh, gods," she moaned, and she collapsed.

Something caught Serena before she hit the ground. Clouds gathered in her eyes. She heard Natalie's voice, but faintly.

"We've got to find shelter. Where can we go?"

But Serena was spiraling down into darkness, and anywhere was better than here.

"Serena, where does Professor Glen live?"

Serena felt her hand rise into the air. It tingled. Something was pressed between her fingers, and her hand fell to the ground on something smooth. Paper. A hand closed around her own. She moved it...she was writing...that was interesting...

Serena slipped into unconsciousness once more.

CHAPTER 15:
BETRAYAL FROM WITHIN

The sound of footsteps caught Julius's attention as he returned to the first chamber of the Crypt. He waved his orb of light toward the stone stairs that led down from the elevator. He took a sharp breath—two figures were descending the steps, a god and a goddess.

Julius clenched his jaw in anger when he recognized the goddess.

Ambrosia.

What was she doing in the Crypt? She had no right to be here without his permission. Was Ambrosia so confident of herself that she could stride into the Crypt and undermine his authority to his face?

And who was the newcomer? Beside Ambrosia was a squat, balding god with frizzy hair and a thick mustache. The blue orb illuminated the god's brown traveling cloak.

The god passed the stacked coffins—and suddenly jumped in fright, presumably hearing their whispers. Ambrosia walked confidently beside him.

Julius crossed his arms and took a deep breath to control his temper. "Ambrosia, what are you doing down here?"

Ambrosia did not look surprised to see Julius.

"This delegate wishes to speak with you." She nodded at her companion.

The god extended his hand to Julius. "How do you do—"

Julius kept his arms crossed. He glared at Ambrosia. "How did you know that I was down here?"

Ambrosia frowned in annoyance. "You were not in your chamber, and I saw that one of the elevators had gone to the lower levels."

"What does that matter to you?" Julius arched an eyebrow.

"I like to know what is going on in the Tower," she said. The blue light cast deep shadows over her eyes. "And it is unusual for anyone to come down here."

"How did you get in?" Julius pressed. "I'm the only one who has the keys."

"Yes, dearest brother," Ambrosia pointed back at the entrance, "but you left the door open."

Julius sneered, unable to muster a comeback.

The frizzy-haired god looked between Julius and Ambrosia with growing interest.

Julius jerked his head at him. "Why did you bring him here? This is a secret place."

"He is from the *Pantheon*," Ambrosia emphasized the last word and gave Julius a knowing look. "He has important business to discuss—the weight of which is worth the intrusion."

"I will be the judge of that." Julius looked the god up and down. "Who are you?"

The god nodded curtly to Julius. "My name is Ewald, and I am a representative from the Pantheon. I've been sent to check the situation here at Mouthrinse."

Julius glared at him. "Mithris."

Ewald frowned and consulted a clipboard. He flipped a few pages, folded them over, and ran his fingers down a long column.

"Aha! Mithris! You're right." He chuckled. "It is, after all, a bit hard for me to see in this darkness. Is there any way," he pointed over his shoulder at the elevator, "that we could move to a place with better lighting? Somewhere friendlier than a spooky tomb, haha?"

Julius didn't move. "What do you want?"

Ewald sniffed and wiped his nose with the back of his hand.

"Well, Julius—it is Julius, yes?" He glanced at his clipboard.

Julius raised his head proudly. "I am indeed Julius, God of Gods, Ruler of Mithris."

Ambrosia rolled her eyes.

"Right, right..." Ewald nodded, writing something on his clipboard. "Well, according to this report, Mithris is in bad shape right now. Your ratings aren't so high at the moment."

Lightning crackled between Julius's fingers. "My *ratings*?"

"Whoa!" Ewald raised his hands in alarm. "Don't kill the messenger! Haha. I didn't write the report—this is from the Pantheon!"

Julius scowled at him, but the lightning dissipated.

Ewald adjusted his brown cloak at the neck. "If you have any questions or concerns, feel free to send them back with me. I'll make sure they get filed and passed along to the right people."

Julius snorted and brushed roughly past Ewald toward the stairs. Ambrosia followed.

"Julius, listen to him!" she hissed.

"I'm listening," Julius muttered, climbing the stone steps. He looked over his shoulder. "So who do I send my concerns to if the messenger accidentally gets locked in a vault?"

Ewald stood still, confused, as the blue orb of light floated away and the chamber fell into darkness.

"Oh, right!" He jogged after them on short legs. "Good joke, haha. So you do have a sense of humor."

Ewald stepped inside the elevator a moment before the doors slammed shut.

"Better light here. No creepy dead voices on the elevator, right? Haha." He smiled at Julius, who ignored him and turned the black dials for the throne room floor.

The elevator began its ascent.

"I'm going to the top of the Tower," Julius said. "You have until I reach my floor to tell me what you want. That's a long climb...but this elevator moves fast."

"Very well." Ewald covered his mouth and coughed. "I'm here to give you an ultimatum."

Both Julius and Ambrosia tore their gaze away from the dials to stare at Ewald.

His eyes widened.

"Or rather, to pass on an ultimatum from the Pantheon," he corrected himself. "That is to say, they're not very happy with the way things are going on Mouthrinse—"

"Mithris." Julius growled.

"—yes, of course," Ewald gulped, backing away from Julius. "As I said, they're exceedingly worried about this developing war."

"The war isn't 'developing.' It's been going on for over a decade." Ambrosia pursed her lips, and Julius shot her a look of annoyance. "The only developing situation is that Artema itself has been invaded, and bombs are falling around the Tower as we speak."

Ewald flashed a brief smile.

"Yes, you have highlighted one of the main problems. This country, of course, contains the planet's central divine presence." Ewald spread his arms to indicate the Tower. "Host countries typically enjoy some kind of patronage. Of course, world wars in general are frowned upon, but when the conflict surrounds the stronghold of the God of Gods, it becomes embarrassing. Makes it look like things are a teensy bit," he pinched his thumb and forefinger together, "out of control."

The cutesy gesture made Julius want to hurt him even more.

"Are you questioning the way I rule my planet?" He stepped toward Ewald, who pressed himself against the elevator door.

The squat god wagged a warning finger, his frizzy hair shaking on his pale head.

"Now, again, it is not *me* doing the questioning, but rather, the Pantheon." He swallowed. "Although I do reserve a few personal criticisms, haha—"

Julius grabbed Ewald by his brown traveling cloak, lifted the squat god into the air, and held him firmly against the door. Ewald squeaked in fright.

Ambrosia grasped her brother's broad shoulders. "Julius, he's a Pantheon official! Put him down right now!"

"Yes, I would put me down right now if I were you!" Ewald demanded in a high-pitched voice. "Because you might not be ruling the planet much longer if you continue with this behavior!"

Julius dropped Ewald to the floor, where he collapsed into a pitiful heap.

"What do you mean?" Julius breathed.

"That's the ultimatum I've been meaning to tell you about." Ewald apparently thought he was safer on the floor, because he stayed down. "The Pantheon will have you removed if you don't remedy this situation very soon. You'll need to—"

"Move aside," Ambrosia interrupted him.

"Yes, precisely." Ewald nodded. "You'll need to move aside."

"No." Ambrosia shook her head. The elevator door opened and Ewald fell backwards into space. "You need to step aside because we're at the top."

Julius and Ambrosia stepped over the unfortunate delegate, who crawled away from the door and picked himself up with as much dignity as he could muster.

Julius stood over him, fuming.

"So the Pantheon is going to take away my throne? What gives them the authority to do that?"

Ewald snorted. "My good sir, 'what gives them the authority'? They're the *Pantheon*! They give authority to *you*." He arched an eyebrow, looking Julius up and down. "And now that I see the situation here, I'm surprised they didn't send someone sooner. The neglect you have shown to your planet—along with your abusive attitude—is more than questionable."

There was a blur of motion. A crack of thunder echoed through the hallway.

Ewald lay on the floor, cradling his broken nose and swearing through the blood flowing over his mouth. Julius flexed his fingers in front of the god's face.

"You're lucky that I wasn't too angry." Julius kicked his unfortunate victim, who yelped in pain.

Ambrosia started to protest, but Julius interrupted.

"What were you playing at, bringing him to me?" He pointed an accusing finger at her. "I can't believe that you entered the Crypt without my permission. Your intrusion comes at a delicate time, dear sister. We'll have a long talk soon—in private."

"Intrusion?" Ambrosia glared at him. "A long talk? How dare you treat me like a child."

"Consider yourself lucky that I am only treating you like a child," Julius said menacingly. "There's been a dirty sneak around the Tower recently. When I find out who it is, they're going to wish I had shown them the same mercy I showed *him*." He curled his lip at Ewald. "But now I must speak with Nikolas about this...unfortunate distraction."

Julius stepped over Ewald and began walking down the hall.

"Oh," Julius looked over his shoulder. "Incidentally, who's going to replace me if the Pantheon decides that I'm no longer fit to be the God of Gods?"

Ewald gathered himself into a crouching position, watching Julius's clenched fists carefully.

"Naddurally id—oh, bodder..." Ewald's voice was muffled by the hand grasping his broken nose. "Thid id murder." He closed his eyes and muttered something under his breath.

His nose glowed—and then cracked loudly.

Ewald swore. He wrinkled his nose for a moment and touched it gingerly. Once he was satisfied, he continued.

"Naturally," Ewald took a deep breath, "since you have no children, the responsibility of ruling Mithris would fall to your nearest relative. Your sister, of course."

"Better late than never." Ambrosia's blue eyes flashed at Julius. "Although perhaps too late for mankind."

Julius gaped at her. "How dare you say such treasonous words! Hold your tongue, goddess!"

Ambrosia's whole body was shaking in anger. "I have held it long enough."

"You've always spoken your mind—and now you reveal it completely! You would replace me as the Ruler of Mithris?"

"Ruler? What ruler is there to replace?" Ambrosia spat at Julius. "A spoiled brat who sips wine and ignores the prayers of a dying world? Yes, I would take the throne if the Pantheon removed you. And Mithris would be better off for it!"

"I am inclined to agree," Ewald mumbled from the floor.

"Shut your mouth before I break it!" Julius pointed a shaking finger at Ewald, who crawled farther away from him.

"You would overthrow me?" Julius looked at Ambrosia as if he had never seen her before. "You filthy traitor! You brought him here, didn't you? To get the Pantheon's help in your little coup?"

"Excuse *me*, sir." Ewald raised a finger from his position on the floor. "I came here on official business, not at the behest of any individual."

"I warned you—" Julius raised a fist of lightning.

"Hold your temper, brother!" Ambrosia shouted, spreading her fingers to create a protective green bubble between Julius and Ewald. "I did not send for him. But the war has gone on for too long. Have you not seen the city burning?" She narrowed her eyes. "It is time for a change. Ewald's arrival is a timely coincidence."

"A timely coincidence?" Spit flew from Julius's mouth. "You expect me to believe that? Timely—just like the release of the Dark Angels?"

"Dark Angels?" Ambrosia blanched. "What are you talking about?"

"Don't deny it! You've done the footwork to overthrow me— now where are your assassins to finish me off?" Julius raised his head and shouted. "Guards! Arrest these traitors!"

"Julius, you are delusional! No one is trying to assassinate you! This is about ruling Mithris—something that you have refused to do. Now either do your job or step aside. The world cannot wait."

"How dare you tell me what the world can and cannot do!" Julius growled. "But then, you always wanted to inherit the throne, didn't you, *older* sister?" Julius jabbed his finger in Ambrosia's shoulder, and she flinched. "I'll bet that's why you were so close to Father. Daddy's little girl."

"Get away from me." Ambrosia slapped his hand aside. "How dare you question my devotion to Father!"

"I question everything about you, you wicked serpent! You've always been ashamed of me, you've been ashamed of my leadership, and you were ashamed of my family!" Julius bellowed at Ambrosia, his shoulders heaving.

His echoing shouts joined the sound of heavy footsteps coming down the hall.

A dozen Guardian Angels came into view, their pale faces gleaming beneath the visors of their plumed golden helmets. The tips of their spears glowed with slivers of red electricity.

Nikolas was at the head of the column.

Julius raised his eyebrows. "Nikolas. Fancy seeing you here."

Nikolas surveyed the scene with interest. "Trouble, my lord?"

"Like you would not believe."

"Who are you?" Ewald stared at Nikolas—and then yelped in alarm as the guards surrounded him and Ambrosia in a fence of spears.

"I am Nikolas, sir." The gray-haired god nodded curtly. "Counselor to Julius, God of Gods, Ruler of Mithris."

"That title is currently under dispute—now hold on just a minute!" Ewald protested as a guard forced his hands behind his back, causing him to drop his clipboard. "You can't arrest me! I'm a Pantheon official and I've done nothing wrong!"

He narrowed his eyes at Ambrosia.

"What did he say about you being ashamed of his family? Aren't you the extent of his family?"

"My family is none of your business," Julius growled.

"He is speaking of his wife and daughter." Ambrosia struggled against the guard restraining her. "His *mortal* wife and daughter."

"Ambrosia, how dare you—"

"Wait—*mortal* wife and daughter? A demigoddess!" Ewald's eyes widened. "Good heavens! Did either of you ever report that?"

"What do *you* think?" Julius spat at Ewald. "It's none of your business what I do on my planet."

"As a matter of fact, it is all of my business, because it is the Pantheon's business what you do on this planet, *sir*. You are not above the law—a fact which you have been unable to grasp. It would appear that you are irresponsible in all areas of your life. It's no wonder that this world is going to hell." He glanced at Ambrosia. "I assume that you had knowledge of this situation and didn't report it?"

"As a matter of fact, I did report it."

"You filthy traitor!" Julius roared.

"It is the law, Julius." Ambrosia glared at him. "One of us has to follow the law, after all."

"Such noble words, coming from a traitor."

"Actually, I believe you are the real traitor." Ewald looked at Julius with disgust. "You betrayed your planet by letting it slip into chaos, and you betrayed the Pantheon by neglecting to report the existence of a demigoddess on your planet."

"My daughter is dead!" Julius screamed in Ewald's face.

"Nevertheless..." He trembled under Julius's fearsome wrath, but he took a deep breath, gaining confidence from the enormous bureaucracy on his side. "You mated with a mortal, you fathered a demigoddess, and, unlike your sister, you failed to report the situation!"

"How dare you—" Julius's fist blazed with lightning as he pulled it back to strike Ewald.

"No!"

A green bubble expanded between Ewald and Julius, sending the latter stumbling back against the wall. Julius recovered his feet and looked around.

"Who cast that spell?" he bellowed.

Nikolas was standing with his arms outstretched.

"My lord, you must not kill him." Nikolas shook his head, lowering his hand. He nodded at the guard holding Ewald. "Release him."

The Guardian Angel let go of Ewald. He fell to the floor, breathing heavily.

"Nikolas," Julius snarled. "How dare you undermine my authority! And what are you doing, guard? I didn't order you to release him!"

The guard was unresponsive. He simply stood at attention against the wall.

Julius stalked toward the angel. "How dare you betray me!"

"Peace, my lord." Nikolas held up his hands. "Everything is under control."

"I should say not." Ewald scoffed, grabbing his clipboard from the floor. "Lord Julius is a criminal. Until Ambrosia is released and he is placed under arrest, the situation is decidedly *not* under control."

"Oh, I think that Ambrosia is where she needs to be. But you're right about Julius." Nikolas shook his head sadly. "Guards...arrest him."

They rushed forward, attacking Julius with a surge of red lightning from their spears. Julius stumbled in surprise as the electricity rippled across his chest, but then he recovered himself, shooting a burst of lightning into the face of the nearest guard. The unfortunate angel crumpled to the ground, smoke trailing from the inside of his mangled helmet.

Julius did the same to another, blasting a hole through the angel's chest and hurling him against the wall.

Yelling with rage, Julius grabbed a third guard, snapped his neck, and tossed the lifeless body to the floor. But the remaining guards hemmed him in from all sides, piercing him with spears and drenching him in electricity.

The energy forced him to his knees, illuminating his entire body. His eyes shone like twin suns. His mouth hung open in agony. The veins in his arms throbbed, flashing through his contracting muscles. His body twisted and flailed under the brutal assault.

Ambrosia screamed, struggling against her captor, but he held her tightly.

Finally, the guards lifted their spears from Julius, and his head slumped forward on his chest.

When he looked up again, his face was pale with sweat and his eyes ached. He stared at Nikolas.

"What are you doing, old friend?" he asked in a hoarse whisper.

"He's obeying orders from a higher power," Ewald declared triumphantly. "You failed to report a union with a mortal that produced a demigoddess. That's a serious offense, according to the Pantheon. Or did you not know the law?"

He tore off a sheet of paper and held it out to Julius.

"Sign this, please."

"And what's that?" Julius blinked wearily.

"It's a statement acknowledging that you have been relieved as God of Gods on Mithris."

Julius laughed bitterly. "I'm not going to sign that, you filthy bast—"

"I can sign it." Nikolas strode forward. "I have the authority to sign documents in Julius's name."

"Nikolas, how could you..." Julius's eyes were slipping in and out of focus. His head lolled on his shoulders. "How dare you..."

"Now Nikolas, if you would, please release Ambrosia so she can temporarily assume the throne of Mithris." Ewald cleared his throat. "I say 'temporarily' because this matter will surely come before the High Council of the Pantheon. They will make a final decision about these shameful circumstances."

"Ah, I would certainly release her," Nikolas bowed deferentially to Ewald, "but for the fact that Ambrosia is also a traitor."

"That's a lie!" Ambrosia screamed.

"Just a moment, my lady." Ewald held up a hand. "I'm sure we can sort this out. Nikolas, what makes you say that? Julius's only accusation was that Ambrosia wanted to replace him. I think we can all agree that would be a good thing."

"Yes, but Julius was correct in accusing Ambrosia of wanting to overthrow him by force." Nikolas scowled at Ambrosia. "She was taking steps to execute her plan...and her brother. She released the Dark Angels from the Crypt."

Ewald opened his mouth in terror. "Dark Angels?"

"Liar!" Ambrosia screamed again. "I have had nothing to do with them!"

"Shouting won't change the facts." Nikolas looked down his nose at her. "And lying won't cover up your assassination attempt."

"I never went anywhere near the Dark Angels."

"Really?" Nikolas raised an eyebrow. "Then why are the coffins open?"

Ambrosia scoffed. "You must have opened them."

"How could I have done so, when you stole my keys."

"What?" Julius raised his head in surprise, wincing with the effort. "But you said I was the only one with keys."

Nikolas looked puzzled. "Surely you misheard me. I said that your keys and mine were the only pairs. Only we can access the Crypt."

"That's not what you—"

"Of course he has keys," Ambrosia interrupted her brother. "He was the Keeper of the Crypt for Father."

"Really?" Ewald looked at Nikolas in surprise.

"Yes." Nikolas nodded. "Lord Aurelius entrusted me with all of his creatures after the War of Chaos."

"Ah, yes. The War of Chaos. Difficult times." Ewald cleared his throat. "Or so I hear, haha. Wasn't around at the time..."

"Difficult indeed." Nikolas turned his attention back to Ambrosia. "As I said, only Julius and I had access to the Crypt. Until Ambrosia stole my keys and released the Dark Angels."

"You are a fool." Ambrosia laughed bitterly. "I do not have your keys."

"Then what's this?" Nikolas leaned over, reaching his hand into Ambrosia's inner pockets.

"How dare you touch me!" Ambrosia screamed, struggling in the guard's grasp as Nikolas searched her. His hand lingered in place for a moment. Then the sound of metal clanked inside her robes, and she froze.

"What could this be?" Nikolas dropped his voice to a deadly whisper. He pulled his hand out, trailing a ring of bronze keys. "Who's the liar, Ambrosia?"

Ambrosia shook her head desperately. "No, this is all a setup! You have to believe me! Nikolas planted the keys in my robes—he made them appear, just now."

"I've seen enough." Ewald shook his head sadly. "No more lies. Lock her in the dungeons!" He motioned to one of the guards, who saluted and led Ambrosia down the hall.

Ewald turned to Nikolas. "What of the Dark Angels? Are they on the loose? Are we in danger?"

Nikolas shook his head and put the keys inside his robes. "The situation is completely under control. I managed to recapture all of the Dark Angels and secure them in their coffins."

"Thank goodness." Ewald sighed in relief. "I don't know where we'd be without you."

Nikolas smiled graciously. "I am only performing my duty to Mithris."

"Yes, and under the circumstances, your duty has temporarily expanded." Ewald scribbled a quick note on his clipboard. "As High Counselor, you will have to be God of Gods until the Pantheon can select a replacement."

"I understand," Nikolas said somberly.

Ewald flipped a page and handed his clipboard to the counselor.

Nikolas signed the paper with a flourish.

Julius struggled against the Guardian Angels with his last reserves of strength, but his efforts were insubstantial. The guards held him steadily.

"Nikolas," he asked weakly, "why are you doing this?"

Nikolas returned the clipboard to Ewald. He dropped to a knee by Julius and looked him in the eye.

"My lord, I'm very sorry. But I'm sure if we follow the law, everything will be made right. For the good of Mithris."

CHAPTER 16:
PROFESSOR GLEN

Serena woke up in a large, soft bed.

She stretched out her hands and felt a wooden headrest. The smooth surface was familiar to her touch.

She opened her eyes to see a white ceiling and a spinning fan. To her left, a staircase led down and out of sight.

Serena sat up. In front of her were bookshelves overflowing with huge volumes. More books and papers were scattered over a desk beside the staircase.

Very familiar. The only thing that would make this place more familiar would be...

Serena's breath caught in her throat as a gray-haired lady ascended the staircase.

"Professor Glen?" Serena was surprised to hear the hoarseness of her own voice.

The middle-aged professor smiled, relaxing her stern features. Her gray hair was tied up in a bun, and she wore a dark green nightgown. The golden morning light reflected in her rimless glasses.

"Professor Glen!" Serena gaped. "It's you! How did I get here?"

"Your red-haired friend."

"But how did she know where to go?"

Natalie appeared on the staircase. "Written directions."

Serena did a double-take at her friend's appearance. Natalie was wearing a pink sweater and gray sweatpants. Serena wrinkled her nose. It was weird to see her without the candy corn costume.

"Wait, aren't those my—"

"Old clothes, yes." Natalie nodded. "They're pretty nice."

"They're sweatpants." Serena stuck out her tongue. "I can't believe I ever wore those."

Natalie shrugged. "I like them. Cozy and comfy." She brought her journal out from behind her back. "And as for the directions, I just had to tickle your subconscious."

"I see," Serena lied. She didn't really see.

"Oh, and by the way." Natalie examined her journal closely, her fingers pressed against a page. "'Waterloo Street' is spelled with one 't,' not two." She looked up at Serena. "You might want to remember that one. I almost got confused and missed our turn."

Serena stared at the journal. "You just used my thoughts to write directions?"

"Yes, you'd be surprised at what memories you can access, even when you're fainting from shock and drifting into unconsciousness."

Images from the previous night flooded Serena's mind.

"It's a good thing you got to me," Professor Glen said. She sat down and pressed her hand against Serena's forehead. "Do you feel all right now?"

"Well enough," Serena answered. "How did you get me all the way from the train yard?" she asked Natalie.

"I carried you," Natalie said simply. Serena stared at her doubtfully, and Natalie looked at her with a mixture of amusement and reproof. "It wasn't the first time, you know."

The professor raised an eyebrow at Natalie. "Yes, you have quite a bit of strength for a...fourteen-year-old."

Serena cleared her throat. "Well, Professor, Natalie actually—"

"—isn't fourteen," Professor Glen interrupted, rising to her feet. "I know. Your friend has filled me in on everything." She stared out of the window for a minute, and then she gave Serena an appraising look. "And your friend has suggested that *I* fill *you* in."

"You two have already talked?" Serena propped herself onto her elbows, then winced as a sharp pain fired up her left arm.

"Careful." Natalie reached out to steady Serena. "And yes, we've talked quite a bit."

"How long have you had? Did I sleep in again?"

"Not really, no." Natalie smiled. "It's around eight in the morning. But come on, you need to get dressed so we can have breakfast. Then we'll talk."

Serena sat at the kitchen table, soaking in the old surroundings of Professor Glen's house. She had never been fond of the place, but the familiarity elicited a certain amount of affection as she poured her bowl of cereal.

Across the round table, Natalie was pouring cereal into her glass cup. When she saw that Serena had poured hers into the bowl, the red-haired girl pursed her lips in thought. Then Natalie poured her corn flakes into her own bowl, which she had already filled with orange juice.

Serena shook her head, trying not to smile. A hopeless effort.

"Can you pass the milk?" Natalie glanced at Serena, acting like nothing was wrong.

Serena handed her the pitcher of milk, and the red-haired girl poured it into her glass. Natalie gulped down the milk, and then she proceeded to eat her orange juice and corn flakes.

"Do you like the cereal?" Serena poured orange juice into her own cup, a smile trembling at the corner of her lips.

"Oh, yes." Natalie nodded, her mouth full. "Very much so."

Professor Glen appeared at the kitchen archway. She had changed into a white shirt, a black turtleneck sweater, and matching black pants. She took a folding chair from the wall and scooted it toward the table.

"Well." Professor Glen folded her hands on the table, eyeing Natalie's bowl. "Enjoying your breakfast?"

"Absolutely. Thank you very much." Natalie waved her spoon enthusiastically, flicking drops of orange juice into her red hair.

"Of course." Professor Glen nodded curtly. "I'm glad to host both of you."

There was a pause. Serena shifted uncomfortably in her chair, feeling awkward in the silence. She had, after all, left Professor Glen's house on a sour note.

She had left without the professor's knowledge.

And she had stolen her car.

A sour note indeed.

Serena tapped her knee, looking at the colorful wooden fish that decorated the walls and the ceiling, trying to avoid the eyes of the quiet people around her.

But when she looked back down, Professor Glen and Natalie were both staring at her.

"Well, Serena." Professor Glen cleared her throat. "I'm glad to see that you're all in one piece."

"Yeah." Serena gazed into her cereal bowl.

"I'm sure Natalie has had a lot to do with that."

"Yeah."

There was another awkward pause.

"I've been taking the bus a lot recently."

Serena winced.

"Look, Professor, I'm sorry about your car—"

"At this point, I'm sure you're sorry about a lot of things." Professor Glen folded her arms. "You put yourself in great danger by leaving Locke City like that."

Serena's ears burned. She felt like a little kid again, sitting at the kitchen table, getting scolded.

The worst part was that she deserved it.

The professor adjusted her glasses and rubbed the bridge of her nose. "But I am sorry too. There are a lot of things I never told you. I hoped you would never have to know them, but that was naïve of me."

Serena shifted in her seat, unused to the professor confessing a mistake.

"Well," Professor Glen sighed, "you know by now that you're a demigoddess."

Serena blinked. Sensible, worldly-wise Professor Glen had just called her a *demigoddess*.

"Yes."

"And you know that your mother, Jillian, was the mortal."

Serena's heart skipped a beat. This conversation was really happening. It was surreal. Professor Glen, the no-nonsense academic, the stern woman she had grown up with, was talking about her birth mother...who had loved a god.

Two worlds were colliding in front of her eyes: the mundane existence of mortality and the supernatural world that had gate-crashed her life.

"Yes," Serena finally answered.

"But you don't know who your father was?"

"No. Do you—"

"And you don't understand why you're being hunted, or how you came to be with me?"

"No, I don't." Serena leaned closer, her curiosity building with each second.

Professor Glen leaned back in her chair and studied her folded hands on the table. Serena glanced at Natalie, who was watching the professor intently.

"Are you familiar with the Pantheon of Mithris?" Professor Glen asked.

"The Pantheon? They're the ones who run everything, right? The ones who sent Natalie?"

"No." Professor Glen shook her head. "That's *the* Pantheon. The one from the Beyond. A 'pantheon' is just the collection of gods within a certain mythology. In this case, it's the mythology that defines our particular world."

Serena raised her eyebrow, confused.

"I'm speaking of the gods that rule Mithris." Professor Glen looked over her glasses at Serena. "Are you familiar with the names of the gods that rule Mithris?"

"The gods of Mithris? Well...not really."

"Oh?" Professor Glen looked disappointed. "I thought you would have picked some of that up, considering that I teach history."

"Not really...sorry." Serena shrugged, embarrassed.

"Well, no matter. At any rate, there are quite a few gods that make up the Pantheon of Mithris. The God of Gods on Mithris was named Aurelius."

Serena caught the use of past tense. "Was?"

"Was. He died."

"Died? How? He's a god."

"It has to do with some very old mythology." Professor Glen waved her hand dismissively. "And if you didn't learn any of the mythology growing up in this house, then it probably won't interest you now, so I'll just tell you the bare essentials."

Serena blushed with a mixture of shame and frustration.

"Basically," Professor Glen continued, "Aurelius died from wounds that he received in the War of Chaos, a great conflict between the gods. After Aurelius's death, his son, Julius, took the throne."

"Julius, okay." Serena nodded. "And he's the God of Gods now?"

"Yes. He's been the God of Gods for fifteen years."

Serena's jaw dropped in shock. "Just fifteen years? Aurelius died within my lifetime?"

"Yes. Julius has only been ruling for fifteen years." She hesitated. "And he's your father."

Serena leaned back in her chair. "My father?"

"Yes, your father."

"Julius? The God of Gods?" Serena gaped. Then she pointed an accusing finger at Natalie.

"Why didn't you tell me that?"

"Tell you what?"

"That my father was the God of Gods! He's the one in charge of everything!"

Natalie furrowed her brow. "Did I not tell you that?"

147

"Oh, don't say that you forgot!"

Natalie raised a finger in her defense. "I might not have forgotten. I could have been withholding that information until the right time. In fact, I think I was—but I can't remember whether I was or not." She pulled her journal out. "Actually, let me check my notes."

"How could—"

"Serena..." Professor Glen interrupted, speaking with a tender voice that the girl had never heard before. Serena almost flinched—the professor's intimate tone was so foreign to her.

"You are the daughter of a *god*," the professor said. "Why does it matter if he's the God of Gods? How does that change anything?"

"It matters a lot!" Serena felt hot with anger. Tears welled up in her eyes. "It matters because it means *my* father is the one responsible for this mess! For the last fifteen years—almost the whole war—he's been screwing everything up!"

She slammed the table with her fist. It was a bad idea, because a sharp pain shot through her hand, and she swore again.

"Don't use that language!" Professor Glen and Natalie said at the same time.

Serena glared at them from under the curtain of brown hair that had fallen over her eyes.

"Okay." Her voice shook. She raised her head proudly, trying to control the resentment boiling inside of her. "So my father is Julius, the God of Gods. What else should I know?"

"Julius has a sister, Ambrosia."

"I guess that would make her my aunt." Serena crossed her arms. "And I'll bet she's a real bi–"

"Don't you say that word!" Professor Glen slapped the table in front of Serena, drowning out her naughty language. "Ambrosia is Julius's sister, and she's the one who brought you to me."

"Oh, okay." Serena wiped her tears away with the back of her hand. "And I suppose she just came up to you one morning and said, 'Hello, this is the daughter of the God of Gods, and you should take care of her and never let her know who she is. I have no good reasons for leaving her with you, but there you are.'" She narrowed her eyes at Professor Glen. "Is that what happened?"

"No." Professor Glen blinked. "That isn't."

Serena swallowed, realizing that Professor Glen's own eyes were wet. She stared at the table in shame, unable to see the professor's display of emotion.

"Then what *did* happen?"

"It was a chance meeting. I had been house-sitting for a colleague, and I was up late grading papers."

Serena could not resist looking up. Even Natalie was leaning closer.

"I had just let the cat out when I saw a flash of light down the street. It was brilliant—brighter than the day, and it sent chills down my spine." Professor Glen stared into space above Serena's head, lost in memory. "I investigated the source and walked down the street to the back of a house. Inside was a terrible scene." She looked at Serena, her face pale. "You were there, with your mother. And Ambrosia was there too."

Serena gaped.

"I remember shivering on the porch, a witness to this sight that no human should ever have seen. Ambrosia was...*magnificent* to behold." She swallowed fearfully. "But there was a scent of great evil on the air. It chilled me to the bone. Your mother was dead."

A sharp pain pierced Serena in the chest, as if she was losing her mother again in this retelling. She bit her lip hard.

The professor blinked furiously. "And Ambrosia was looking right at me, making me feel so *mortal*...so small and insignificant and..." She shuddered. "I tried to leave, but she motioned for me to come inside. I couldn't refuse."

"And what did she do?" Natalie whispered.

"At first she was very angry. She was terrifying—beautiful and terrifying. She stared at me, and her eyes seemed to drill into my mind. I quailed under the gaze of those eyes." Professor Glen shuddered. "She brought us out of the house and made us stand across the street. Then she set the house on fire."

"She set it on fire? With my mother still in it?"

"Your mother's body," Professor Glen said gently. "She was gone, Serena. It was like a funeral pyre."

Natalie stirred in her seat.

"Forget the funeral pyre!" Serena said angrily. "Ambrosia was just destroying evidence, wasn't she?"

"You can call it that, and I wouldn't argue. The gods have strict rules about marrying mortals. Ambrosia was ashamed that her brother got involved with a human. She wanted to erase what she perceived as a stain upon the gods."

"So I'm a stain?"

"I'm trying to explain the gods' perspective, Serena," Professor Glen said impatiently. "And you need to understand that if Ambrosia wanted to destroy *all* of the evidence, she would have killed you. And me. But she didn't kill us. Instead, she told me to take care of you."

Serena looked down at her lap, twisting her fingers together.

"And did she say anything else?"

"She told me that I was never to speak of what I had seen," Professor Glen said, and Serena detected a tremor of fear in her voice. "She told me that you were the daughter of the god Julius, and that I was to take care of you, because you couldn't live with her or your father."

Serena felt anger bubbling inside of her again.

"But why not? Why couldn't I have lived with them? She was my aunt for god's sake! Did you ask her?"

"Do you think I was going to question a goddess?" Professor Glen's voice cracked, and Serena knew then that the professor really was afraid.

She ran a hand through her gray hair. "You can't just question the gods."

"They're sure raising a hell of a lot of questions for me!" Serena fell back into her chair, crossing her arms again.

Professor Glen shook her head regretfully. The tired lines darkened under her eyes. "Serena, I'm sorry about all of this. All I ever wanted was to be straightforward and give you the best." She looked imploringly at Serena, but the girl would not meet her gaze.

The three of them sat in silence for a few minutes. Then Natalie cleared her throat.

"Was that the only time you saw Ambrosia?"

"No. She visited my house every year, in secret, asking after Serena."

Serena uncrossed her arms. "Asking after me? How did she know where we lived?"

Natalie raised an eyebrow at Serena, who spread out her arms indignantly. "Look, the gods have already proven their incompetence, okay? I can't assume they know anything."

Professor Glen rapped the table to regain the girls' attention. "I showed her! She wasn't so negligent an aunt that she didn't care to see where her niece would be staying. And she came back each year to see how you were doing. She was very interested to know that you were doing well."

"And that was it?" Serena scowled. "She just wanted to make sure I was eating my vegetables?"

"No." Professor Glen adjusted her glasses. "She also wanted to make sure that you weren't showing any divine potential. That you didn't have powers you weren't supposed to have as a mortal."

Serena rolled her eyes. "Except that I'm a demigoddess."

"Right," Professor Glen conceded. "But she also wanted to make sure that you were staying in Locke City. Her instructions were very specific that you stay in Locke City."

"Why?"

"Because of the geographic magic!" Natalie slapped the table triumphantly. "I knew it!"

"Geographic magic?" Professor Glen repeated, confused.

"It's magic associated with a certain place," Natalie explained. "Ambrosia probably set a concealment spell over Serena, centered around Locke City, that made her undetectable to all divine beings. That way, Julius wouldn't know that Serena was still alive and he wouldn't come looking for her. The spell would also protect Serena from whoever wanted her dead."

"That explains why she was so vehement that you never leave Locke City." Professor Glen's expression was grim. "And why she was furious with me when you finally did."

"Furious with you?" Serena looked alarmed. "She visited you after I left?"

"You left a few days before the fifteenth anniversary of your mother's death. Ambrosia always visited on that night. When she came this year, I was terrified. I had to tell her that you were gone." She blanched at the memory.

Regret filled Serena's chest—she had put the professor in a terrible position.

"But there was nothing that either of us could do," Professor Glen continued. "She couldn't look for you because her absence would be noticed at the Tower. I couldn't look for you because I had no car...and no idea where you'd gone."

Serena's heart sunk at the hurt in Professor Glen's eyes. She tried to think of something to say, but no words rose to her lips. She looked away in shame.

"So...Ambrosia was trying to protect me?"

151

"Yes." Professor Glen studied Serena from over her glasses. "Not such a nasty goddess after all, is she? Full of contradictions, perhaps, but well-meaning at heart."

Natalie crossed her arms and sighed. "And if you hadn't left Locke City, Ambrosia's spell would have continued to conceal you."

"But she should have known better—she restricted me to one lousy city! I'm not a dog that you can keep on a leash! I'm a human being! Of course I wanted to leave."

"It was never a foolproof plan," Professor Glen agreed. "But Ambrosia must have thought it was the best way to keep you safe. Maybe she never figured out what to do when you grew up. Or maybe she thought the threat would disappear."

"Apparently she never figured anything out. And the threat didn't disappear. Even though the Dark Angels are gone, whoever is trying to kill me is still out there, probably at the Tower of the Gods. And that's where we have to go."

The three of them sat in silence for a moment. Natalie checked her watch.

"Speaking of the Tower of the Gods, would now be a bad time to remind you that we're running out of time?"

"I need to get some air." Serena got up from her chair. It made a horrible noise sliding across the tiled kitchen floor. She crossed the living room, opened the front door, and slammed it behind her before collapsing on the front step.

CHAPTER 17:
ALWAYS THE INNOCENT

Serena buried her face in her hands. Why was everything so complicated?

The world kept getting more dangerous, the gods less understandable, and Serena more involved with all of it. She was learning just how tightly her destiny was intertwined with the planet's.

Destiny. She snorted.

Did she really have to go to the Tower of the Gods?

What was she going to say to her father?

Thanks for screwing up my life by having me.

Thanks for the war.

Thanks for nothing.

Her hands were digging into the ground beside the front step, and she realized that she was pulling up chunks of earth. She dropped the grass, clapped her hands together to shake off the dirt, and wiped her hands on her jeans.

She looked up at the houses around her. Only the children had been evacuated, but the entire city had an unnerving silence about it. The children seemed to have taken all the light and joy with them. But the adults continued to work. Someone had to keep the city running, to power the plants, to work the lines, to turn out more planes and guns.

So more people can die. Serena shook her head bitterly.

Then she noticed the newspaper lying out on the lawn. Professor Glen hadn't picked it up in all of the morning excitement. Serena rose to her feet and walked slowly across the grass to pick up the paper. She pulled it out of the plastic sleeve and examined the front page.

Her heart skipped a beat when she read the headline.

"Train Carrying Evacuee Children Bombed. No Survivors."

Serena's mind went numb. She examined the large photograph underneath the headline. It showed the mangled wreckage of a passenger car. Resting beside the shell of the car was a teddy bear, torn and burned by the flames.

Serena knew that teddy bear. She instinctively felt for the ribbon around her hair. It was still there, soft and tender.

She staggered. Her knees hit the grass beneath her. She tried to stand up again, but she swayed, unable to find her feet. She fell forward, planting her hands in the dirt.

Charles. Emma.

She stumbled back to the house, and Natalie opened the door.

"Serena, I—" Natalie stopped when she saw the look on Serena's face. "What's wrong?"

Serena collapsed onto the front step in front of Natalie. The newspaper fell out of her hand. Natalie dropped to her knees and held Serena up.

"Serena, what's wrong?" Natalie asked, panic creeping into her voice.

"No!" Serena shook her head, eyes watering. Her lips trembled. "No, no!" She closed her eyes and shook her head fiercely.

"What is it?" Natalie picked up the newspaper and scanned the headline. "Oh gods." She fell back onto the front step and held Serena tighter. Her voice broke. "Oh gods!"

"No!" Serena screamed, breaking free of Natalie's embrace and stumbling through the open door. She fell into the living room, bowed over with grief, her face pressed against the carpet as she screamed like a wounded animal.

"No, not Charles! He was just a little boy." She pounded the floor. "Not Emma, not Emma." She pulled the ribbon from her hair, squeezing it tightly, soaking it with her tears.

She had a dim impression of Professor Glen standing in the doorway, her hand over her mouth in horror. But Serena paid her little attention.

"No, please, no!" She shook her head, looking up at the ceiling. She felt arms around her, but she fought them off, her voice pleading. "Oh gods, no! Why the children? Why the children?"

She fell back to the ground, images swimming in front of her burning eyes.

Charles, with his black hair, his sweet smile, and his balloons. Emma, with her precious brown curls.

She remembered the feel of Charles in her arms. His tiny body against hers when he cried, when he missed his poor mother who had already died. Another victim of the war.

More and more victims.

Serena pressed her face against the carpet floor. If she could explain how Charles and Emma were so sweet, so innocent, maybe someone would make everything okay again.

She could feel Natalie and Professor Glen around her, could hear Natalie sobbing. Serena swallowed, choking on her own tears, trying to breathe, and producing high, desperate sobs instead.

She gripped her head tightly. What was there to be done? Charles and Emma were dead.

What kind of a god would let that happen?

She breathed, deeper and deeper, trying to control herself.

Finally, Serena stopped shaking. She felt a terrible emptiness welling up inside of her. The grief felt like exhaustion. Serena raised her head slowly, her eyes red like fire, her face stained by tears.

She felt older, spent.

She coughed violently, rising to a sitting position, wrapping her arms around her knees.

Charles and Emma were dead. She held the wet ribbon in her hands, the ribbon that had belonged to Eugene, the ribbon that Charles had given to her. She felt its softness in her fingers, and an aching pain threatened to overwhelm her again.

Serena wanted to stay where she was forever. It would be indecent to ever smile, to ever laugh, to ever move again. Children were dead, and there was no sense in pretending that anything could ever be all right again.

She raised her eyes reluctantly to see Professor Glen and Natalie sitting in chairs beside her. Natalie's green eyes were shining with tears. Professor Glen was sitting back in her armchair, her hands folded in her lap, a solemn expression on her lined face.

Irritation mixed with the other emotions boiling inside of Serena. Why hadn't the world stopped? Why were they still sitting there, waiting patiently, as if Serena could just get up and keep going?

Professor Glen rose from her chair and knelt on the floor. She put her hand warily on Serena's shoulder, who did not shake it off. Serena felt tense, ready to rebuke the professor for saying, "Everything is going to be okay," or "I'm sure they're in a better place," or something empty like that. She was almost disappointed that Professor Glen kept silent. She wanted to vent her anger. Her lungs were ready to burst.

Serena stared up at Natalie, noting the terrible grief on her face. She remembered the balloons that Natalie had conjured for the children. Natalie loved children. The red-haired girl wrung her hands in her lap, and she turned away when she saw Serena looking at her.

Serena glanced at Professor Glen, who was still waiting patiently to see what Serena would do next. And suddenly Serena needed to get up. She rose to feet, feeling dizzy for a moment. The agony was lifting from her mind like a cloud, to leave her in a momentary state of unfeeling.

But that's what she wanted to feel: numb and blank. Serena wiped her eyes and walked toward the hallway.

"Where are you going?" Natalie sniffed loudly from the living room.

Serena stopped, leaning against the wall.

"I don't know."

Natalie sighed with a shuddering breath, and Serena heard her rise to her feet.

"We still have to go to the Tower, Serena."

Serena shook her head, staring at the ground. She wanted to yell at Natalie for suggesting that they could just move on, but her emotion was spent. Her voice was nothing but a whisper.

"Can't you just leave it, Natalie? It's over."

"No, it's not," Natalie whispered back. She walked up next to Serena. "That's what's so terrible about it. There's more to come. More children will die the same way that Charles and Emma died."

Serena flinched at the sound of their names, but Natalie continued to talk in her firm, quiet voice.

"We have to speak with the gods. We have to get them to stop this war. You have to get your father to care about mankind again."

Serena turned around to face Natalie, her expression impassive. Natalie leaned closer.

"The gods aren't going to change anything on their own. They need us. That's why I'm here." She reached out to hold Serena's hand. "That's why we're together."

Serena sighed.

"I know..."

"Know what?"

Serena swallowed.

"...that you're right."

Natalie nodded.

"It's just that..." Serena's eyes felt wet again. Her voice was almost inaudible. "It hurts."

Natalie nodded, blinking, as more tears rolled down her cheeks. She enveloped Serena in a hug, and the two girls held each other tightly.

CHAPTER 18:
THE TOWER OF THE GODS

"Do you know where the Tower of the Gods is?"

Professor Glen opened the front door for the girls as they stepped outside.

"Not precisely." Natalie tapped her umbrella against her rain boots, having resumed her usual attire. "But a place with such powerful magic will be hard to hide. My umbrella and I can find it, just like we found Serena."

"Good luck then." Professor Glen waved. The girls walked down the front steps onto the sidewalk.

Natalie held her umbrella in front of her, the tip facing forward.

"What are you doing?" Serena asked.

"Probing for magic." Natalie closed her eyes, and they walked down the length of an entire street.

Serena watched Natalie patiently for a few moments as mist fell from the gray clouds above them. Her patience waned quickly.

"Is it working?"

"Shh." Natalie held a finger to her mouth, still holding the umbrella with her other hand. Then she stopped abruptly and swung the umbrella around to her left.

Serena jumped aside. "You almost hit me!"

Natalie opened her eyes, pointing with her umbrella.

"It's that way. Let's go."

She broke off at a run, Serena following close behind.

They walked past shops and restaurants, most of which were empty, save for a few patrons. Some of the businesses were closed, their doors and windows boarded up. Broken glass peppered the streets, and fires still smoldered in the wreckage of damaged buildings. A few stretches of neighborhood were totally bombed out.

The few people outside bustled past the girls without sparing a second glance. It seemed that no one wanted to be in the open for too long.

The girls picked their way around fallen stoplights and burnt-out vehicles. Natalie led them deeper into the heart of the city, where the buildings were taller.

They occasionally heard the sound of an airplane overhead. They ducked under shelter when this happened, but no bombs fell.

"Must be the Arteman Air Force," Serena said after the third time.

Natalie nodded. "Still, I don't care for us to be seen. Especially not by soldiers. They might find a reason for us not to be where we're going."

The girls ran from building to building, avoiding patrolling military jeeps as they moved into the heart of the city. They passed a power plant and saw civilians with hard hats shouting orders at each other. Their voices sounded nervous.

They entered a neighborhood near the train yard, and Serena wondered how many train workers had been killed in the bombing. Those trains hadn't run by themselves, but now they weren't running at all.

Natalie raised her hand to stop when they reached a massive lot enclosed by a wooden fence. It looked completely abandoned, but big enough to hold an enormous building.

Maybe an invisible skyscraper.

"I've been downtown loads of times, but I've never really noticed this place before." Serena watched as Natalie felt along the wooden fence. "I guess I figured they would build something here eventually."

"That's probably what everyone figures, if they notice it at all." Natalie ran her hands along each board, edging slowly along the sidewalk.

"What are you looking for?"

"An opening. It's probably concealed by magic, but I'll be able to find it eventually." Natalie raised her umbrella to tap a segment of the fence.

"Or you could try the door," Serena said. "It looks unlocked."

Natalie turned around to see Serena pointing a little farther down the fence.

Natalie shrugged. "I guess we could try the door."

Serena managed a brief smile.

The girls walked inside the lot. The ground was broken and torn, like a construction site in progress.

"This is definitely it," Natalie whispered. "Can you feel the magic?"

"I feel something," Serena said thoughtfully. Then she looked down at her feet and stepped around Natalie. "Oh, that was it. I was standing in mud."

Natalie rolled her eyes.

"Good job finding this place, if you're sure it's the right one," Serena said. "Now, how do we get into the Tower?" She rubbed her shoulders anxiously, feeling exposed while standing in this huge lot. "Is it below us, you think?"

"No." Natalie let her umbrella rest against her legs, feeling the air with her hands. "I think we're probably standing right next to it. Maybe we're already in."

"Well that's helpful." Serena kicked a clod of dirt. "But how do we get *in* in?"

"In in?"

Serena shrugged, feeling embarrassed at the way she phrased the question, but a smile was forming on Natalie's lips.

"Now you're thinking just like me." Natalie grinned. "How do *you* think we get in?"

Serena hesitated. "Well, there are no doors."

"Very good." Natalie nodded encouragingly. "So what do we do?"

"I don't know...announce that we're here?"

"Is that a question or a statement?"

"A statement. We're here."

As soon as the words left her mouth, the outline of a door gleamed in front of them. Natalie grabbed Serena's hand and pulled her under the archway. The ground shifted beneath their feet, and Serena felt herself moving upward.

The feeling was unsettling. Serena didn't know if she felt more or less comfortable when an elevator materialized around them. A metal floor solidified beneath their feet, and a glass tube encased them as the streets below faded into the fog.

"We'll have quite an entrance." Natalie tapped the newly-formed elevator door with her umbrella. A series of black dials were spinning beside the elevator door, the numerals getting larger and larger as they rose into the air.

Finally, the elevator began to slow down. Serena braced herself against the sides, expecting a bump at the top, but the elevator came to a smooth stop. The door opened soundlessly, revealing a wide corridor that stretched out of sight.

Serena felt an uncanny feeling, a mixture of terror and awe. They had entered the domain of the gods.

It was very clean.

Natalie stepped out of the elevator confidently, looking around as if she owned the place. The corridor seemed to be empty. Natalie turned left and disappeared out of sight. Serena hesitated in the door.

Then Natalie peeked her head around the corner, right in front of Serena's face.

"Well, are you coming?"

"Yeah, I guess." Serena shook the nerves from her head and stepped into the corridor. It was wide, with a panoramic view of the skyline. Doors lined the opposite hallway, but they were all closed. The girls walked down to the end of the hallway, entering a much bigger room with an enormous statue of a god that stretched from floor to ceiling.

The god was dressed in full body armor. An enormous hammer rested at the statue's feet. Serena noted a lightning bolt engraved on the head of the hammer. An inscription on the pedestal below the statue read, "Aurelius."

Serena would have gazed upon her grandfather's face, but it was too high to see clearly. The letters on the inscription were as tall as she was. She felt miniscule.

Her sense of unease grew with each moment.

Natalie was lost in concentration, scanning the many doors that led out of the cavernous room.

"Come on, Serena. We've got to keep moving. We need to find the throne room. And I wonder where everyone is...?" Natalie stared up at the high ceiling, where stars floated above them, twinkling in their radiance and splendor.

"Is that the universe?" Serena stared at the imitation of the heavens.

"The whole thing? Not hardly. But we're over there."

Serena tried to see where Natalie was pointing amid the countless lights.

"Which ones are you pointing at?"

"The cluster of tiny dots circling the big, shiny one. The big one is your sun."

"That one?"

"No. More to the left."

"There?"

"No. Try to follow where my finger's pointing."

"Let's just say it's that one. There are too many...and they're all too small."

Natalie laughed.

"Everything in the universe is small when you see it from the right perspective."

Serena felt her confidence slipping by the moment. The whole place screamed of her insignificance. She cleared her throat nervously.

"Natalie, why do you think they'll even listen to us? I'm an eighteen-year-old girl—"

"Demigoddess."

"And you look even younger than me."

"But I'm a Phoenix Guardian. And I'm older than some of these gods." Natalie waved a dismissive hand at the gigantic room.

"But where are the gods anyway? This is a pretty big building. It seems like the Tower would be swarming with them."

Natalie put her hands on her hips. "Just how many gods do you think there are?"

"I don't know. Enough to fill a Tower of the Gods?"

"They only assemble if there's something important going on."

"Like what?"

"An assembly." Natalie winked.

Serena rolled her eyes.

"Once a year, all of the gods gather to discuss the affairs of the world. The rest of the time, the gods are ruling over their respective countries and continents."

Hearing about the gods in the Tower made them seem so real. They *were* real. The thought intimidated Serena, overshadowing her like the starry ceiling.

"So...what's my purpose here again?" Serena's hands were cold with sweat. She wiped them on her jeans.

Natalie reached out to hold Serena's shaking hand. Serena trembled for a moment, but the strong warmth of Natalie's hand had a calming effect.

"You're going to see your father." Natalie smiled. "You're going to help him care about humanity again. You can mediate between the gods and men. Who better to make them understand the human condition than someone who's lived as a human all her life?"

She patted Serena on the shoulder. "You're in the right place."

"I couldn't agree more."

Serena jumped at the sound of the male voice behind her. She turned around to see an older man in glowing white robes. Long gray hair fell across his face, and his eyes were full of triumph. He grabbed Serena's arm with a vice-like grip.

"Natalie!" she screamed, trying to break free of the old man's grasp. She turned around to see Natalie—and her heart jumped into her throat.

Another man in a helmet and armor held Natalie by the arms. Her umbrella had dropped to the floor. A second guard picked it up and examined it curiously.

"Hold onto that," the old man ordered the guard, who saluted smartly. "Take her." He nodded to a third guard, who relieved him of Serena.

The old man stood before the girls. A grin spread across his face.

"This is an unexpected twist, but I think it will prove to our advantage. You have arrived at an opportune moment, Serena, daughter of Julius. Come with me."

CHAPTER 19:
SKELETONS IN THE CLOSET

Julius sat against the cold walls of his cell. A foul odor hung in the dark dungeon, and a constant drip of putrid water grated on his nerves with each passing minute.

He had been locked in the dungeon for more than a day. His body ached from the torture of the spears, but his humiliation and anger overshadowed the pain.

Julius shook his head furiously. He had been betrayed by his sister and overthrown by his closest adviser. How could this have happened?

Ambrosia and Nikolas had been with him from birth. Ambrosia was flesh and blood. Nikolas had served Julius's family since the War of Chaos.

But Ambrosia had grown tired of his leadership. Nikolas had deceived him. The closest bonds had come untied, and Julius's final foundation had been swept out from under him.

"Julius, you need to listen to me."

He twitched, as if shooing an irksome fly. Ambrosia had been trying to talk to him for the last day.

"Listen to me!"

He tried to block out her voice. He stared at the bars of his cell, silently cursing whatever gods had forged such powerful metal. If only he could break out now...and kill them all. But he was trapped, in his own dungeon, on his own planet. The bars that imprisoned him stood as monuments to his failure.

"Julius! I am trying to tell you something!"

"Have you no shame, goddess?" Julius spat at the ground. He raised his head to look at his sister in the cell across from him. Her dirty, blonde hair fell over her face and shoulders.

"I did not betray you. I never meant to hurt you."

Julius snorted and turned his back to her, scuffing his sandals against the rough stone walls.

"Listen to me, you fool!"

"What's worse, Ambrosia? Betraying your brother or denying it?"

"What betrayal are you talking about?" Ambrosia slapped the bars in frustration. They responded with a dull, hollow ring. "Can you really blame me for wanting to save Mithris? Are you blind to the burning city outside? That is what the entire planet will look like if we do not intervene soon. I am sorry if you think that makes me a traitor, but someone has to lead. You have neglected humanity for too long."

Julius turned around and glared at her. "And that justifies murdering your own brother?"

"I will tell you one more time—I did not release the Dark Angels! I never tried to murder you!"

The ferocity of Ambrosia's tone made the hair rise on the back of Julius's neck.

"Then why did you have keys to the Crypt?"

"Did you pay any attention to what happened? If I had stolen the keys, how would Nikolas have entered the Crypt to discover that the coffins were open? How would he have locked up the Dark Angels again? With the keys he did not have?" Ambrosia's voice dripped with sarcasm. "You and Ewald just swallowed his lies when he miraculously found the keys in my robes. How convenient for Nikolas, the High Counselor, the Keeper of the Crypt, to find his keys on the last obstacle between him and the throne."

Julius felt a twinge of hesitation. What if she was telling the truth?

Ambrosia narrowed her eyes. "Nikolas made you believe that I was a traitor, did he not? He told you what you already know—that I am unhappy with the way you are ruling—and then he made it look like I was seizing power. He set me up."

"I think you set yourself up." Julius scowled. "You wanted to be the Ruler of Mithris. 'Better late than never,' you said."

Ambrosia flinched. She started to speak, but Julius interrupted her.

"You're right about Nikolas. He warned me against a conspiracy. He planted ideas in my head that you were the traitor. He made me curious about the Dark Angels. I investigated the Crypt and discovered that the coffins were empty." Julius didn't disguise the bitterness in his voice. "Then you played right into his hands by speaking your mind."

Ambrosia crossed her arms. "And you played right into his hands by believing I was the traitor."

"You were very believable." Julius gripped the bars menacingly. Then he took a deep breath. "But tell me, if Nikolas was the one who unleashed the Dark Angels, where are they? Why haven't they attacked me?"

"Nikolas did not release the Dark Angels to kill you. He released them to kill someone else." Ambrosia hesitated. "Just like he did fifteen years ago."

"What?" Julius's eyes widened.

Ambrosia winced, turning her head away. She stepped back from the bars, retreating into the shadows so Julius couldn't see her face.

"It was not a house fire that killed your family. It was a Dark Angel."

"What? How do you know?"

"Because...I was there."

"You *what*? You were there when Jillian and Serena died? You could have saved them!" He groaned. "You as good as murdered them! I told you to let them stay in the Tower with me—"

"Do not ever accuse me of murdering them! I tried to keep them safe." Ambrosia pointed an accusing finger at Julius, and there was pain in her voice. "Nikolas was acting suspicious that night. He had taken a strange interest in your family...strange for someone who despised the union as much as Father and me."

"What?"

"Yes, Julius. Nikolas was ashamed too. He never showed it around you because he wanted you to like him. He probably knew that Father's days were short, and he wanted to ingratiate himself to the heir to the throne. I realized too late that your family might be in danger. I went to the house to see if they were safe."

Julius stared intently at his sister, listening hard.

"When I arrived, the Dark Angel was already there. He had killed your wife, but Serena was still alive."

Julius felt the floor drop out from under him.

"And you just let her die?"

"No, I killed the Dark Angel." Ambrosia hesitated again. "And I saved your daughter's life."

Julius struggled to find words.

"You saved her? But then...how did she die?"

"She did not die. She is still alive."

The words lingered in the air like a cloud. Julius held his breath as the revelation sunk into his mind.

She's still alive.

Serena...my daughter...is still alive.

A drop of water struck the floor by Julius's foot, waking him from his reverie.

"But you told me that she was dead!" Julius yelled, and Ambrosia jumped in fright. "You told me that same night that both of them were dead! You lied to me!"

"I lied to you to protect her!"

"And to make sure that I could never see her again!" Julius tore at his hair. "What have you done?"

"I protected her," Ambrosia pleaded. "And Nikolas believed the deception too. He stopped hunting your daughter. He thought she was dead. Your daughter was safe, living with a mortal."

"But why didn't you tell me about Nikolas?"

"Because then I would have been forced to tell you what really happened. And because Father died that night and my whole world fell apart." Ambrosia bit her lip. "Besides, I did not have any evidence against Nikolas. Only strong suspicions. And he has not caused any more trouble for the last fifteen years. I thought it had all gone away."

"You thought it had all gone away..." Julius shook his head in disbelief.

"She was *safe*, do you hear me? And you were free to rule Mithris, free to be the god you were supposed to be!"

"How dare you!" Julius beat his fists against the bars. "How dare you decide whether I see my family! How dare you decide to hide my daughter from me all these years!"

"Someone had to make the decision! Someone had to decide what was best for Mithris, and it was not going to be you. You made the mistake when you had a child, and I had to clean up the mess."

Julius glared at his sister, his blue eyes full of anger. "The 'mess' you speak of was my family. *Your* family!"

"And I was the one who saved it from complete destruction." Ambrosia pointed at herself. "I saved your daughter's life."

Julius shook his head. "But you failed!"

"What?" Ambrosia flinched. "What do you mean? I left her with a mortal—a good woman. I made sure that Serena was taken care of, that she was raised in their fashion. I checked up on her every year. I set a concealment charm over her to make sure that Nikolas could never find her."

"A concealment charm?" Julius scoffed. "You thought that she would never leave the city?"

Ambrosia swallowed. "I thought that—"

"No, that's the problem! You weren't thinking! She left Locke City, didn't she? And Nikolas was waiting. He must have noticed, year after year, when you left to see her. We've both underestimated how cunning he is. You thought you could visit her in secret, but he must have suspected you. He never believed that she was dead, not without the bodies for evidence. Then she left Locke City—and your little spell failed."

Ambrosia shook her head desperately. "No...that is not my fault..."

"That's what happened, isn't it?" Julius snarled. "A young girl decided she didn't want to live in the city anymore, and Nikolas started hunting her again!"

Ambrosia grasped her head in her hands, bowed over with grief.

"You as good as killed her!" Julius screamed. "And I never got to see her! I never got to hold my daughter again!"

Julius ground his teeth. It was torture, knowing that he could have had a life with his daughter. Fifteen years ago, he had been told that Serena was gone forever. Learning that she had been alive was like losing her all over again.

And now the Dark Angels were going to murder Serena, if they hadn't already.

"Julius, you have to forgive me. You have to believe I was trying to do the right thing."

"Every time you try to do the right thing, you make everything worse! Why not let me know that she was in danger so I could protect her—and bring her here to live with me?"

Ambrosia hesitated, and Julius snarled, shaking his finger at her.

"*That's* why, isn't it? Because you didn't want her living with me! The shame would have been too great! Even though her life was in danger, you still couldn't let her live with me. And when you set the concealment charm, it wasn't just to protect her from Nikolas. It was to keep her separated from me!"

Ambrosia's eyes shone with tears. She shook her head, but her denial had lost all conviction.

"I...I still did not want...I am sorry." She covered her face again. "I just wanted everything to go back to normal."

Her last word was a pleading note that rang desperately in the cold air.

"Nothing will ever go back to normal. You've made sure of that."

"You have to believe me," Ambrosia said weakly. "I have done everything that I can."

"To ruin us."

"I never wanted Jillian or Serena to be hurt! I just wanted them to have their place, like we have ours."

Julius shook his head. "And who are you to decide places?"

Ambrosia opened her mouth to speak, but the words failed on her trembling lips. She covered her face and slumped against the wall.

Julius brooded in the corner of his cell, burning in anger against his sister.

He cursed under his breath, hating Ambrosia for trying to do what she thought was right. It would have been more satisfying to believe that she had done this out of malice.

But to know that she felt remorse—he had listened to her weeping—sent his emotions into deeper turmoil. He loved Jillian. He had wanted a life with her. But Ambrosia obeyed a law that forbade love between gods and mortals.

How could two people pursue what was right and still come into such sharp conflict? How could right be so wrong?

Julius closed his eyes, hoping that sleep could bring relief to his troubled soul.

He had just drifted off when a clang reverberated through the dungeon. He heard footsteps running down the stairs toward the cells.

A torch blinded him as a group of people came close. Julius squinted, raising his hand to block the light.

"Who's there?" he asked warily.

"A most interesting development, Julius," Ewald responded. "You and your sister are to come with me immediately. No tricks—or the guards will give you another round with the spears."

Julius blinked, lowering his hand as his eyes slowly adjusted to the torch's bright glow. He heard the creak of hinges, and his own door swung open.

Two Guardian Angels grabbed him roughly by the shoulders, holding his hands behind his back. Three more stood in front of him, their spears poised, ready to stab him in the chest at the first sign of trouble.

Julius sneered. "What now? Nikolas wants to execute us?"

"No." Ewald shook his head, and his cold bureaucratic eyes glinted in the torchlight. "Your daughter is here to see you."

CHAPTER 20:
HAMMER AND SPEAR

Natalie struggled against the grip of the Guardian Angel as he pushed her into an enormous room similar to the one they had just left. This chamber had a high dome with arched windows, revealing a breathtaking view of the starry night sky.

Beside her, Serena was struggling against her captor. The god ahead of them stepped lightly, reveling in obvious excitement. As the group walked, Natalie tried to edge her guard toward the one who held her umbrella.

She was running out of time.

If she closed her eyes and shut out the other sounds, she could hear the ticking of her watch. It was getting louder, and she had so little time left. Mere hours. It was going to happen soon, and Natalie wanted to make sure that she made every second count.

The god held up a hand to stop them in the center of the room. Across the way, a door opened. A balding god with frizzy hair entered, followed by two guards. His face lit up with happiness when he saw Natalie and Serena.

"Absolutely fascinating!" The newcomer clapped his hands. "And you're sure that it's her, Nikolas?"

Nikolas nodded. "Of course it is, Ewald. You can sense her power. She's the one."

Ewald gazed at her for a moment, awestruck. Then he looked at Natalie.

"And this one? Who are you, young lady?"

"You should let me go." Natalie tried to pull her arms free, but the guard tightened his grip.

"Careful!" Ewald raised a warning finger. "I wouldn't try to escape. You could get hurt. Let's skip the silliness and get to the information. Your name?"

"I'd like my umbrella back, please."

"Of course. But answers first." Ewald wagged his finger.

"Natalie Bliss. Now can I have my umbrella back?"

"You won't need it indoors, haha." Ewald winked. "Now who are you?"

Natalie scowled, eyeing her umbrella. Then she shrugged. "Just a friend of Serena's."

"A very powerful friend, I would guess." Ewald looked Natalie up and down. He glanced at Nikolas. "Another demigoddess?"

"No." Nikolas frowned, stepping up to Natalie. "Her magic is much older."

Nikolas raised his hand to touch Natalie's face. He closed his eyes and pressed his finger against her forehead. She stared at him, defiant and unflinching.

Then Nikolas fell back with a cry. He shook his hand as if it had been burned.

"A Phoenix Guardian?" he gasped.

Natalie raised her chin proudly. "Who wants to know?"

"Excuse me?" Ewald cleared his throat, looking from Nikolas to the red-haired girl.

"She's a Phoenix Guardian." Nikolas narrowed his eyes at her.

"A Phoenix Guardian? Are you sure?"

"Look at her. A little girl by appearance...but so much more. She's too powerful to be anything but a Phoenix Guardian. Besides," Nikolas sucked his finger, "she *knows* fire."

Natalie gave him a smug smile.

"A Phoenix Guardian?" Ewald swallowed nervously. "Who sent you, young lady?"

"Isn't it obvious?" Nikolas arched an eyebrow. "The Pantheon."

"Then why didn't I know anything about it?"

"Oh, come now, Ewald." Nikolas rolled his eyes. "Since when have the departments of the Pantheon communicated clearly about any affairs, internal or external? Besides, you know the Phoenix Guardians have always been a little rogue."

"Ah, yes." Ewald frowned. "Always expecting special privileges and poking their noses into other people's business."

Natalie shrugged again. "We try to watch out for the universe."

Ewald stroked his chin thoughtfully. "What exactly is your mission here?"

"Could you release me first?" Natalie smiled sweetly.

"Well, I would, but the situation at the moment is a bit complicated, haha. You see, we've just discovered that Julius has a daughter—which would, of course, be you." Ewald nodded to Serena. "That's a no-no to the Pantheon, so Julius has been removed as Ruler of Mithris. In regular circumstances, his sister

Ambrosia would have taken the throne. However, she was caught in an assassination attempt on her brother. The scheme was just uncovered the other day."

Natalie raised her eyebrows and glanced at Serena, whose face registered the same surprise. Ambrosia tried to assassinate Julius?

"So it's all a very big mess, haha." Ewald wrung his hands. "Speaking of that, let's bring the prisoners in."

He waved at his two guards, who turned and walked briskly through the door behind them. They emerged a moment later, followed by ten more Guardian Angels. Two were restraining a goddess, whose beautiful blonde hair was dirty with grime.

Ambrosia, Natalie thought.

Two more were restraining a god—Julius, clearly. His white toga was wrinkled and stained, his short black hair was tussled, but his eyes were fierce and alert.

The other eight guards surrounded him, watching him warily, spears at the ready.

The angels pushed their captives to the ground a short distance away from the girls. They forced the gods into a bow, but Julius jerked his head up immediately.

"Serena, is that you?" He gazed hungrily at her.

A Guardian Angel promptly jabbed his spear into Julius's back, electrocuting him with red energy. Julius screamed. His mouth and eyes glowed white as the shock illuminated his body. Then the angel withdrew his spear, and Julius's head slumped onto his chest with a groan.

"Julius!" Ambrosia shouted, straining to move closer to her brother.

Another guard hit her across the face with the butt of his spear, cutting her lip. She spat blood onto the floor. Then she took a deep breath and glared defiantly at her attacker.

Natalie glanced at Serena, who looked dizzy with emotion. She was seeing her father and aunt for the first time...and Natalie could hardly imagine worse circumstances.

"Stop this nonsense!" Ewald waved his hands. "Bring the prisoners over here. It's time for Julius to meet his daughter."

"That's the God of Gods?" Natalie asked reproachfully. "What have you done to him?"

"I believe it would be more appropriate to ask, 'What has he done to himself?'" Nikolas shook his head sadly. "Julius is merely suffering the consequences of his actions."

"And who are you, exactly?" Natalie looked the god up and down.

"I am Nikolas, High Counselor, formerly to Aurelius, and now to his son, Julius." He tilted his head thoughtfully. "Or perhaps I should also say 'formerly' to Julius as well, due to these most recent and unfortunate circumstances."

Serena's voice shook. "But I don't understand. Why would Ambrosia betray him?"

"I did not betray anyone." Ambrosia spat at Nikolas. "Do not listen to him."

The guard hit her again with his spear. She laughed—a frightening sound that raised the hair on Natalie's neck.

"You cannot keep us down forever." Ambrosia's mouth was bloody as she stared at Nikolas, her head swaying slightly.

"I understand that," he answered grimly, "which is why you will be dead before long."

"Dead? Now wait just a minute." Ewald put his hands on his hips, looking from Nikolas to Ambrosia.

Ambrosia chuckled, wincing in obvious pain.

"How are you going to kill us? With the fools that you have turned against us?" She jerked her head at the guard beside her. "After all, they are only angels with shiny toys...and you are not a fighter."

A smile spread across Nikolas's face. "So it would seem."

He turned to Ewald.

"Have you finished the message informing the Pantheon of Julius's treachery?"

"That he failed to register his daughter? Yes, I sent it, but—"

"And you explained that he has been replaced as God of Gods?"

"Yes, I did, and I included a notice of your temporary status as Ruler of Mithris. The paperwork has been sent, and I'm waiting for their response." Ewald ran a hand through his frizzy hair. "But Nikolas, answer my question. What's this about killing?"

"I'm going to kill them, Ewald."

"Sir." Ewald glared at Nikolas sternly, tucking his clipboard under his fat elbow. "These traitors will be taken to the Pantheon for trial and sentence. I will not stand by and watch you murder them."

"Don't worry." Nikolas walked over to Ewald and placed a hand on his shoulder. "You won't have to watch."

He pulled a knife from his robes and shoved it into Ewald's stomach.

The fat god squealed in shock, but Nikolas stabbed him again before he could react—once, twice, three times.

Blood poured from the wounds. Ewald fell to his knees, eyes wide and mouth trembling.

He gargled something incoherent.

Nikolas inclined his ear. "What's that now?"

Ewald's skin was deathly pale. His eyes were wild, like a trapped animal before the slaughter.

He mouthed the word, "Why?"

"Ah," Nikolas said, standing upright. "Because these are difficult times."

He pushed Ewald's head forward, lifting his blade against the god's fat neck.

Then he slit his throat with a quick jerk of the wrist.

Nikolas released his grip, and Ewald collapsed onto the floor. Blood oozed from his neck.

Serena screamed.

"Nikolas! What have you done?" Ambrosia yelled.

"Ambrosia, out of everyone here, you should be the least surprised." Nikolas waved his knife reproachfully at Ambrosia, flicking blood onto the floor. "You know I unleashed the Dark Angels. You know what I'm capable of. I will take whatever means necessary to do what's best for Mithris."

He wiped the knife on his robes. "I already have fine qualifications to take the throne, but why risk being replaced by an inexperienced Pantheon god with no prior interest in this world? I arrived ages ago with Aurelius, and when the Pantheon learns that I withstood your murderous coup, my credentials will look even stronger. The Pantheon will reward me for bringing you to justice after you murdered poor Ewald." Nikolas brushed his gray hair out of his eyes and smiled confidently. "I will take my place as the permanent Ruler of Mithris and give this planet the leader it deserves."

He snapped his fingers, and a sound like the ringing of chimes filled the air. In response, a tremendous boom shook the floor.

"What was that?" Serena screamed, staring down at the shaking ground.

Nikolas laughed. "Something more than angels with shiny toys. The true treasure of the Crypt: a fire giant. He'll make good sport of you."

Serena trembled violently in her guard's strong grasp. "A fire giant?"

Natalie felt her heart plummet into her stomach.

Ambrosia's voice shook with rage and disbelief.

"Nikolas, why? The fire giant could kill us all!"

"He's a temperamental one for sure, but I can handle him." Nikolas waved a dismissive hand. "I am, after all, the Keeper of the Crypt. I've been taking care of these wicked creatures since Good Lord Aurelius and the First Gods used them in the War of Chaos. I know Aurelius's personal collection very well. But don't let me get ahead of myself." He raised a warning finger. "I left a few passages open for the fire giant, but it will still take him awhile to find his way up here. In the meantime, we'll talk."

"What is there left to say?" Julius glared at Nikolas with bloodshot eyes.

Nikolas walked up to him, leaning down until his face was at eye level.

"I want to kill you, Julius. You're a spoiled, rude, disrespectful, short-tempered little boy. You disgraced us all with your short assemblies and debauchery." He slapped Julius across the face. "Siring children with humans is wrong. It defies nature. A god should know better. Gods who mate with mortals are not fit to rule planets."

Nikolas stood, holding his hands behind his back. He walked to Ambrosia and lowered his face to hers.

"I'm going to kill you too, Ambrosia. You're too clever and I never liked you." Nikolas ran his hand through her blonde hair. "Although I do confess to a certain level of desire. I've watched you for centuries, and I've been unable to do anything about it. Daddy's girl." He smiled. "But Daddy is long gone, and brother can't protect you."

Nikolas pressed her hair against his lips and kissed it.

Ambrosia jerked her head away from him. "Don't touch me, you filth."

Nikolas punched her in the jaw. Ambrosia breathed heavily, blood dripping freely from her mouth.

"You've been hit in the mouth a lot tonight." Nikolas patted her on the head. "A few more insolent words and your jaw will be broken. Then I won't be able to hear you beg for mercy before I kill you."

Nikolas turned around to look at the girls. Serena quailed under his gaze.

"Oh, Serena," he chuckled, shaking his head. "To think that I ever considered you a threat to inherit the throne. I realize now that your powers are insignificant. You must take after your mother more than your wretched father."

His face was full of contempt. "You're weak and irrelevant. You wouldn't even have made it this far if not for your Phoenix Guardian friend. She fought all of the battles for you, didn't she?"

He glanced at Natalie, who merely blinked in response. She was too focused on moving closer to the guard who held her umbrella. During all of the commotion when Nikolas had stabbed Ewald, the angel with Natalie's umbrella had repositioned himself next to her guard.

The guard was resting her umbrella against the floor, and the umbrella point was inches from Natalie's toe. With each passing moment, she moved her foot closer to her umbrella, almost imperceptibly. When her toe finally made contact, Natalie closed her eyes and thought very hard of an adjective. She needed the guard to release her arms. The umbrella could provide the proper motivation if Natalie could find the proper adjective.

Ah. There we go.

Hot.

No one likes to hold hot hands, especially if those hands have burst into little balls of flame that ignite the rest of your body.

The Guardian Angel released his grip with a cry of surprise. In that moment, Natalie grabbed her umbrella from the other guard's grasp.

She scooped it up and turned around, opening the umbrella to blast the burning Guardian Angel across the floor. He slammed headfirst into the wall on the other side of the room. The guard's helmet might have saved him from the head trauma, but his armor was insufficient to prevent the smoking hole that Natalie had made in his chest. He slumped to the ground, his sightless eyes still wide with shock.

Before anyone else could react, Natalie's umbrella had ignited into white flames, and she had thrust it into another guard's chest. She pulled the umbrella out with a quick jerk, and he collapsed to the floor in a clatter of armor.

"Kill her!" Nikolas pointed at Natalie.

STEVEN THORN

The guard holding Serena let her go to lunge at the red-haired girl. Two more guards rushed at her with spears raised.

Natalie dived to her left, evading the angels' attack and shooting two well-aimed bursts of flame at the guards holding Julius. The shots found their targets, and the shock from the blasts gave Julius enough time to spring free of his bonds. Julius turned around to grab one of his captors in a headlock.

The other angel grabbed Julius from behind, but he was focused on the one in his grasp. His neck muscles bulged with the strain as he tightened his elbow against the guard's neck, pushing the angel's head forward. Suddenly, he grasped the top of the angel's helmet and twisted it sharply to the right. A sickening crack reverberated through the room. The guard fell lifeless to the floor.

Julius threw his arms back, grabbed the other guard by the shoulders, and threw him bodily into the air. In a blur of movement, Julius picked up a fallen spear and hurled it at him. The spear caught the angel through the neck. He hit the ground face-first, his head bent at an unnatural angle.

Julius's body shone with a fearsome light as he whirled around to face the guards between him and Ambrosia. Five guards stood in front of her, their spears sparkling with red electricity. The three remaining guards ran to protect Nikolas, who was shouting desperate orders.

"I am the Son of Aurelius!" Julius bellowed. "The Lightning Hammer strikes again!"

Julius swung his arm back, and a glowing hammer materialized in his hand.

The first Guardian Angel charged him with his spear. Julius sidestepped right and swung the hammer into the angel's chest. The hammer broke through the guard's torso with a booming thunderclap. The Guardian Angel flew across the floor, smoke trailing from his blackened armor.

The next angel lowered his spear and charged. Julius swung the hammer back across his body and broke the guard's spear. He continued his swing, raising the hammer over his head and bringing it down upon the guard's skull. The hammer crushed the angel into the ground with a blinding flash.

The remaining three angels huddled close together, their spears leveled at Julius. He advanced slowly, his shoulders heaving. The guards stared at the lightning hammer, which emitted sparks of electricity as it waited for its next victim.

The Guardian Angels broke and ran.

Natalie fired shots at the three angels who had charged her—and tried to keep out of their spear reach. She had lost sight of Nikolas in the melee, but she saw Julius dispatch his first two guards. That left how many? Her mind calculated furiously as she ran, sending another series of blasts at her enemies.

Two already...another full in the face! That's three...almost hit that one! Two that Julius got...a third with his hammer...a fourth...

Ambrosia escaped from her guards while Julius fought them. Flashes of red and white electricity crackled in the air, mixing with the frightening booms of Julius's weapon. Ambrosia sprinted through the confusion to reach Serena, who was shaking on the floor with her hands over her head.

But where was Nikolas?

A blow to the back of her head forced Natalie to the ground. She turned over to see a Guardian Angel standing over her, his spear poised menacingly. Natalie tried to point her umbrella up at the guard, but he kicked her hands away and pinned them to the ground.

Then he stabbed her in the stomach.

Natalie's world exploded in a rush of pain. Every inch of her body burned in agony—electric claws raked the inside of her skin and ripped through her spine. Her head was forced back as a suffocating pain bludgeoned its way through her jaw and into her brain.

*Think, think hard...*She commanded herself to stay calm, but black flares were erupting in front of her eyes. Her very mind threatened to flicker and die.

The spear was electrocuting her to death, and she felt a horrible pain in her stomach as the guard pressed his weight onto the weapon. The spear was killing her...death was flowing into her, washing her life away...

The spear is the killer.

Her whole body tingled. She saw the edge of a precipice. She was tipping over.

It's killing me...killing me...

Falling—

Could you change a pronoun like an adjective? Redirect the action?

She dropped into the chasm of death—air rushed past—

The spear isn't killing me—*it's killing* him!

Natalie's senses returned in a rush. The screams of the Guardian Angel filled her ears, and his face erupted with a blinding light. He stumbled to the ground, red energy shooting out of his own spear. The electricity coursed through his body, crumpling his armor like burnt paper.

Then the lightning stopped, and the guard collapsed, a smoking, lifeless shell.

Natalie turned onto her side, reaching out for her umbrella on the floor and finding it. She cried out in pain as she laid it across the gaping wound in her stomach.

She hoped that her damaged umbrella could heal the wound—and quickly, before someone finished her off.

Another guard appeared ready to do so. He stepped into Natalie's blurred vision, a grin spreading across his pale, gleaming face. He hoisted his spear up, ready to plunge it into her neck—

—and Natalie swung her umbrella into his face.

The Guardian Angel exploded into a burst of orange and yellow flames. Natalie placed her other hand on the handle, increasing the flow of fire, and the guard's armor melted away like thawing ice. He screamed as waves of shimmering heat overwhelmed him. Then he was gone.

Natalie's arms fell back onto her chest. The umbrella clattered to the floor beside her. Her breathing was ragged.

She didn't need a watch anymore to tell her that time was short.

With a terrible groan, she pulled the umbrella up and across her stomach, willing herself to be healed. Fully repaired or not, the umbrella had to heal her. Or she would die.

Natalie's mind raced furiously. She had killed five guards now...and who knew how many Julius had killed...

Then a piercing scream split the air.

Natalie lifted her head, looking around wildly, trying to see what had happened.

She saw Ambrosia lying on the floor, pale and unmoving. Her blue eyes were wide with shock. Blood poured from a wound in her chest.

She was dead.

"No!" Natalie screamed, and then she clutched her stomach and winced.

Beside Ambrosia's body, Nikolas held Serena like a shield, his knife pressed against her neck.

"Let her go, Nikolas!" Julius yelled.

"Not likely," Nikolas winked, his face glistening with sweat.

Natalie strained to lift her head again. Julius circled warily, the hammer poised in his hand.

"All I have to do is hold out long enough for the fire giant to come," Nikolas said. "He'll make short work of you."

"Natalie!" Julius glanced at the red-haired girl, waving a hand in her direction. "I'll save Serena! You see to the fire giant!"

"'See to the fire giant'?" Nikolas laughed. "She's not in a condition to see anything for much longer."

"No, no, I can stand." Natalie groaned, trying to sit upright. But she doubled over in pain. All of the nerves in her body were on fire.

"Natalie." Julius's hand stretched out to her even as he circled Nikolas. "Don't be afraid."

The counselor sneered in derision. "You're not going anywhere, Phoenix Guardian!"

He shook Serena roughly. She was crying hysterically, unable to look away from Ambrosia's limp body.

Natalie's mind spun, the pain forcing her eyes shut. As Julius spoke, she felt a cool wave pass over her stomach, a soothing balm that numbed the pain. She opened her eyes to see that Julius was twisting his fingers slowly in the air. As he moved his hand, the wound on her stomach closed, and her breathing became normal again.

Nikolas curled his lip.

"You best run along, Phoenix Guardian." Nikolas pointed his knife at Natalie, who stumbled to her feet with great effort. "Julius and I have a lot to talk about before I murder the last member of his family."

Natalie hesitated, swaying on the spot, before Julius yelled at her.

"Natalie, go! I'll see to my daughter, and to this traitor!"

His eyes blazed with a fearsome light. Natalie nodded, tightening the grip on her umbrella while the fire giant's heavy footsteps thundered beneath her.

She took a last look at Serena—whose eyes were wide with terror—before turning around and sprinting out of the room. She ran through a hall and down a sweeping flight of stairs, following the sounds of the fire giant that boomed louder and louder.

CHAPTER 21:
FATHER

Nikolas pressed his knife against Serena's throat. She whimpered in panic as the tip pricked her skin. A pearl of blood dribbled down her neck.

"Let her go, Nikolas!" Julius commanded. He circled his enemy slowly, his hammer poised to strike.

"You're not in a position to be giving orders anymore," Nikolas sneered. "I'll decide how this goes—and if you don't stand still, my fingers might twitch and bury this knife in your daughter's neck."

Julius stopped moving. He clenched his hammer in both hands, searching for an opening in Nikolas's defenses.

"There's nothing you can do. You may have killed all of the Guardian Angels, but you and I are at a stalemate." Nikolas smiled. "I'll tell you what's going to happen: I'm going to enjoy this for a few minutes. Then I'll kill your daughter. And then I'll kill you too."

Julius licked his dry lips and tightened his grip on the hammer. "And if I don't like that option?"

Nikolas shrugged. "We could just wait for the fire giant to kill you. He'll be here soon. You might have bandaged the wounds of your Phoenix Guardian friend, but she's in no condition to fight a fire giant."

Julius blinked sweat out of his eyes, his mind racing for ideas. Everything was happening too fast. He tried not to look at the body of his sister, shock still etched on her beautiful face. Blood shone from the wound in her chest.

Julius's heart twisted like a wet rope.

Ambrosia was dead.

"She really was beautiful, wasn't she?" Nikolas prodded Ambrosia's shoulder with his foot. "But so proud."

"Don't touch her!" Julius took a menacing step toward Nikolas, who jerked Serena back. The girl shrieked in terror.

Julius stretched out a hand toward his daughter. "It's going to be all right, Serena!"

"It's not going to be all right, Serena. Don't listen to him." Nikolas grabbed Serena's hair and shook her roughly. "I killed your aunt and I'm going to kill you too, you bastard."

Nikolas spat, as though ridding his mouth of a nasty taste.

"You know, it didn't have to end this way." He shook his head at Julius. "You might have been a decent ruler. You could have moved on after finding out that your family was dead. But," he sighed, "Ambrosia lied to both of us, and you were too emotional to forget your affair. Such an immature little boy—to mate with a mortal and then punish the world when you suffer the consequences. Ruling a planet is a huge responsibility, but you didn't even try."

Julius took slow breaths, his eyes darting from Nikolas to Serena. He flexed his fingers anxiously, wondering if he could hit Nikolas in the head with a bolt of lightning. Nikolas was taller than Serena. His neck and face were fully exposed above her right shoulder.

"For fifteen years, I watched you lose credibility in the eyes of the Pantheon...and in the eyes of every god and goddess on this planet," Nikolas said. "It was only a matter of time before you lost the throne. And I was ready when you did." He winked. "Good things come to those who wait. I thought I would have to hurry things up a bit, but you let the world fall apart at a reasonable pace."

Julius took a chance—shooting a thin burst of lightning over Serena's shoulder at Nikolas's forehead.

But Nikolas was ready. He threw up a green energy shield to block the bolt, which sizzled harmlessly against the barrier.

"Steady there!" Nikolas yelled, shaking Serena roughly. She whimpered as Nikolas dragged her back. "No interruptions, please. I want to insult you thoroughly before it's all over."

"You've said enough already." Julius clenched his teeth, swinging his hammer in slow arcs. Tendrils of electricity crackled as the hammer whirled through the air.

Nikolas gave Julius a reproving look.

"I know you're stronger than me—and your father's shiny hammer can do nasty work. But if your daughter is dead, what does it matter? Just sit tight until the fire giant arrives." He grinned, full of confidence, flaring Julius's anger even more. "Surely you have some questions for me to pass the time? Like how I turned the Guardian Angels against you? It was a masterpiece of manipulation to convince them that you were a threat to Mithris. And yet you disappoint me with your silence. No sense of curiosity."

Julius shook his head. "The only thing I'm curious about is how loud the crack will be when I break your thick skull."

Nikolas laughed in derision, and Julius quivered with rage.

He glanced at Serena, and the sight of her terrified face tore his heart in two. Serena's blue eyes pleaded silently to him underneath a curtain of disheveled brown hair. He gripped the hammer so tightly that his muscles burned.

"It's torture, isn't it?" Nikolas whispered. "Watching her suffer like this? Maybe now you realize the consequences of your actions. You brought her into the world to die, Julius. The passion that you had with your woman—that you so disgustingly described to me—has led to nothing but hurt."

Julius was about to retort when he noticed that Serena's skin had gone deathly pale. She looked like she might pass out at any moment. She had fallen limp in Nikolas's arms, and her eyes were rolling to the back of her head.

"She's fading. She's going to die, just like her mother. Just like Ambrosia." Nikolas's eyes widened. "Just like you."

Julius felt suffocated. His head spun with anxiety as Serena's head lolled to one side. He couldn't allow the last member of his family to die. Not his precious daughter, not when they had just been reunited.

He gazed intently at her face. She was so much like Jillian. Her lovely, long brown hair. Her beautiful blue eyes.

Emotion swelled inside Julius's chest. This was his daughter, and he had lost fifteen years with her. He was not going to lose any more.

"Your father is coming up with a plan to save you," Nikolas whispered in Serena's ear, loud enough for Julius to hear. "But is that any comfort? He abandoned you once before."

Serena's eyes flickered open—a flash of white as she took a sharp breath. Her body trembled from head to toe.

"A good father would have searched the entire world for his daughter. But Julius didn't care to look for you."

"That's a dirty lie, Serena!" Julius swung his hammer in large circles. It hummed loudly, shining brighter and brighter. "Ambrosia told me that you were dead!"

Nikolas's mouth brushed against Serena's ear. She shuddered at the touch. "He's a failure as a father. He's a failure as a god. He abandoned you, and he let the world slip into bloodshed and chaos."

Serena's eyes fluttered rapidly, sweat pouring down her face.

"Surely you've lost loved ones in this war? Do you know who's to blame?" Nikolas turned his knife toward Julius. "Him."

The accusation pierced Julius in the chest. His heart burned with anger and grief, opening to the pain he had suppressed for so long.

He started to speak, but a voice interrupted him—crying loud inside of his head.

Father!

Serena!

Father, save me!

"You're the one to blame, Julius!" Nikolas yelled. "First for the war, and now for the death of your daughter."

Father!

A torrent of emotions flooded his heart. It was a prayer...from his daughter.

Save me!

Julius swung his hammer faster and faster, making it a glowing white blur at the end of his arm.

"Stop spinning your toy and put it down!" Nikolas commanded. "Or I slit her throat right now."

But Julius continued to swing the hammer, throwing his entire body into the motion. The weapon rumbled, making a noise like growing thunder. Julius felt the sound reverberate in his chest. He swung harder. Sweat poured down his brow.

"Your choice, Julius. You killed her, not me." Nikolas pushed Serena's head forward, pressing the edge of his knife against her throat. "This is the end."

Julius brought the hammer forward on its final revolution— and let go.

Nikolas's eyes widened as the hammer flew through the air. His mouth opened in dismay, and a shield of green energy shimmered in the air to protect him.

But it was too late.

The lightning hammer broke through the half-formed barrier with a deafening boom. The hammerhead missed Serena's shoulder by an inch, sailing by to shatter Nikolas's face.

The weapon passed through the god's skull, trailing bolts of electricity, and hurtled across the room to bury itself in the wall behind him.

Nikolas's arms fell from around Serena's shoulders, and then his headless body collapsed to the floor.

Julius had no time to watch his enemy fall. He rushed forward to catch Serena as she dropped to the ground, unconscious. He caught her before she landed, cradling her in his arms.

He lowered his daughter gently to the floor. She felt deathly cold. Her face was pale and her eyes were shut tight. Julius held his head over her mouth, pressing his ear against her lips.

A flutter of air brushed against him. And another.

Her chest rose and fell.

She was alive. Fear and delight overwhelmed him.

Julius took a deep shuddering breath. Tears ran down his face as he stroked Serena's beautiful brown hair.

It was just like her mother's.

CHAPTER 22:
THE VALLEY OF FIRE

Natalie followed the booming sounds of the fire giant until she found herself back in the chamber with the statue of Aurelius. She glanced at the colossal figure that dominated the right side of the room, and then she scanned the multitude of doors around her. Her eyes focused on two in particular, directly across from Aurelius. Judging by the noise, the fire giant would come through one of those.

The shining stars and planets overhead flickered with each step that the fire giant took. Natalie felt a tingling down her spine as the creature's magical presence drew near.

She assumed a fighting position, left foot in front of her right, staring down the two massive doors across the way. Natalie doubted any doors would be big enough to admit the fire giant, but he probably wouldn't mind.

Natalie's watch ticked rhythmically against the deep growls of the approaching monster.

Time was almost up.

She patted her umbrella nervously.

"Just one more show, old girl."

The repairs to her umbrella had worked so far, but she wondered if it could survive the coming battle.

She was about to find out...

The fire giant made his entrance in an explosion of flame—incinerating the door and crashing through the wall. Broken stone rained down upon the floor. The fire giant shook his head like a dog, clearing his shoulders and back of debris.

Natalie had expected *big*, but the monster was over six times her size. She should have prepared herself for "huge" or "massive"...or "giant."

Who would have thought?

Natalie took a deep breath, trying not to panic while her brain registered the fire giant's scale. If her mind hadn't been frozen with shock, she might have tried to remember if she had faced a giant before.

As it was, Natalie felt like the floor was dropping out from beneath her. That made it hard to concentrate.

The fire giant's dark red skin was cracked like dry mud. Fire shone between broken pieces of flesh. The monster sniffed the air warily, exhaling jets of flame from his nostrils. Then he reared to full height, stretching out his arms and flexing fingers as thick as Natalie's waist.

The fire giant tilted his head, considering Natalie. Then he roared menacingly, causing her hair to fly about her head. Heat waves billowed from the monster's mouth. His teeth were black like sharpened obsidian. His eyes and mouth glowed with shifting hues of yellow, orange, and red. A ridge of spikes trailed down his spine.

Natalie stepped back slowly, tightening her grip on her umbrella. She hoped that her stomach injury wouldn't be a handicap in the battle, because the odds were already stacked against her. Julius had done much to seal the gash, but she didn't want to think about what could happen if she got wounded there again.

Then again, any blow from the monster could be the end of her.

Natalie forced herself to stare back at the fire giant's eyes. The hot embers gleamed in his rough, round head. She wondered if a few centuries of imprisonment had dulled his killer instincts or weakened his power.

Probably not.

The fire giant slammed the ground with his two fists, roaring like an enormous ape. Then he broke into a run toward Natalie. The ground shook beneath heavy footfalls, sparks flying as massive feet hit the smooth floor. The fire giant swiped at her with a three-fingered hand, smoke trailing from his forearm. Natalie dropped to the floor just as the hand passed overhead.

The fire giant recovered his balance with alarming agility, planting his feet and swinging at the girl with a backhand.

But Natalie was already running around the fire giant toward the ruined doors. She fired a few bursts of flame from her umbrella tip, hitting the monster on the chin and shoulder. The giant shrugged the blows off, growling—the sound like a thousand bricks sliding over each other. He turned around and lunged, slamming fiery fists into the floor where Natalie had been a moment earlier. Smoldering holes remained when the fire giant withdrew his hands and regained his footing.

Natalie slapped at the edge of her raincoat, which had caught fire from the giant's burning blow. She pointed her umbrella at the blaze, starving the fire of oxygen until it dissipated. Then she resumed a defensive position in time to realize that the fire giant was standing directly overhead.

Feet spread apart, Natalie pointed her umbrella up at the fire giant like a sword. The monster hesitated, snorting a gust of flame from his nostrils.

Natalie licked her lips nervously. The fire giant spread his own legs and lowered his shoulders, ready to pounce. The monster was clearly savoring the moment. He could crush her immediately if he just fell on top of her.

Still aiming her umbrella at the fire giant, Natalie glanced at her watch to see how much time she had left.

Just enough.

The fire giant roared again, and Natalie felt the intense heat billowing from his mouth like a torch, a smothering blanket of death.

He jumped at her with all fours, arms and legs wide, poised to pummel her into the ground. Natalie flicked her umbrella above her like a whip.

The point of her umbrella burst with a sphere of red light, sending a shockwave in all directions. The energy met the fire giant in the air like a wall, knocking him onto his enormous back. He skidded on the ground, gouging a trench as waves of crimson energy tore up the stone around him. He howled as the power of the Phoenix Guardian washed over him, pinning him to the floor like a gale-force wind. Electricity crackled from the tip of Natalie's umbrella as the sphere faded away.

The last red waves dissipated into nothingness. Natalie took a deep breath and stumbled backward. The entire stone floor was cracked from the attack, broken like ripples of water. The statue of Aurelius creaked and groaned, its foundation compromised by the shockwave.

Natalie felt dizzy. Spots erupted in front of her eyes, and exhaustion tugged at her muscles. She looked back at the fire giant to see that he was regaining his feet. Her lip quivered in fear. It wasn't over yet.

Natalie raised her umbrella again, feeling her legs tremble. Her heart skipped a beat when she saw that one of the tears in the red canopy had reopened. The strain of the magic was taking its toll on the umbrella.

Be strong, Natalie. Stand your ground.

She blinked back sweat from her eyes, remembering a field of sunflowers and a girl who had stopped to help her.

The fire giant growled, sending shivers down Natalie's spine. She tried not to think about how big the fire giant was...and how thin and fragile she was.

The monster circled Natalie warily, his shoulders heaving, the fire between his cracked skin glowing brighter as he took deeper breaths. Then the fire giant threw back his head and roared, shaking the walls and ground. The broken floor under Natalie shifted, and she nearly lost her balance.

But then the fire giant slammed his fist into the ground, and Natalie did lose her balance. The floor split in half, a widening crack growing from the fire giant's hand to where Natalie had fallen. The crack was like a trench of fire, fed by the fire giant. A torrent of death rushed through the ditch of stone, straight for Natalie.

The flames ran closer and closer—and Natalie regained her feet just in time. She jumped out of harm's way, rolling on the floor to her right as the trench carved a path where she had lain.

The monster had anticipated Natalie's jump, and he slammed another fist into the ground, slicing a parallel trench of fire through the stone. But Natalie was ready too, and she jumped to the left in plenty of time—

—realizing too late that she had jumped between the two trenches.

The flames rose on both sides to create an impenetrable wall of fire, cutting off everything else from view.

All she could see was the cracked, grinning face of the fire giant staring at her through the valley of fire. The monster raised his hands, higher and higher into the air, and the flames rose with them, as though he were conducting an orchestra of death.

Then he stepped forward, walking toward Natalie between the shimmering walls of heat. The red-haired girl took a step back, sweat pouring from her brow in the increasingly hot space. She glanced behind her. There was still a gap between the two walls. The damaged statue of Aurelius stood at the end, flanked by the trenches of fire.

Natalie broke into a run toward the statue. A monstrous shadow overtook her, and she dropped to her knees, sending a blast of flames from her umbrella tip. She heard a ripping noise as the tear in the umbrella grew wider.

194

Natalie's shot missed the fire giant, who had jumped her to land in front of the statue of Aurelius. With his back to her, the monster slashed the ground with his hand, uniting the two trenches and sealing off the exit. The fire giant turned around to face Natalie, grinning with cracked obsidian teeth.

Natalie looked the way the fire giant had come. He had already sealed off that side. The valley had become a rectangle—a fiery box—and she was trapped. This was the last stand.

The fire giant advanced slowly, savoring the kill.

Natalie swallowed, holding her umbrella above her head and pointing it at the fire giant. She felt her journal through the raincoat with her free hand. She closed her eyes, letting the memories fill her mind, feeling their power.

A fireman with an umbrella...

The footsteps of the giant boomed in her ears, reverberating through her chest.

"Clotted cream...do you know how to drink tea?"

The monster's roar forced Natalie's eyes open. She gazed into his wild, flickering eyes as he lumbered slowly toward her. The monster's face was like a flaming brand, burning itself into her vision. But the memories still swam in her head, fighting against her fear.

"Jillian...that's your mother's name."

A tongue of fire swept out of the creature's mouth, licking the black, obsidian teeth.

Charles and Emma...precious children.

The giant was less than fifteen feet away. The heat was suffocating.

"Next time, don't just leave me, okay? If we have to go, let's go together."

And Serena wiped my cheek with her shirt sleeve...

Natalie held her umbrella with both hands, tightening her grip, mustering her last reserves of strength.

"That's why we're together."

"I know...it's just that...it hurts."

The fire giant stood over her, flexing his fingers for the kill, but a smile came to Natalie's trembling lips.

She remembered.

Strength.

The fire giant let loose a howl of rage, shaking Natalie to her bones. The monster bared his teeth, throwing his head forward to devour her whole. Natalie raised her umbrella to meet the fire giant, opening it with a rushing sound like tornado.

He might have been a fire giant, but Natalie was a Phoenix Guardian.

With a deafening rush of wind and heat, the flaming walls were sucked into Natalie's umbrella and funneled into the fire giant's face. A torrent of fire rushed through the tip of her umbrella, pumping a spray of concentrated magma into his mouth. The giant staggered and fell to his knees. Natalie twisted her umbrella in her hands, increasing the flow of fire rushing down the monster's throat.

The umbrella itself ignited, and Natalie gasped. New tears in the canopy joined the first hole. The handle grew hotter and hotter, threatening to disintegrate at any moment—but Natalie held on, pressing the advantage against the fire giant.

Smoke billowed around Natalie's feet, and the ground trembled violently. The handle burned like hot coals, and Natalie screamed from the pain—but she had to hold on, just a few seconds longer.

The surface of the ceiling cracked. Fragments of stone dropped onto the floor—and onto the damaged pedestal supporting Aurelius's statue. The colossal icon tottered and fell upon the head of the stunned fire giant.

The monster's head burst apart like a volcanic eruption, crumpling under the weight of Aurelius and the power of the Phoenix Guardian. The statue shattered the giant's body, shooting sparks and embers onto the broken floor. His final roar of agony lingered in the air for a long moment.

Then there was silence, and nothing remained of the fire giant but the glowing fragments of his corpse.

Natalie dropped her flaming umbrella. It crumpled to the ground, trailing smoke—a tangled mass of wire and burnt fabric.

She whimpered in pain, her shoulders and arms throbbing. Her hands burned in agony from the umbrella's final act.

But it was over...she had won...

Tired.

She swayed for a moment, her knees buckling...

And then Natalie collapsed onto the sooty ground.

She felt the ashes beneath her face and chest. Beside her ear, Natalie's watch ticked slower and slower.

And Natalie knew that it was time.

CHAPTER 23:
THE PHOENIX

A tremendous boom shocked Serena back into consciousness. She opened her eyes to see Julius kneeling in front of her.

"Natalie!" Serena gasped. She gripped her father's arms. "The fire giant!"

"I know. We don't have much time." Julius helped Serena to her feet. "I think I know where they are."

Julius took his daughter's hand, leading her out of the chamber and into a long hallway.

They ran down a wide flight of stairs, passing intricate sculptures and painted bas-reliefs. Serena's heart pounded against her chest. She tried to block out the worries in her mind—they would make it in time to save Natalie. They had to.

She followed her father through a set of golden doors, finding herself on the landing of an enormous spiral staircase. The size of it took her breath away. Serena arched her head back, trying to see the top, but it was too high.

Julius led her down the stairs. She grabbed the railing, struggling to keep up with her father's fast pace. Her shoes slapped on the granite steps. She looked over the edge again, trying to see the bottom, but it was too far below.

Serena frowned in spite of herself. "You'd think they'd have an elevator with a place this big."

Julius glanced over his shoulder. "An elevator?"

Serena blinked, embarrassed that she had spoken out loud.

"We do have an elevator—but the chamber we want is right here." Julius pointed ahead. "I think this is where the noise came from."

Serena followed his gaze to see the same room in which Nikolas had captured her and Natalie.

She held a hand to her mouth as they ran into the room, which was unrecognizable from the one she had seen a short time ago.

The high walls were torn and broken. It looked like someone had taken a plow to the stone floor. The colossal figure of Aurelius lay on the ground in pieces, surrounded by a field of ashes and burning embers.

Julius surveyed the destruction and gasped in disbelief. Across the way, something of monstrous proportions had battered through the walls, adding more debris to the mess.

Serena pressed her hands to her lips, walking around the shattered Aurelius, hoping against hope that Natalie was okay. She held her breath, dreading the sight of a broken umbrella or a torn raincoat. With each glimmer of yellow and red, she flinched, afraid of what she might see...

Even on the ground, the statue was huge, obscuring a fair portion of the chamber. But as Serena rounded the ruins, she saw someone on the ground.

A yellow raincoat. Flaming red hair.

"Natalie!" Serena sprinted toward her friend.

"Serena, wait!"

Serena heard her father's shout, but she ignored it, stepping around stones and dodging holes to reach Natalie.

The red-haired girl laid face down, her head resting against her left arm. Serena knelt beside her friend, noting the loud, slow ticking of Natalie's golden watch.

"Natalie, are you okay?" Serena leaned down next to Natalie's ear.

Natalie did not move. Her whole body was dirty with ash. Serena wrung her hands, looking her friend up and down for signs of injury. They were easy to find. Her pink shirt was blood-stained at the stomach, and the edges of her raincoat had been singed.

"I'm going to move you, okay?" Serena gently lifted Natalie, cradling her head as she rolled the girl onto her back.

"Serena, don't move her!"

Serena looked up, startled, to see Julius standing beside her. Sitting next to Natalie's limp body, Serena felt numb and confused.

"I just...she's hurt. She's..." Serena took Natalie's hand, checking for a pulse. When she didn't feel anything, she pressed her forefinger harder against Natalie's wrist.

"Come on, Natalie, be alive. Stay with me." Serena held her ear to Natalie's lips, listening for a breath.

Nothing. Hot tears collected in her eyes.

"Come on..." she pleaded.

Julius knelt across from Serena, taking Natalie's hand reverently in his own.

"Serena...I think your friend..." He swallowed. "I think she killed the fire giant. What a courageous girl."

"I know." Serena's lip trembled. "But she's not gone, is she? Can't you do something for her?"

Julius caressed Natalie's hand, looking from her face to Serena's.

"I'll do whatever I can."

"Thank you, sir..." Natalie interrupted softly. "But there's nothing more to be done."

She opened her eyes and Serena cried with delight.

"Natalie!" Serena squeezed Natalie's hand, kissing it in relief. "You did it! You beat the fire giant—you're alive!"

Natalie gave her a tired smile. "But not for much longer."

Serena brushed a strand of hair out of her teary eyes.

"What?" she stammered. "What do you mean 'not much longer'? Julius—my father—he can heal you. You're safe now. Everything's going to be okay."

"It is going to be okay." Natalie nodded weakly. "It's going to be okay because I fulfilled my mission. It's over."

"Of course it's not over, don't say that." Serena was surprised at the anger in her own voice, but Natalie was being stupid. "You have to save the world, remember? You need to stop the war."

"No." Natalie shook her head. "You're the one who has to stop the war. My mission is done. I took you this far, reunited you with your father. Together, you'll bring peace to the world. Father and daughter, you are the link between the mortal and the divine." She took Serena's and Julius's hands and brought them together. "But my time is up."

Serena stared at Natalie, stunned.

"But you're wrong—I don't believe you." A lump rose in Serena's throat. "I don't..."

Natalie smiled at her, and Serena resented the understanding behind those beautiful green eyes.

"That's what the ticking clock is about, Serena. My time has been running out the whole time."

"No, Natalie." Serena released her father's hand and brushed Natalie's red hair. "I need you."

"I know." Natalie held Serena's hand to her ashen cheek. Her voice was heavy with fatigue. "I don't want to leave you. But you have your father now. You and he need to rebuild your lives...and rebuild the world."

Serena's hands trembled. Natalie held them tighter.

"That's your destiny, Serena. You have to be the mediator. You have to make sure the gods care about humanity."

"But you have to be there with me." Serena's voice cracked, tears dripping onto Natalie's raincoat. "You can't just leave me, not when we were just becoming..."

"Friends?"

"Friends." Serena managed a watery smile. "Sisters."

Natalie beamed. She reached into her coat pocket and pulled out her journal and pink pen.

"This journal has everything in it. All that I have seen, all that I have heard. Where I have been, who I have known. Memories and connections are what make us who we are." She gazed deep into Serena's eyes. "You're part of this journal, just like you're part of me. You have to read it, do you understand?"

"But—"

"Serena, promise me that you'll read it. Write in it. Record the memories of our time together. Promise me?"

"I promise." Serena nodded, taking the journal and the pen.

"Read it." Natalie's green eyes shone. "And remember me, Serena."

She let go of Serena's hand gently, motioning for her and Julius to stand.

"You're a good friend. Take care of the journal. When you read the words, I'll be there." Natalie smiled, a tear tracing its way down her cheek. "Now let me go."

Serena's vision swam in tears as she stepped back from her friend. She felt a hand on her shoulder, and she turned to see Julius standing beside her. She took her father's hand and grasped it tightly.

"Serena?" Natalie whispered.

"Yes?" Serena's heart jumped in her chest.

"Remember me."

Serena bit her lip. "How could I forget?"

Natalie smiled one last time. Then she closed her eyes and folded her arms across her chest.

Serena listened to the rhythmic ticking of Natalie's watch grow louder and louder, filling the room. With each passing moment, the clock slowed down. Finally, it stopped with a ping that echoed through the still chamber.

Natalie's body burst into flame, and Serena screamed.

Soon Natalie was enveloped in a blur of orange and yellow. Her face was obscured by the blaze, but Serena could see the yellow raincoat and white boots stripping away, consumed by the sudden heat. For one last moment, Natalie lay before her, and then her entire body was lost to the fire.

Serena dropped to her knees and covered her face, unable to see anymore.

"Look, Serena! Look!"

Serena heard the surprise in her father's voice as he gripped her shoulders.

She opened her eyes again to see the silhouette of a tremendous bird. It flew in the rising flames, above the ground where Natalie's body had lain.

"The Phoenix Guardian," Serena gasped, clasping her hands in front of her face.

The phoenix called out with a sound that reverberated through Serena's body and sent shivers down her spine.

The chamber flashed with a blinding white light. A tremor ran beneath their feet, and the air was stripped of sound. Serena could see Julius yelling beside her, but she couldn't hear anything. The lights winked out, casting them into total darkness.

A powerful wind knocked them onto their feet. Serena winced as her elbows scraped against the hard floor.

Then her ears popped, and the sound returned in a rush.

The lights in the room came back on. The air grew cold.

There was no more phoenix...and there was no more flame.

Natalie was dead.

Serena rolled over onto her face, her shoulders shaking as she sobbed. She had tried to hold the tears back, but now they ran unrestrained.

She felt hands on her back—heard comforting words.

"No!" she screamed, fighting her father's hands away. "Leave me alone! No!"

She pounded the ground with her fist.

Natalie couldn't be dead.

Serena looked up at the spot where her friend had been. A pile of ashes remained, glowing faintly. As Serena watched, the ashes swirled into the air and funneled into the journal in her hand.

Serena examined the book. The bird which normally appeared on the cover was gone. In its place, a pile of ashes rested on the bird's nest.

But it wasn't a nest after all. It was a funeral pyre.

Serena shook her head. They had only been together for a short time, and now Natalie was gone.

Natalie, who had loved her like a sister, and protected her, and told her the secrets that Serena needed to know.

Natalie, who had a red umbrella, a yellow raincoat, and those shocking white rain boots.

Natalie, who didn't know how to drink tea. Or start a car. Or hold a conversation with a normal person.

Natalie and her magical adjectives.

Natalie and her beautiful, flaming red hair.

Natalie was gone.

Serena opened the journal to a back page, where she found a list of words under the heading, "Nicknames." She read them, laughing in spite of herself as tears dripped onto the hard floor.

"The girl who fell from the sky."

"You!"

"Firefighter."

"Candy corn."

Serena pulled Natalie's pink pen out of her pocket and wrote at the bottom of the page.

The Phoenix Guardian.

The pen hovered above the page. Her lip trembled as she wrote one more name.

My friend.

*

Serena sat on the hard stone floor for a long time, staring at the journal. She gave a start when Julius touched her shoulder— she had almost forgotten that he was there.

"I'm sorry about your friend." Julius knelt beside her. "She was very brave. And it's clear that she loved you very much."

Serena looked back at Natalie's journal. She took a deep, shuddering breath. The pain was so heavy.

Julius grasped Serena's hands and caressed them gently.

"Natalie was right, you know." Julius cleared his throat. "About you being the mediator between gods and men. Her mission wasn't in vain. I want to be there for the world...and for you."

Serena looked at Julius. Her breath caught at the hope and desperation in his eyes.

"Will you forgive me? Will you be my daughter?"

Serena's chest swelled with emotion. She felt his hand in hers, felt the strength, the divinity, the tenderness, the love.

The father...

She squeezed his hand.

"I've always been your daughter."

Julius smiled. His blue eyes shone with emotion.

"I love you, Serena."

He kissed her forehead and held her tightly.

Serena did not say that she loved him. She could not, perhaps, say those words just now. There was too much hurt clouding her mind. The skies would clear one day, but not today.

For now, it was enough to hold him, and to be held.

EPILOGUE
(SEVEN MONTHS LATER)

Serena woke up to the sound of the radio.

"Good morning, Locke City! Today is the first day of spring, and we're expected to have a beautiful start to the season. The sun hasn't risen quite yet, but the forecast calls for a sunny day with a pleasant breeze. For the first time in years, the weather just keeps getting better—and so does the news. As top world leaders converge today on the capitol to discuss international disarmament, the mood..."

Serena rubbed her eyes and threw the covers off. She stared at the digital clock on her desk. The green digits glowed in the darkness.

5:39.

She was running late.

Serena stumbled through the darkness to her closet, where she grabbed a light blue shirt and a white cardigan. She sat on the floor, pulled on a pair of blue jeans, and tied her shoes.

She grabbed her purse and a leather-bound book off her nightstand before running down the stairs.

"Good morning, professor." She strode across the living room to the kitchen, where she grabbed a banana from the countertop.

"Good morning, Serena." Professor Glen looked up from her newspaper and set her cup of coffee onto the round kitchen table. She smiled at Serena, the light reflecting in her rimless glasses.

"I have to run." Serena grabbed a juice box from the refrigerator and slammed the door shut again. "Special errand. Probably won't be back until late."

Professor Glen brushed her gray hair out of her eyes. "Shall I call Mrs. Winters so they have a replacement for the after-school program today?"

"No need—I told her and the kids yesterday."

"I see." Professor Glen returned to her newspaper. "All right then. Be safe and have a good day."

"Thanks, professor," Serena called over her shoulder as she opened the front door.

She closed it and ran down the sidewalk, dodging tired businessmen in suits. Their briefcases bounced against them as Serena brushed by with a quick, "Excuse me! Sorry!"

The sun hadn't risen yet, so the yellow glow from the streetlights illuminated her way as she rushed past the dark windows of shops and cafés.

Serena stopped at a curb, waited for a truck to pass, and then ran across the street to a crowded bus stop. She made her way through the crowd until she stood under a small sign that read, "Downtown City Center."

She waited impatiently, bouncing on either foot to keep herself warm. A few commuters backed away from her, irritated by the show of energy so early in the morning.

Her bus arrived, the doors sounding their distinctive "whoosh" when they opened. She showed the driver her pass and took a seat near the front.

Moments later, they were off again. She watched the shops go by as the bus picked up speed in traffic. The colors of the passing buildings blurred together—blue, yellow, green, pink.

She glanced across the aisle at a young man's newspaper. The headlines read, "Teuten and Viran Officials Discuss Reconstruction of Sydney."

Serena smiled. Ever since the war had ended last year, political tensions had eased across the globe. Hardline politicians had been replaced by leaders who were willing to compromise and negotiate. For the first time in decades, the phrases "humanitarian relief" and "rebuilding" were more important than "conquest" and "expansion."

Pundits had called the transformation, "Nothing short of miraculous."

Indeed.

With a second chance, Julius had proven to the Pantheon that he could rule Mithris after all.

Serena stared out of her window, watching a playground pass by. She thought of the children who would be there later in the day, and something twinged inside of her chest.

She sighed deeply, leaning back against the tall seat and pulling a white ribbon out of her cardigan pocket. She tied the ribbon in her hair, making a ponytail and remembering a little boy at a train station.

She caressed the ribbon in her hair. It was so soft.

Blinking her eyes, Serena reached into her purse and pulled out the leather-bound book. The cover was almost blank, except for the faded picture of a funeral pyre on the front.

Serena opened the book, scanning the pages that she had read carefully over the last seven months. The book was so familiar to her. It felt like a friend, and yet there were still sections of the journal that she hadn't read. The stories seemed to stretch on forever, and Serena hardly dared to believe half of them.

But with Natalie, you never knew.

Serena had written in the journal. She hadn't intended to write much, just what pertained to Natalie. That had been more than she had expected. But once she started writing, she found that she had a lot to say.

She had even written about Ambrosia—about how she wished she could have known her. It would have been nice to talk...to have a relationship with the aunt who protected her.

Some things in life could not be restored. And yet, a strange peace came from writing those thoughts down.

The journal was inviting.

It always had room for more memories.

When Serena got off the bus, she thanked the driver and ran down the street until she reached an abandoned construction site. She walked alongside the tall wooden fence, making sure that no one else was looking. When she was sure the coast was clear, she slipped inside an unlocked gate.

The old hinges creaked when she closed the gate.

"I'm here," she whispered.

The outline of a door gleamed in front of her, and she stepped under the shining archway. A whooshing noise sounded behind her, and then she felt herself flying upward. She watched an elevator solidify around her. The skyscrapers of Locke City faded away like dripping watercolors as the Tower of the Gods materialized into view.

A bell chimed, and the elevator doors opened. Her father, Julius, was waiting just outside the elevator. He smiled and opened his arms.

"Hello, Father." Serena stepped forward to give him a quick hug. His white robes were warm and inviting. "Is everything ready?"

"Yes, come over here." Julius pointed to a doorway at the opposite side of the room. He took her hand and led the way.

A panoramic window stretched around the building to their left, showing a brilliant view of the eastern skyline. The tops of the skyscrapers were lined with red and yellow from the morning light peeking over the horizon.

Serena turned away from the sunrise when they reached the far end of the room.

"Are you sure this is better than driving?" Serena looked uncertainly at the door in front of her.

"Absolutely." Julius nodded. "The Portal is how I used to visit your mother. We can go anywhere in the world."

"I don't have an address though." Serena bit her lip. "I just know the general location."

"If you can visualize it, that will be enough." Julius turned a dial on the wall. The door opened noiselessly and they stepped inside.

They entered a pure white room. Serena held her hand up to shield her eyes from the brightness.

Julius patted her shoulder. "Just think about where you want to go."

Serena closed her eyes and remembered, feeling the journal in her hands.

When she opened her eyes again, the picture of a highway and a field of sunflowers swayed in front of her. She reached out to touch the image—it looked like a floating veil of water.

"That's it," she whispered.

Serena blinked as the image swayed even more. Wind blew against her face. Her feet felt like they were falling asleep. She flexed her tingling fingers, overwhelmed by the sudden flood of sensations. All around her, the air seemed to solidify and press against her—

—and then all feeling was gone, and she was weightless.

Her mind spun into dizziness...she closed her eyes again...

She and Julius were standing on the highway in front of a field of sunflowers.

They couldn't see the sun, but the low-lying clouds were tinged with orange and red.

Serena took a deep breath. This was the same place that she and Natalie had met so long ago.

And yet not so long ago.

Julius looked around them. "This is the place?"

"Yes." Serena walked into the sunflowers, pushing aside the tall green stalks.

She didn't expect the clearing to still be there, but she moved ahead to the general spot where Natalie had landed. Or crashed, rather. She failed to suppress a smile at the thought.

She stopped abruptly in the middle of the flowers and pointed to the ground. "Here, Dad."

Julius nodded and waved his hand in a sweeping arc. Serena heard a deep sigh on the air, and the sunflowers parted, moving aside as though stepping out of the way. They made a small circle, wide enough for someone to lie in.

Serena knelt down and took out the journal. She opened it to the front and read a passage out loud.

"I spend my entire life learning how to live. Then I die. And so, in this journal, I will remember all that I have seen, all that I have heard. Where I have been, who I have known." Serena stood, gazing at the words on the page. "Write it down. Remember."

She closed her eyes.

"You wrote in your journal that spring is the time of new birth. Those who are remembered will live on. You have been remembered, Natalie Bliss. Spring is here. Rise from the ashes."

She placed the journal reverently on the ground, suddenly conscious of her heartbeat. It sounded steadily in her ears, and then it accelerated—louder and louder. She took a deep breath as all of the flowers around her began to glow. The sun cut through the early morning clouds, bathing the sky in golden light.

On the cover of the journal, a small bird lifted its head from the funeral pyre.

A crack sounded high above, echoing around and through them. The journal opened, an unseen wind flipping through the pages. Serena *felt* the sound as the pages turned rapidly.

Beams of light shot up from the book. A cascade of colors fell around them, creating a shining dome in the field of flowers.

A beautiful cry rose up from the ground, reverberating inside of her chest. The radiant form of a phoenix rose up from the journal, unfolding its wings with a joyous sound.

Serena gasped, choked with emotion. She wiped her eyes, feeling her father's strong hands on her shoulders. She turned around to look at him, beaming with expectation. He smiled back at her.

The phoenix sang out once more, and then Serena and Julius shielded their faces from that light that consumed their vision. All of the sound was taken away—Serena's ears popped—and when she lowered her arm...

...she saw someone standing in front of her.

Flaming red hair fell across the girl's face.

She looked about eleven years old.

She was—Serena's heart caught in her throat—wearing a yellow raincoat, blue jeans, and, of course...

...white rain boots.

Serena smiled. "Candy corn."

The red-haired girl tilted her head, a curious smile spreading across her face.

"Candy corn?" She held out her hand to Serena. "Is that your name?"

Serena shook her head. "My name is Serena."

"Serena. That's a pretty name. It's nice to meet you. My name is..." Her smile faltered. "Well, I'm not actually sure what my name is."

Serena handed her the journal. "It's all in here."

The girl took it cautiously, turning it around to examine the cover. There was a gleaming phoenix on the front, its wings spread wide.

"That's a pretty bird." She stared at the shining picture. "I like birds. What is this bird called?"

"It's a phoenix. And you can open it. It's your book."

The girl raised her eyebrows in surprise. "My book?"

"Yes." Serena nodded encouragingly. "Do you know how to open it?"

The girl put a hand on her hip. "Of course I know how to open it. It's a book."

She slid her finger across the lock and turned to the front page. She stared at it for a moment. Then she looked back at Serena.

"This isn't my book."

Serena started. "What do you mean?"

"It says here, 'This book belongs to Natalie Bliss.'" The girl looked up at Serena. "This is Natalie's book."

"But that's your name." Serena nodded reassuringly. "You're Natalie Bliss."

"I am? That's excellent." Natalie beamed. "'Natalie' is such a beautiful name. And 'Bliss' sounds very happy. I feel very happy."

Natalie squeezed her shoulders together, delighted. She flipped through the book and scanned a few pages. She stopped halfway through to read a passage.

"I love this handwriting. It's so pink and full of hearts." She turned another page. "Wait a minute!" A look of dawning comprehension lit up her face. She took a deep breath and stared at Serena. "I think..."

Serena swallowed, waiting—hoping for what would happen next. A breeze blew past them, lifting Natalie's flaming red hair so that it caught the morning sun.

Natalie's green eyes twinkled.

"I remember you."

AUTHOR'S NOTE

This is the second edition of *The Phoenix Guardian*. A few typos and sentence structure issues have been fixed. Certain paragraphs have been modified, deleted, or added to make some chapters flow more smoothly. Nothing in the overall story or plot has changed. A casual reader would be hard-pressed to notice the differences, but the changes have improved the book.

The largest additions were in chapters 9 and 11, in Natalie and Serena's interactions with the soldiers, who now have names.

I also modified the cover titles and added a dedication and an acknowledgements section.

Thanks for reading.

ACKNOWLEDGEMENTS

My mom and dad, for encouraging me to major in professional writing, reading my stories, proofreading this book multiple times, and proofreading it again

My brother, for encouraging me to be a writer before I considered it a serious pursuit

My sister-in-law, for enjoying my books, and for providing graduate level feedback

Mel Odom, for teaching me seven straight semesters, mentoring me for four as a teaching assistant, editing this book multiple times, feeding me pizza, and teaching me that a man has to live by a code

Adam LaDine, for taking me on his road trip from Oklahoma to Massachusetts in 2011, and for reading early drafts of *The Phoenix Guardian* and insisting that Natalie's raincoat was green, not yellow

Alyssa Grimley, for printing the book so I could proofread the second edition, and for loving chapter seven

Andrew Chandler, Andrew Middleton, Caleb Holt, Kailey Gillman, and Pat Santucci, who listened to my initial novel idea at the Eagle and Child in Oxford, England, summer of 2011

Caleb Holt, for buying the book first, and for inviting me to the *other* library to celebrate his birthday (and the publication of *The Phoenix Guardian*)

Carli Lewis, for a drawing of "Waldo Reed and the Totem Mountain" that made me think again about the girl on a flying umbrella

Daniel Kordek (daekazu), for his excellent cover illustration and titles

Don Carmichael, for telling me that my book was replete with cardigans, and for walrus

Dr. Carlisle, for knighting me at the Thai restaurant in Colorado Springs, reading my stories, and telling me to get to work on the next one

Kyle West, for recommending the professional writing program at OU, and Jelani Sims, for demanding that I *stay* in professional writing

Noah O'Hair, for proofreading the book, and for putting my autographed book on the shelf next to his esteemed authors

Robert Byrd, for proofreading the book, and for believing in its potential

ABOUT THE AUTHOR

Steven Thorn was born in Virginia, USA. He and his brother were homeschooled through high school by their mother, a former public school teacher in California and Florida.

Steven received his Bachelor's and Master's degrees in Professional Writing from the University of Oklahoma, his dad's alma mater. He is a musician and recording artist. He enjoys studying history, mythology, and religion. His other pursuits include football, soccer, tabletop games, and perfecting parallel structure. When he's not writing or doing his annual pushup, he's pondering the mysteries of the universe.

Visit his website at www.steventhethorn.com.

Read his thoughts on life, liberty, and the pursuit of happiness on his blog: steventhethorn.blogspot.com.

You can also follow him on:

facebook.com/steventhethorn
instagram.com/steventhethorn
twitter.com/steventhethorn
youtube.com/steventhethorn

Made in the USA
Coppell, TX
18 June 2020